Desire of the moth

[a novel]

Champa Bilwakesh

P.O. Box 200340
Brooklyn, NY 11220
www.upsetpress.org

Established in 2000, UpSet Press is an independent press based in Brooklyn. The original impetus of the press was to upset the status quo through literature. UpSet Press has expanded its mission to promote new work by new authors; the first works, or complete works, of established authors—placing a special emphasis on restoring to print new editions of exceptional texts; and first-time translations of works into English. Overall, UpSet Press endeavors to advance authors' innovative visions, and works that engender new directions in literature.

Cover art by Chitra Ganesh / www.chitraganesh.com
Book design by Wendy Lee / wendyleedesign.com

Library of Congress Control Number: 2014957114

ISBN 978-1-937357-94-8
Printed in the United States of America

This Novel is for Shubha and Nikki, my heartbeats.
Kechu, for your love and support.

To the memory of my parents, Visalakshi and
Krishnamurthi,
and my dear elder brother, Balu.

The desire of the moth for the star,
  Of the night for the morrow,
The devotion to something afar
  From the sphere of our sorrow

Percy Bysshe Shelley

prologue

Whenever she recalled home, it was not the painted teak pillars of the front stoop that Sowmya remembered. Not the small front gate or the patch of earth under it, smoothed and hardened by sprinkling of water, nor the daily changing pattern drawn on it with powdered rice: a blooming lotus one day, or a peacock dancing the next. Nor was it the small porch sheltered by a stoop where her father read the newspaper in the morning, although she always saw his form buried in a fragile space in her somewhere, only to tear forth in shards of glass at unexpected times.

What she remembered then of the small village of Ponmalar, by the bank of the Kaveri, was the particular way the morning light fell on the enclosed courtyard at the center of her father's house. This light dropped no shadows. She was ten years old and her home was her world and it was still whole.

There was no sunlight that particular morning of the brand new year, 1928. Because it was a wintry January, it dawned gray and cool. Sowmya sat on the edge of the single step that led down from the main hall into the paved courtyard. She hugged her knees to her chest for warmth and watched her mother, Janaki. She was moving in the thin light, singing a familiar hymn in a barely audible voice. Her sari shifted slightly when she moved and revealed a smooth calf, and the shape of her belly swollen with the new baby. Sowmya could already imagine her little sister, a tiny hand nestled in her own as she led the child on their rounds during the winter festival. Delighted by the displays of toy people in every house in the neighborhood, they would collect the loot of sweets, ribbons, and glass bangles handed out in small sacks for the price of a song.

Janaki was now laying fresh wicks in the clay lamps arranged on a tray. She placed the lamps in the niches that were scooped out on the four sides of the urn that stood in the courtyard. This urn held the dusty green tulasi shrub. Nourished with sprinkling of water and whispered desires, it grew tender branches and tiny seedpods. Her mother claimed that the shrub bestowed conjugal bliss.

"What is conjugal bliss, Amma?" Sowmya called out to her mother.

Janaki stopped what she was doing and looked at her daughter for a moment. She bit down on the smile that rose to her lips and returned her attention to the lamps and began lighting them. Drops of brilliance lit up the urn which, with its edges scalloped and tipped with russet paint, now looked like a bride dressed in finery in that morning's gray light.

"Sowmya! Come here, child." Janaki called.

Sowmya approached her mother. A dot of red kumkum

between Janaki's brows brightened her face like the glow of a full moon. Janaki cupped her daughter's chin and tilted the girl's face, smoothed down the tiny wayward strands of hair at her brow. Sowmya smelled the odor of cut vegetables in her mother's hands. From the kitchen behind them Aunt Meenakshi sneezed.

With a hand at her back, Janaki guided her daughter towards the shrub.

"Close your eyes, and pray. Say please. *Please* let me have a good husband. That is conjugal bliss."

Sowmya closed her eyes and pressed her palms together. She rolled the word *husband* in her mouth. Hiding it under her tongue like sugar-candy, she imagined him. Only a few months ago, soon after her tenth birthday, the family from Thanjavur had arrived to conclude the engagement. Sowmya's parents had exchanged flowers and fruits with the parents of the groom-to-be, known with affection as Ramki. He was seventeen. The wedding was to follow in January when the sun transitioned into Capricorn, on a day when the juxtaposition of the stars and planets were deemed perfect by the astrologer. The couple was sure to be blessed with a long and fruitful marriage, he said.

"Say it, child," her mother's voice urged.

Always faceless because she had glimpsed him only for a moment, Ramki appeared to her with jasmine garlands draped over his broad shoulders and chest. She felt a rumble of joy in her young breast, but she said nothing.

●   ●   ●

Soon after the engagement, Sowmya's father, Natesan, ordered the silk saris from Kanchipuram. They were delivered in two large canvas covered bundles and would be distributed as gifts for all the women attending. The bride's saris arrived separately, a dozen of them in deep hues, one for each occasion that was going to fill the days of the wedding. Not a single one was white.

Daily for several days before the wedding, relatives and friends of the Natesan family started arriving from the surrounding villages and towns. They came from as far away north as Madras, and even Calcutta from where Sowmya's cousin Niru arrived with her mother.

The women helped Janaki and her younger widowed sister, Meenakshi, in the kitchen. Soon the Natesans' house filled with the smell of syrup of jaggery, and of lentil wafers frying in sesame seed oil. Sowmya and Niru spent all their waking moments together and in the morning woke with their thin limbs intertwined.

On the morning of the wedding Sowmya stood in the open courtyard when night had not entirely lifted. Aunt Meenakshi had earlier unclasped Niru's hands from around Sowmya, woke her up, oiled her hair, and washed it with powdered sheekai pods, with a final rinse of turmeric-tinted water. Her wet hair was now finger-combed until all the snarls were undone and the damp hair hung down to her hips, heavy and fragrant with crushed herbs and seeds. Outside the musicians were tuning the pipes of the nadaswaram and the drums.

Sowmya's eyes widened at the heavy brocade that was brought out, its color that of the sea. She turned around and around as instructed while the women tied and tucked and draped her in it. Finally when they were done with the sari she seemed to drown in it, as the bride had neither the breasts nor the hips to give shape to the sari. But she loved it nevertheless, all the attention, the glory. Her cousin Niru, still in her rumpled nightclothes, her face bearing marks of sleep, watched slack-jawed. Sowmya grinned at her with glee and a little pity. She was stepping into a world that was still half hidden and mysterious and for that reason also one of privilege, full of color and fragrances. She looked at her feet. Her toes were stained russet with marudani. Both her palms had large circles of stains as did her fingertips. The stain on her nails would glow coral for several months after everything else had faded.

The musicians blew a tune of joyful welcome through the nadaswaram. The drums beat. Sowmya tripped over the cumbersome folds as she was led to the wedding platform that was festooned with pendants of mango leaves. One of her uncles hoisted her up to the platform, where Sowmya sat beside her father. Ramki's father flanked Ramki. Kamala, his mother, stood behind them watching their only son, their beloved, performing his most important and sacred rite. An invisible force had emptied out Kamala's womb year after year and finally, when she was thirty-nine years old, she conceived Ramki, a miracle, the lifeblood for the family tree. Her fingers twitched to reach out and stroke his shoulder. This girl sitting across from him better fill the house once again with life.

Ramki's handsome face was full of intent as he leaned forward and repeated the mantras the priest instructed him to chant. *May the gold-winged god bring your heart to dwell within me. Let no evil eyes bring death to thy husband. May you give birth to heroes.*

Sowmya thought of little boys with swords drawn against evil demons jumping out of her belly. She quickly placed a hand over her mouth, once again tested the word *husband* on her tongue, and moved it to the inside of her cheek.

Following the priest's instruction whenever he called for her, Janaki stood behind her husband and poured water here, or a handful of rice there. Diamonds sparkled on her nose and ears as she bent down, her face so close to Sowmya, strands of damp hair pasted to her flushed and sweaty cheeks. The pregnancy had made her mother's eyes sink into her cheeks, but still how resplendent she was in her new silk!

Across the courtyard aunt Meenakshi watched the festivities from behind the window-bars of the women's room. This was where the women in the family gave birth and also where they sat out the three days of their monthly seclusion, a room of pollution. Meenakshi had cut her own hair after her husband died. She had taken a sickle to her hair one day and chopped it off in clumps. She was only fifteen at the time, five years younger than her sister

Janaki. Meenakshi's in-laws wrote that she was becoming obstinate, hiding in corners with a slate and charcoal and pretending to write. This was trouble they did not need, *please come and get your sister.* So Janaki and Natesan had fetched Meenakshi back to the only home she knew. Sowmya could not remember now when the barber started coming every other month to shave her aunt's head clean.

Sowmya stroked the gold bangles Meenakshi had given her as wedding presents. These were what was left of her own dowry. They glowed among the glass bangles that were stacked on Sowmya's wrists. A strange feeling of shame and biting sorrow tightened her throat. She looked up at Meenakshi smiling at her from the women's room, carefully hiding herself so bad luck would not taint Sowmya. She smiled back at her aunt.

For the next three days Sowmya sat next to Ramki every morning, while he fed the sacred fire with melted butter and his chanting. Afterwards she played hopscotch and hide-and-seek with her cousins who numbered in the dozen. Small concerts were arranged for the pleasure of the guests after dinner. On the final night, a troupe from Melattur arrived to stage a musical drama in the terrace. The all male troupe was dressed in brightly colored garments and jewelry, their faces beautifully made up. By the flickering light of the oil soaked flambeaus, they mesmerized the audience with their dramatization of *The Sulking of Satyabhama.* Sowmya watched them dance and mime the story of Krishna, the dark-skinned god, charming the milkmaids and getting chided by his wife, Satyabhama. In between the verses the dancers would tap out rhythmic patterns to the beat of the drum. Sowmya craned her neck to see better their nimble movements and the patterns their feet made. Later, much later, when recalled the festivities of her wedding she would remember these dancers.

With the three tight knots that Ramki tied in a yellow string necklace, Sowmya became his wife. He kneeled in front of her, lifted her middle toe and slipped on the silver toe-rings. She looked down at his naked young shoulders revealed by the sliding garlands, gleaming as though oiled. When Ramki straightened he stood barely two inches taller than Sowmya. From this day onwards she would use only the formal form of address when she spoke to him. This thought and the downy moustache growing on Ramki's face made her want to tease him. She grinned. Ramki broke into a smile and then quickly composed his face into a serious frown.

Later that night the wedding party arrived at the temple for a propitiation ceremony for the deity. At the end of the offerings, just before they returned home, a devadasi appeared for the final Offering of the Lamps. Sowmya had grown sleepy by this time but was struck by the woman who was about the same age as her mother, but from a different world. Her spine straight, chin up, the woman walked tall as she went past them. Her long braid, which she had trimmed with tassels decorated with flowers, swung to and fro across her hips in a way her mother would have never allowed. Musicians accompanied her. She sang a prayer, crouched down on her knees to touch the floor and then her eyelids. Her feet together and toes angled in opposite directions, on slightly bended knees, the woman began to dance to the sprightly beat of the mridangam. With combinations of steps where she struck her heels on the floor, flexed and crossed them, she moved in intricate patterns, tapping the ground with such lithe grace that it seemed effortless. Her arms formed angles, her fingers gestured, she moved her shoulders and neck. Sowmya stood up, ignoring people tugging at her skirt to make her sit down. Finally the woman sang, bidding the Lord of the *Temple on the Hills* to retire for the night. She picked up the seven layer lamp that was lit with dozens of tiny flames and waved it in the air for the deity.

As Sowmya walked home that night with her cousins she stuck her arms out and imitated the steps and gestures the devadasi made. Immediately she felt Janaki's firm grip on her shoulder, stopping her. *"Behave!"*

But when she was alone in the bathing room Sowmya continued to try out the movements of the dancer and discovered an exquisite bubble that filled her chest when she danced.

The wedding canopy came down. Ramki departed with his family and entourage to Thanjavur to wait for Sowmya to come of age. After the ceremonial bath to mark her first bleeding, she would join Ramki at his parents' house and begin her life as his wife.

For a long time after Ramki's departure, Sowmya recalled the fun and festivities of the wedding days, remembered every detail of the myriad kinds of sweets, the colorful new saris, and the varieties of her new jewelry, the dancers and the dance. But the smoke in the wedding altar that had made her eyes smart seemed to have also obliterated part of her memory because, try as she might, she found she could not recall her husband's face. Yet, the recall of the brown of Ramki's arm, and the firmness of his clasp as he led her around the fire, would suddenly overwhelm her with its clarity. A small pocket of air would expand right between her ribs. She would gaze down at the toe-rings that shone with new polish and wonder if this was conjugal bliss.

Six months after the wedding, Ramki came to Ponmalar with his father, Hariharan. There was a revenue dispute that needed to be settled. They sat with Sowmya's father on the front porch and strategized ways to approach the British officer over this matter.

In a small alcove below the staircase in the front hall, Sowmya was dressing her two wooden dolls in red velvet. She placed them in the horse cart. Her cousin Niru, who was visiting, brought out the English doll and her porcelain tea set from Calcutta. The two girls planned the dolls' wedding.

Words such as *Swaraj* and *Simon Commission* reached them through the window above Sowmya's head. A woman called Parvati Devi was charged with inciting riots over the Commission's arrival and took her baby with her to jail. Ramki's response to her father made Sowmya pause. His voice was full of sweetness and manliness. Earlier, at dawn, the three men had performed their morning prayers in the courtyard. Holding the tips of their right fingers to the nose, eyes closed, the men sat erect and recited the *Gayatri Mantra*. When Sowmya brought the water for their ceremonial offering, she was struck by the handsome shape Ramki's arms and shoulders made. The bright white line of his sacred threads that angled down from left to right across his sand colored chest aroused a giddy curiosity in her.

From the street the vegetable vendor called: *Fresh and tender greens, amma!*

Sowmya walked over and stood in the dim corridor that connected to the front porch and peered into the street. Dust swirled in a column of sunlight that angled in and fell in a rectangle on the floor. In that glare of bright morning light a man's left foot dangled. From the way he jiggled it and the rosy color of his young toenails, she knew it was her husband's. It was not quite clear to her yet as to how she was supposed to relate to him, and it remained an unresolved mystery when, later that afternoon, young Ramki died.

chapter I 1932

The priest who officiated the *amavasya* ceremony was new. He was young and zealous. He looked askance at Sowmya when she brought in the flowers and inquired pointedly, "How old is the child?"

Janaki turned to see whom he was referring to. Her eyes filled with dismay when they alighted on Sowmya. She signaled to Sowmya, *Leave!* Sowmya had become accustomed to being vanished, to be disappeared. She stepped into the women's room.

A little later when Janaki paid him off and the priest left he must have stopped at the front porch to talk to Natesan because suddenly the voices from there grew sharp, heated.

Janaki rushed out to the front porch where the two men were talking. Sowmya followed. The priest was saying something about the sacramental offering for the ceremony.

"Soiled," he said, by the widow's touch. Now had she only observed the vows, observed the pollution and purity laws, this desecration would never have occurred.

"A Brahmin widow's karma is to take her vows. Our elders were not fools," the priest said. "These laws that they set down are not insignificant that can simply be ignored. The girl is not a child anymore to be sin free. She is *fifteen!*" Natesan should arrange to have Sowmya's hair shorn as soon as possible, he said with certainty, and have her dress appropriately.

Natesan fixed his reading glasses that were sliding down on his nose, and with a flick of his wrist straightened the morning newspaper and raised it over his face.

The man was not deterred by this dismissal. "You are the elder, there is nothing I need to tell you," he said to the newspaper.

Janaki left her space at the window in a rush. Sowmya pressed closer to the window.

"Why would she enter the kitchen and touch the food for the sacrament?" Janaki charged at the man, diamonds glinting on her flaring nostrils. "Are we such barbarians?" She pressed on, her righteousness silencing the man who appeared to visibly diminish in size in front of her mother. "We have no propriety? My sister Meenakshi and me, do we look to you like cripples unable to do the necessary work? *She* does not touch the offering," she said and dropped a ripe mango, golden and sweet like a bribe, into the priest's hand. "From our own tree, please take," she said.

The young priest looked at the fruit in his hand, rolled it as if to weigh it. His long abundant inky hair was pulled back into a knot and half his face was covered in beard. Until his pregnant wife delivered he would not shave. Without glancing at Janaki he placed the fruit at the stoop. His eyes met Sowmya's watching from the window.

He straightened the cloth shawl covering his chest and left without bidding goodbye.

But after the man left, and after Sowmya had swept up the wilted flowers and leaves from the central courtyard, and cleared the burnt cinders from the sacramental fire, Janaki's face remained grim. It seemed as though the temple elephant was trampling the courtyard and nobody knew how to deal with it. Sowmya was the culprit who had let him in.

Later, as Sowmya cut vegetables and helped aunt Meenakshi prepare the evening meal, her father, her dear brave father, rested on the canvas easy-chair in the courtyard. Janaki sat close by, sari draped over the twins as they fell asleep on her lap. She spoke softly, barely a murmur. Sowmya leaned out the kitchen doorway slightly but could not hear her. But in the quietness of the descending night Natesan had knitted his hands together, and with his head bent over them, listened. Seeing her parents confer so quietly intrigued Sowmya, and she knew in the hollow of her belly that this was a conversation she dare not interrupt.

"What's your mother saying?" Meenakshi asked softly.

Meenakshi was leaning over the stove roasting eggplants, holding them by the stem over the coals, turning them around deftly. The sari she draped over her shaven head had slipped down and sweat glistened on her smooth bare skin. Sowmya imagined the steel crescent that the coconut man used to shave the green husk, leaving a thin film of the pale and moist coconut shell, slicing through her aunt's hair, *chisk, chisk*. The barber had come that morning very early, slipping in by the back door with his box of tools, and drawn a pail of water from the well, rinsed his tools and set them out to dry at the rim of the well. When Sowmya went there to brush her teeth in the morning, she looked at the tools, at the waiting man, and her throat had seized with aversion and horror.

Sowmya swiped her sweaty brow with her forearm. "Nothing, aunty."

The next morning Janaki came in where Sowmya slept and spread a sheet on the floor. She removed from the almirah all of Sowmya's silk skirts, all the wedding saris, the sage and aqua blue with the temple border, the lotus colored one with the bottle green border, the crimson with the black checkered border—every single one of them she tossed to the sheet on the floor.

Sowmya had not been allowed to wear these saris after Ramki's funeral, but they had remained there all this time, periodically aired out, refolded with neem leaves between the layers and put back on the shelves.

Sowmya grabbed the tumbling saris that swirled like water on their way down, gathered them up to her chest. "No, no, no! Amma, please, *please!*" The saris slipped out of her hands as she tried to gather more. "Please, what are you doing?" She fell on them, pressing her angry tears to the colors, the gold, the russets, the blues. "Why must you take these from me? I look better in them than you! Why are you so *jealous?*"

Janaki stopped in mid action, looked at her speechless.

Immediately Sowmya wished she could take back the words but a trap-door was closing over her head, and if she could somehow get those saris back from her mother everything would be all right between them, back to the old times when her days had clarity and made sense. She reached up and pulled the sari from Janaki's hand. It was the sacred blue, the color of Lord Rama, the very sari that she had worn the day Ramki had arrived at Ponmalar with his father.

Janaki had helped her dress that morning, pleating and tucking the folds, and brought the end drape around her hips and tucked one corner neat and tight at the waist. Sowmya had served the morning meal to the guests, the rustle of the crimson border brushing at her feet, and later played dolls with Niru dressed in it. She had begged Janaki to let her keep the sari on for the rest of the day, and was still feeling like a princess when they brought Ramki's body home from the river bank and laid him in the courtyard.

His face was bruised and bloated beyond recognition. The long ebony hair was tangled with twigs and sand. What possessed him to go for a swim in the river in the middle of the afternoon? Swollen with monsoon rains, the river was treacherous in July. The banks were particularly rocky where it flowed near Ponmalar. He was struck unconscious by a blow to the head and was carried away by the currents. Villagers had found him floating face down several yards from the bathing ghats.

Fate, the men muttered as they stood with their arms folded after giving the to Sowmya's family. *Who can bargain with fate?*

They looked at Sowmya in her blue silk. The musings and murmurs quietened and came to rest on her like flies. Later still, the new sari splashed with water, she helped wash Ramki's poor body and prepare it for the cremation.

Sowmya looked down at the sari which was in a tight twist in her hand.

Meenakshi appeared at the door. She had pulled the drape of her sari, which appeared to be the color of mud, over her head tightly to cover its nakedness.

"Please, Amma!" Sowmya whispered fiercely, feeling her aunt's presence at her back. "Don't take them away. They are mine, aren't they?"

Sowmya turned and looked up at her aunt who had locked eyes with her sister. Clutching the blue sari Sowmya got up on her knees and wound her arms tightly around Meenakshi's hips.

Janaki abruptly turned around and left the room. It was then, in that flash of movement when her mother's shoulder vanished from her sight, that Sowmya knew all was lost. Still she quickly folded up the saris, those bright shining objects that were her talisman, and laid them all back one by one on the top most shelves. Only when she was all done did she turn around, and saw Meenakshi watching her without saying a word. Meenakshi reached out and touched Sowmya's cheek, brought up the thin gold necklace that was hidden among the folds of her sari out and around her neck and fixed it so the pendent rested at Sowmya's throat. She patted it gently, saying nothing.

Next morning when Sowmya opened her almirah she felt as though the door had slammed into her face. All the colors had been replaced with pale cotton saris.

●   ●   ●

"New?"

Sowmya tightly twisted the end of her voile sari around her finger and stood at the door to the women's room. Her mother was dressing. It had been two weeks since the battle over the saris.

"Amma, is it a new sari?"

Janaki's fingers rapidly pleated the luminescent silk, its two-toned color that of the golden beetle. She tucked the pleats against her waist, which was now expanding with another pregnancy.

Sowmya's fingers twitched to tear the sari off her mother and wear it herself, feel the swish of the new silk glide over her arms. She wanted the garland of jasmine that circled around her mother's braid and to pin it up her own hair, line her eyes to brilliance with kohl as her mother had done, retrieve all of these to herself.

"Where are you going?"

Sowmya asked knowing fully well that along with Natesan and the twins, Janaki was getting ready to attend a wedding and a feast. There were never any invitations to festivities for Meenakshi or Sowmya. Young and widowed, denied the full glory of womanhood, they would naturally be full of envy and malevolence that would turn every festivity into charcoal. No, there were no invitations for them and their attendance was never required at any happy event.

"Sowmya, listen. Look at me Sowmya, are you listening? Take those two little donkeys, bathe them and get them dressed, will you? They have been playing in the dirt outside all morning, and look at them. All caked with it."

"When did you get this? I haven't seen it before."

"Sowmya, go *now*." Her mother's wide eyes pleaded. Sowmya looked into them without mercy. Finally Janaki rustled out of the room past her.

Later, after she had bathed the twins and dressed them for the outing, Sowmya passed by the prayer room. Janaki was seated on the floor, her eyes closed, her lips moving in recitation. Sowmya released Jaya and Uma who were squirming, and the children ran outside to resume their play.

The prayer space was lit by the flickering glow of the oil-lamp. Taking central place in the altar was the celebration of the Cosmic Couple's wedding: Cast in bell metal, Shiva and Parvathi shone in their timeless embrace, their ancient smiles lit by lamplight. In front of them was a small stone icon of Ganapathi, Sowmya's favorite elephant-headed and pot-bellied deity, the Vanquisher of Sorrows, the Lover of Sweet-dumplings.

Sowmya sat down by her mother on the floor, pressing her knees into Janaki's soft, warm side. A small trickle of perspiration ran down the side of Janaki's face.

Sowmya stared unblinkingly at the flickering flame. How large and uncouth her limbs had become. Her interior had taken fearful shapes beyond her control, and its heat had coarsened her skin with pimples. She knew the cure for this condition. *Conjugal bliss.* She had lost so thoughtlessly the one bequeathed to her. Widowhood, like a deformity, was forever. No man would marry such a bearer of misfortune. Not for her the colors and the fragrance. Bit by tiny bit, day by day, her mother leached, sieved, removed all the things that would make her desire or be desired, forcing on her the life of a nun, a *sanyasin.* Be good now, better luck next life.

In front of the altar was a basket with a few blossoms remaining at the bottom. Wilted, rejected blossoms, unsuitable to be woven into the garland that was decorating the altar. Sowmya picked up a flower and tossed it towards the altar.

"Sowmya!"

She tore the petals off an oleander and tossed.

"Stop that. Please!"

Janaki's voice was hoarse, as though she had been crying.

Sowmya grabbed the basket and threw the contents into the altar. The flame flickered wildly. A sharp intake of breath from Janaki. A stinging slap came flying from her hand. In the flickering shadows her mother's face was unrecognizable. It could have been a stranger's.

Sowmya fled from the room, clutching her cheek.

"Sowmya, come back here. *Sowmya!*"

Sowmya ran up the stairs to the terrace.

In the hot days of summer the room upstairs gradually gathered heat. It held it oppressively within its four walls, barely releasing it at night. No one came up here during this season unless necessary. Sowmya's cheek throbbed as if it would squirt blood if she touched it. The humidity made her eyes melt. She flung open the door to the terrace.

Across the sun-bleached terrace, against the cloudless sky, the temple tower rose like a small hill. The brightly painted yakshis, demons, gods and humans carved over the tower's four sides were visible even from where she stood. Two huge gilded wings, as if ready to take flight, topped its crown.

Sowmya tip-toed quickly across the hot terrace to the center where a wall on all four sides enclosed a rectangular opening. Leaning over it she looked into the central courtyard below. Her mother called towards the kitchen for Meenakshi.

She walked to the edge of the terrace where tree branches shaded a corner. Carefully she perched on the narrow parapet wall. She walked her fingers up the length of her braid, loosening it, feeling the shape of the muscle at the nape, the bones beneath the skin. If she pressed them very hard, would they break?

On the eleventh day of Ramki's funeral her head would have been shaved clean, just as Meenakshi's was done this morning. Before dawn the women had come to the house to get her up and to prepare her. But when the barber arrived Natesan had turned him away at the door. Amidst loud murmurs of protests he had refused to let anyone touch Sowmya's hair. "A child, only a child," he had cried, his face crumpled into the towel he pressed to it.

Sowmya had seen her father lift a hundred pound bag of rice onto his shoulders. No one could match his swift footwork at stick fight competitions, he would tell Sowmya. Although she had never seen this, she believed it to be true. She could see him as a youth swiveling the long bamboo pole in his hands, the arc he would draw on the sky. He was like a banyan tree to the women in the house, a shelter forever and ever. It had frightened her to see him cry, and she had started to weep as well. After a few moments Natesan had folded his palms in prayer. "Please go," he told the people, their neighbors and family. "There is plenty of evil in this world. Sowmya is not the cause."

But another transformation had come over her father that was more gradual. He began to draw his grief close around his shoulders, sinking into himself. And the day Sowmya's body had declared itself with blood he retreated even further from her. Had Ramki's unnatural death not occurred, Sowmya would have been feted and sent off to her husband's home with great joy and celebration. From that day forward she belonged to them and he would have discharged his duty as her father. But now a young single woman in his charge was like holding live coal on the palm of his hand. The things expected of him and expected of Sowmya made her father furious and yet helpless. As the head of a house full of women, disobedience from any one of them became unendurable for him. His face, always open and kind, closed like a fist with deep frown lines.

Sowmya pressed her hands into her eyes until she saw light sparks. Every inch of her skin itched as though it had ruptured and sprouted wings that flapped uselessly. She imagined splitting that horizon and flying beyond and over where there were towns and cities that lay in every direction from Ponmalar, and hover like a bird over the sea that lay to the east.

She had once asked Meenakshi why she allowed it, why could she just not refuse to get her head shaved?

"Nobody is forcing me to do this, I *want* this for myself. This way everybody knows what is what, there are no suspicions and no fear. It gives me freedom to do what I please, come and go as I please."

Meenakshi was resting in the afternoon after all her chores were done, her head on a small wooden platform, not caring that her sari had slipped from her head, deeply absorbed in reading the three newspapers that she brought from the market daily. Later in the afternoon she would spin the raw cotton that the Congress people brought for her, which when spun into skeins, she would take to the *khadi* depot. She indeed had freedom to go about in the streets, more so than what Sowmya had. It had become quite impossible for Sowmya to leave the house with the heavy censure hanging over the Natesan household.

Meenakshi then dropped what she was reading and looked at Sowmya for a full minute. She sat up and touched her face. "But this is not for you, my sweet," she had said. "Times are different now, and you must never submit to this. Never."

This was something Sowmya had never heard her mother say. Meenakshi had also arranged, with Natesan's approval, for a relative from her late husband's side, young man named Mani, to come tutor Sowmya. Mani was a student at St. Joseph's College in Tiruchi and he came only sporadically, without notice. He left as suddenly, referring to meetings that were a mystery to her, with people that she did not know. She would wish then that she could, by magic, slip into his skin and go into that world with the easy abandon that he displayed. She envied him for the simplicity and ease of the trousers that he wore, the stories that he held within his slight frame and thin limbs, for the way he seemed possessed with some kind of hope. Names of towns and cities that he talked about opened up like a pod full of seeds inside her after he left and made her want to sprout wings and fly away.

Sowmya plucked a leaf off the branch that hung low over the parapet and dropped it. It slowly spiraled down where two women stood at the gate. They wore black hoods that covered their hair.

Natesan stood behind the gate, holding it slightly open, or maybe slightly closed.

"All the houses on this street, and the next," Natesan Aiyar pointed over his shoulder, "we are *all* Brahmins here, this is the *agraharam*. You can try the quarter on the east side, or over there, outside the village. But here, here no one will let you inside. We have no use for these," he said looking at a pamphlet that they must have given him. "We are simple people, we have our own way of doing things." He joined his palms together, *goodbye*.

The women's black shoes made a rasping noise as they walked away from the gate. Their white cotton saris barely covered their ankles. The black hoods and trains slowly became small. The pamphlets her father clutched in his hands behind him flicked nervously as he watched the receding figures. How thin had her father's shoulders become.

"Child," he said later when he saw Sowmya downstairs. "Get me some buttermilk, will you?"

She handed him the glass of buttermilk, wanting to touch his hand in mutual reassurance, and yet frightened by the way he avoided her touch. It was then that she knew that his hands were slowly getting slippery, withdrawing from her hold. Or was it that *her* hands had engorged and bloated and become too cumbersome to hold? In any case they were all getting lost a little bit every day and there was no rescue. None.

The full weight of what Natesan carried on those shoulders came to her on the following day when the letter arrived from Ramki's parents.

chapter 2

It was an overnight journey to Thanjavur from Tiruchi. Ponmalar lay another hour away from the city. At the station Mani hired a cart pulled by two mangy bullocks.

The river was the saving grace for this excruciatingly slow trip. The cart track ran along the Kaveri, which turned the delta's fields to emerald lakes that glittered in the morning sun while it meandered its way towards the Bay of Bengal. Mud banks that divided the paddy fields were planted with palm trees. The trees' slow dance against the blue sky made time seem meaningless. There was no use fretting. The cart would get there when it did, provided the wheels didn't get stuck in some ditch. He stopped the cart man from prodding the pathetic animals and resigned himself to the man's hands and the bullocks' will. The temperature was rising rapidly.

It was mid-day when he paid off the man at the village market. There was the smell of hay and green things wilting in the heat. He stopped at the temple flower shop and picked up a couple of yards of the rose-tipped jasmine.

Even before he turned the corner at the Ganapathi temple, he trained his vision at the second floor terrace of the Natesans' house. Rain or shine the girl, Sowmya, waited there. He touched the bag slung on his shoulder, thinking of the books he was carrying for her. By unspoken agreement between him and his cousin's widow, Meenakshi, he had become the girl's tutor.

He had arrived at Ponmalar for the first time four years ago, in July of 1928. His late cousin's pension from the South India Railway was arriving at his uncle's address. Mani decided to get the signature of this cousin's widow, Meenakshi, so the funds would transfer to her here, where she was living with her sister.

He found the family in the midst of mourning the untimely death of a young man, Natesan's son-in-law. It was the afternoon of the tenth day of mourning. What that meant made him queasy. He could not very well turn and go back, so he stayed the night in that sad house. When dawn broke a silent band of widows arrived to strip the terrified girl of the wedding pendants from her necklace, break her glass bangles, wipe the red kumkum off her brow, and shave her head. He knew the routine having observed his own mother's torment at his father's death. It was he, at the age of ten, who had to recover the sacred yellow thread from his mother's neck and drop it in the pail of water, and he did so unable to look at her face or meet her eyes while performing the dreadful act. She died a few years later and he stopped performing altogether any rites associated with being a Brahmin. A wail broke through the muffled noises from inside, a struggle. He lay on his mat in the outside porch, welling with helpless anger. Finally he got his things together and left for the train station.

Only on a later visit did Mani learn how Sowmya's father, Natesan, had resisted the pressure mounted by the agraharam, the closeted community of Brahmins, to make Sowmya observe the final widow's vow——get her head shaved clean. This was the last step to complete the pretense that the widow was now shorn of any connection to her body and would live in the purity of her mind, like a nun. The ghastly truth was Natesan would never be able to find a decent Brahmin to marry his widowed daughter within his community or outside, since she was now forever tainted by her own misfortune. Had she been properly blessed her husband would have had a long life and survived her. The solution for this intolerable situation was to force sexual abstinence on a girl who had not even fully matured, and what better way than deny that she had a body? And yet Natesan had firmly refused to allow this final abomination and this filled Mani with hope. He looked upon Natesan as a comrade even if they were not in the battle in quite the same way.

After that he came to visit his cousin's widow as often as he could, and over these years he had not only become a tutor for Sowmya, but also made himself a place among Natesan's family. Natesan took a vicarious interest in Mani's work, and so he always had some piece of news, some gossip, to give the older man. He ran small and big errands for the women. He carried Sowmya's twin sisters around when the little ones needed calming. Mani knew that Natesan saw him as a son he did not have. An orphan himself who grew up as his uncle's ward, he quite willingly took on the mantle of the son.

The entire family drew to Mani eagerly to hear the stories he carried to this small village here on the river bank which stood unperturbed (and therefore also unaware) by all that was happening in the rest of the country. He told them about the ambushes and the killings in Bengal, in the Punjab, about the Indian policemen who opened fire on a crowd of Indians. His throat tingling, he told them of women under the gun and barred from the exit, who then threw their babies into the well before following them into it in desperation; of meetings in the Madras beach at night, where a thousand voices rose in a new anthem that frightened the British Government. He showed them a photograph some reporter had taken, which was never published but was only passed from hand to hand like this. An open *maidan* near the Marina beach. The crack of the sturdy stick on skull. Men and women step up clutching their white Congress caps as the one before them fall bleeding, who are then carried away by volunteers who attend to their wounds. The march to the sea at Vedaranyam in disobedience of the British law against making salt, where three hundred satyagrahis were beaten and arrested.

As he expected, Sowmya was leaning over the parapet wall when he turned the corner. He gave no signal of acknowledgment, barely even looking up, as he walked towards the house. The image of the skinny girl in the pale sari never failed to raise a feeling like that of a welt in his throat, but it also made his heart thud in a disturbing way. So this cultivated indifference was essential to make his coming and going possible under her mother Janaki's watchful gaze. It would not do if Sowmya were to develop some kind of improper affection for him. Besides it was also part of the way he had planned his own life. This left no space for bonds he could not afford. Like a wife, for instance. He had already been in jail twice, although only for a few days at a time. He was prepared for anything at any time.

Natesan had added a second story to the house and so it stood a little taller than the rest on the street, providing a nice look-out from the corner of the terrace. From where he stood outside the small gate, he could look right through the tunnel of dark corridor to the inner courtyard of the house, a brightly lit rectangle of space that smelled green, of moss.

Natesan stood at the gate when he reached the house, as though he was expecting him. He was dressed in a fine zari-bordered veshti and a white shirt, ready to go somewhere.

"*Oho ho*! Mani master! Come in, come in. What's new, what's all the news?"

"Hello, Uncle!" Mani stopped to take his slippers off at the gate. "They have banned all marches. College newspaper has been shut down, because we filled whole pages with nothing but arrests. Meetings are announced on pavements with chalk because flyers are banned." He told

Natesan about the violent shape the resistance to the Simon Commission was taking in the north.

But he did not tell him of the two schoolgirls sentenced to life for shooting a British officer. They were sisters of a man he had met at a work-camp once. This man was now in hiding, and it was better not to know his location.

"They are breaking heads in Tiruppur too," Natesan said and turned when he heard footsteps behind him. Janaki. "Praksam's in jail."

Janaki sparkled in her new sari. She held the squirming twins, three year old Jaya and Uma, by their shoulders. The Natesans were leaving to attend a wedding and a feast, which meant he would get some time with Sowmya and Meenakshi alone.

With a whoop Jaya pulled free and ran towards Mani. He scooped the child up and onto his shoulder where she perched happily. Uma stood back shyly peering from behind her mother's sari folds.

Janaki smiled and nodded a greeting at him. He carefully removed the packet of the flower garland from his shirt pocket. Janaki shot a wary look at him. Bringing flowers into a house with two young widows banned from any adornments was risky. Too late.

"Flowers, aunty," he said.

She made no movement towards accepting it. He waited. Suddenly from behind him Sowmya stepped up and reached for it.

"Meena! Come here and take the flowers inside!" Janaki called to her sister.

"I'm coming, coming! Oho ho, Mani! When did you—" Meenakshi looked at the flowers in Sowmya's hands. "You all leave, it's getting late. Have a good time," Meenakshi said. "Give my inquiries to Savithri. What a relief it must be for her now, getting a wedding necklace around that girl of her's finally, chubby and all—"

Janaki shoved Uma towards the waiting cart. Mani plopped Jaya next to the cart man. He slapped the bullock on its flanks. "Get going, brother," he told the man, and waved as the cart moved away.

Inside, he crossed the courtyard to the corner, tipped the large brass urn there and splashed some water over his face and feet, washing them.

When he wiped his face with a handkerchief and turned, Sowmya was next to Meenakshi on the swing that hung in the wide gallery that served multiple purposes. She was pushing the swing with her feet, at a good clip. The two women were flying through the air. The forbidden flowers were squashed and jammed now into Sowmya's dark braid. Stars in the night sky.

Mani had come with a mission. It had taken shape after a conversation with his friend Balakrishnan when Mani had gone to pick up the book for Sowmya, the advanced English reader. Balakrishnan was on the staff at the mission school and would sneak these books to him from their reserve.

Along with a dozen other Brahmins, single and married, Balakrishnan had recently been converted by the Anglican Church. This had shocked Mani at first. Was it just naivety or loneliness that led them to this? Like most people he too had imagined that conversion required eating meat and drinking wine. Instead, he found his friend living a life in a colony of Brahmin converts observing every purity and pollution law of his Brahmin upbringing. The mission was going to send Balakrishnan as superintendent of their schools in Jaffna. The condition was that he arrived with a wife, as a family man. With his conversion to Christianity the usual network of family connections through which a bride materialized had vanished for his friend.

"What about that girl—the one you tutor?" Balakrishnan asked him, handing over the book.

Mani was struck speechless. Although there were regular orations and scholarly scolding everywhere about the need for social reform and widow-remarriage, he personally did not know a single person who had got his widowed daughter, a sister, or a cousin, remarried. Sowmya was getting on to fifteen.

"Yes. Yes! Why not? I will. I'll talk to her father."

He knew that his proposal would be received, if not with outright derision, with polite reserve and silence. And now the Natesans had gone, and would not return until late at night. Maybe tomorrow when everyone was relaxed after the morning coffee he would approach Natesan. When for just a moment it occurred to him to think of what Sowmya's reaction would be, the thought quickly evaporated. How could anything be worse then rotting slowly in a place like this?

Mani drew water from a clay pot and drank. *They can all turn their back on Sowmya, things can happen in a flash.* From where it came he didn't know, but the thought stung him. There was no time to lose.

"My friend, he's leaving soon. Going to Ceylon," he said.

"Ceylon?" The women said in unison.

"I will have to figure out another way to get you your books."

He pulled out the reader and an exercise notebook from his bag, laid them on the swing next to Sowmya. .She broke the speed, brought the swing to a halt, and picked up the book.

The book was part of a series. The cover had three European children singing, their mouths opened in Os. Titled *Songs the Letters Sing.* Inside were colorful pictures of children picking apples.

Sowmya ran a finger beneath the words, forming them on her lips.

Mani picked up the notebook. "Bharathi's poems. Bharathi had fled to the French Pondichery when he wrote these. I have copied them down for you. They came to arrest him just a few minutes after he fled."

"For writing poetry?"

"Yes, that too. They charged him with seditious activities. They closed down his magazine office in Triplicane."

She opened the notebook. He had sat in the fading evening light in his room at the hostel and carefully shaped the Tamil letters around the poet's lament, *When will freedom come, when will this thirst quench?*

"Bharati's favorite poet was an Englishman named Shelley," he told her. He had written down on a page one of Shelly's poems that he had memorized.

Sowmya traced each word as he read them out to her. *The desire of the moth for the star.*

"What does your hostel look like?" Sowmya asked in the evening while Meenakshi poured batter onto a griddle, making *dosai* for Mani. Mani sat crosslegged with them on the kitchen floor, Sowmya next to him.

"It's a building. I have a room, a cot, table and chair. I share it with another student. There is a canteen where we eat."

"Whom do you share your room with?"

"His name is Gopal, we have known each other for a long time, from the time we were little."

"Then who is Balakrishnan?"

Mani dipped a piece of dosai in chutney. This was an unexpected opening. "He . . . he works at the mission school."

He waited for Sowmya to ask some more.

"How do you get there?" she said.

"What?"

"To Ceylon."

"A boat, you have to cross the ocean in a boat."

"*Aiyo!* Across the ocean in a boat?" Her eyes widened.

"It's a big boat. People do it all the time. Yes, it is far and can be lonesome. He's looking for a woman to marry, so he can take his wife with him."

He panicked that the Natesans may be returning and there may not be another suitable moment. He had to set forth boldly.

"Doesn't he have a family?" Meenakshi turned the pancake on the griddle and spooned some oil over it.

"Yes he does. Comes from a village near Madurai. His father is the head priest at the temple. But who is going to give their daughter to a Christian?"

"Christian?" Meenakshi placed the spatula down and looked at him. "He became a *Christian?*"

The sound of a cart that had stopped at the door. Mani heard voices in the street.

"He was asking about Sowmya. He wants to get married, and he is willing . . "

He could not see Sowmya but could feel her stiffen. Meenakshi placed the pancake on a plate and pushed it towards him, giving him a quick glance.

"What do you think Uncle will say?"

Meenakshi stirred the batter. She turned and glanced at Sowmya. "What do you think anyone will say? In a few years, he will have to get Jaya and Uma married. It's easy for you to talk, Mani. Be careful of what you say. Don't cause trouble with your ideas. "

"So? Sacrifice one life for two."

Mani knew what Meenakshi meant. How could Natesan afford to risk alienating the same community from which he would seek future grooms for Jaya and Uma? Getting a widowed daughter remarried would be scandelous enough, but to a man who has converted? That would be even worse than marrying out of caste; that would be like marrying an outcaste. It was hopeless, he knew, but still worth an attempt. Nothing to lose. He would wait for an opportune moment. Tomorrow.

"You just teach her to read and write. A woman has opened a school in Madras, to train women to become teachers. Marriage is not everything." Meenakshi poured the batter on to the griddle and drew the ladle over it, spreading it thinner and thinner. Small bubbles covered the pancake.

After dinner Mani left to meet a friend and it was late when he returned to the Natesans house. He expected everyone to have retired but the lights were on and the front door was wide open into the night, which was highly unusual.

He found the three women sitting in the inner courtyard. No sign of Natesan. The kitchen, which Meenakshi would have by now washed out, and stacked the pots and pans gleaming on the kitchen shelves, was in disarray. The charred remains of the firewood in the stove remained untouched.

Meenakshi handed Mani a telegram that had arrived earlier. "From Thanjavur," she said.

Sowmya's in-laws lived in Thanjavur.

"Letter is from Hariharan's wife, Kamala. They want Sowmya to come and help for a while. She has fallen ill," Janaki summarized, "the mother."

Mani unfolded the letter.

"Mani, they want us to send Sowmya to help," she looked at him as though he would have a solution for them. "How can we send her, Mani? Sowmya's father . . . he's so . . ."

Such a request in time of such need could not be refused, Natesan had insisted. When the women protested Natesan had become furious and walked out. The women were waiting. Nothing could be done until he returned and made the decision.

A half hour passed before Natesan returned to the court-yard. He looked disheveled in a way Mani has never seen him before. Something unpleasant was working in him. Mani braced himself.

"What has happened has happened," Natesan said. He spoke rapidly looking at no one in particularly and to all of them. "You can ask why, why, why, all day you can ask why, who knows the answer? Why should it be Sowmya's destiny to live with a bare face at such a tender age? Why should it be mine to live to see my daughter's life wasted like this, every day, every single day? Maybe it is my sin, your sin," glancing towards Janaki who buried her face in her sari. "Sowmya's karma!"

He looked directly at Sowmya now. His dark irises swam in liquid fear one moment and fury the next. "If they want your help they have a right to ask, we have an obligation. Don't disobey me, Sowmya!"

Disobey? Would this girl ever disobey her father? How did she come to be so wicked? Mani watched Natesan become someone he did not recognize, like a cornered animal.

"You stay for the ceremony," Natesan said his voice softer now. "Help out and return. Shaving the head and all that—there is no need for it, even Hariharan cannot—I will talk to him. There are ways of getting around all that, times are changing." He waved his hand vaguely, dismissing the thoughts. "This trip, this cannot be avoided, it is your duty."

"Duty? How long does the living atone for the dead?"

Natesan's face twisted with anger and shock as he whirled around at Mani.

"What makes you think you own her body and soul, to ship her off like this because *they* want her?" Mani pressed on.

Natesan pointed to the door. "Get out! You have no more business in this house."

"I will go, I will go!" Sowmya spoke for the first time. She put her hand on her father's chest. "Appa, I will go, please don't be angry. I'm not afraid. I will go and help."

"But Sowmya *can't*!" Janaki jumped up. "She can only—she's not—how can she? They are—that man Hariharan—Such terrific orthodoxy—How can Sowmya help in the kitchen? Won't they—"

"Appa, I will go. I will go, don't worry. I'm not afraid at all."

Mani looked at the girl. She would do as she said. She was beautiful and strong.

● ● ●

Mani picked up his bag and came outside. The cart summoned for him waited at the street, the cart-man's bee-di glowing in the dark. The bulls patiently swished their tails. A hurricane lamp hung at the side of the cart.

Mani threw his bag inside the cart and was about to get in when Meenakshi came out. She drew close, whispered something. He leaned closer.

"Do something, Mani, *do something for that girl,*" she hissed. "You *must.* Talk to your friend, that Christian. If she goes there . . . I am so afraid."

For a long time after Meenakshi left his uncle's house as a widow, Mani had remembered her with mixed-up feelings. He was twelve and boarding with his uncle to attend school. He heard but did not pay attention to the harsh scolding Meenakshi received from the other women in the house. Bits of memory would surface and rise in flashes years later as he went off to college: the young woman reading quietly in the dim light in the kitchen; the sounds of her weeping behind locked doors of the pantry, the ugly stripe of red blister on her arm one day. The cause of these burn marks would suddenly emerge like a revelation and he would stop whatever he was doing and freeze, aghast at the cruelty of the people he had lived with, and at his own mindless indifference to her misery. He had returned from school one day and saw her standing in the dark corridor, her head shorn in clumps. She had done it to herself. Soon after that Janaki had come with Natesan to take her sister home.

In the light of the cart's lamp Meenakshi's eyes were bright. Her thin white sari covered her smoothly shaved head. It was hard to believe she was only five years older than him, she looked older. He wanted to put his hand around her shoulders, tell her he would save her, save Sowmya, whatever meager means he had was all theirs. Instead he turned his back to her and then looked towards the house, his eyes stinging with anger at his own inability. Sowmya stood at the porch, holding a damp towel to her head.

"My address is on the notebook," he told Meenakshi as he climbed in. Even in the dark he saw the furious shine in her eyes. "I wrote it down before I left." He pointed his chin towards the porch. "Make sure she has that when she leaves. And give her some money." He took everything he had in his pocket and gave it to Meenakshi.

She tucked it all back into his pocket. "I will find something. You get something to eat and pay for the cart."

The cart driver threw away his beedi, prodded the bullocks with his stick. The animals' pale flanks shivered once. The bells jingled, and they set off. The hurricane lamp swung and soon the small house faded in the distance. The image of the two women at the stoop remained two pale ghosts.

chapter 3

The fortress-like walls at the Big Temple were painted with alternate stripes of white lime and red earth. Small sitting bulls were sculpted on its rim at regular intervals. In the wide-open space inside the temple gates was the *vimana*, the central pillar that towered to the height of seven palm trees stacked one on top of the other. One hundred and seven paragraphs, as directed by the king Rajaraja, were carved on the pillar. Sowmya read:

For my Lord dances here within an areola of thirty-one five tongued flames. Within the sound of his rattle He holds the world at balance.

The Nandi, a sitting bull carved out of single black rock, was housed in a stone temple. Tall as a building, its jet black surface shone as though oozing oil. Its huge eyes gazed across the length of the brown earth and blue sky that separated it from his Lord Pashupati, the Guardian of Animals.

In the inner sanctum of the tower the Deity had risen in a black vertical monolith rock from the earth. Women stood several rows deep on their side of the sanctum waiting for the showing of the lamps, and Sowmya joined them. The air was warm and fragrant with sandalwood, flowers, and the smoke of incense. The priest's voice was raised in adoration.

As the copper sun at a red dawn
Appear before us Oh Destroyer of Sorrows.
We see you and are blessed by this Beauty.

Decorated with three horizontal stripes of silver, a ruby in the center, and draped with garlands the sacred pillar was lit by the skylight above.

The bells sounded and the priest lifted the seven-layer lamp and waved it in a circle in front of the deity. A murmur of prayers went up around her. Sowmya took in the blessed sight, folded her hands in prayer. But when she started the familiar hymns they wouldn't come to her, and instead she was gripped by grief and despair and desire all converging in a tidal wave. She had not eaten anything since morning, and when she closed her eyes, the hall spun around her.

She opened her eyes and saw the young priest standing before her, the holy ash between his fingertips, swaying a bit as well. She extended her hand when her legs became steady again. He dropped the holy ash into her cupped palm and moved quickly down the line of waiting worshipers.

She came out and stood in the bright sunlight. She felt a little queasy, not only due to the heat and the gnawing of hunger, but at the consequence that awaited when she got home. Kamala, Ramki's mother, would be furious. Sowmya was sent to fetch the homeless widow, Ranga, to cook for the ceremony tomorrow. Ranga was old, tonsured, and could be allowed inside the kitchen safely, unlike Sowmya who was not properly purified, polluted beyond measure, and not fit for anything. Kamala had pointed all this out for her. "Your father, he thinks you're still a child. Letting you go on like this. *Sin it is!* For seven births he will pay!"

Sowmya thought of her father, paying over and over for his sin, because she had so carelessly lost Kamala's only son.

But when Sowmya reached the priest's house where Ranga slept at the front stoop for the night, they were preparing a funeral bier to carry the old woman out. The priest had found her dead in the early morning when he opened the front door. Shook up by the sight Sowmya had stood not knowing what to do next. When the early morning music of the nadaswaram came from the famous temple she had impulsively followed the sound there.

Sowmya walked towards the east corridor. Dancers in various poses covered the walls, their hand gestures and ornaments sculpted in vivid detail. A woman was shown from behind, as she twisted around, lifting one bejeweled foot off the floor. A woman leapt. A row of musicians here on one wall, and Sowmya looked closely at the mridangam, a flute, and a man playing the veena, a boy with tiny cymbals on his fingers. Any moment they could all come alive and fill this gallery with dance and music.

She turned the corner and walked past walls painted in colors of persian blue, coral, crimson, and green. Lord Shiva at Play. Here He is, kneeling down to the child Kumara, listening to the cosmic secret whispered to him. Here is Paravathi in her fearsome penance for Shiva's love. Shiva's fury scorching Kama, the god of desire, who is then resurrected by Parvati. Desire is Life. Here is the divine family, with Ganapathi, created out of her own skin and love by Paravathi.

At the end of the corridor a panel capped the exit archway. A mortal couple dressed in fine clothes and jewelry. The man was approaching the woman who had decorated her hair with garlands of flowers. He had a mustache that made him look happy and he was about to place a hand on the woman's shoulder. Did the woman smile in anticipation of the warmth and weight and size of his hand? *Say please. Please let me have a good husband. That is conjugal bliss.* She smelled Janaki's hands, her voice. Yearning for unkown things lost forever stabbed at her throat.

The afternoon service had ended and the main sanctum closed. It would reopen later in the evening. The courtyards had become vacant except for a few people, pilgrims from the villages. Gathering in small clusters they began to spread a sheet in the halls and galleries and opened their lunch carriers.

Sowmya too sat down to rest a bit on the open field shadowed by the temple towers. She knew Kamala would be waiting but she was also afraid to go home and face her.

The sky above the shrine was darkening with rain clouds. Sowmya leaned on her elbows, threw her head back. She was floating slightly above ground, weightless with possibilities. She was just one of the travelers who were around her, resting awhile in mid-journey to some place else far away. She wanted to open her mouth and say something loud to the sky above. The words filled her, but their sharp angles only stuck and pierced at her throat.

Three women, with lustrous hair edged with jasmine, walked toward her. They seemed like sisters, jostling each other, all with the same dusky cheeks rounded and shiny with laughter. Sowmya wanted to smile at them, fill her mouth with glee as well. But the women suddenly became quiet and passed her with their eyes averted from her bare face and pale sari, the marks of widowhood.

Sowmya buried her face in her knees. It was hard to believe that it had been only two days since she left her father's home in Ponmalar. The night before she left, it had sprinkled rain, and at dawn when she got into the cart with her in-laws who had arrived to fetch her, the sky was dark and overcast. Her father had stood in the mist with his arms across his chest. Her mother and aunt Meenakshi huddled together behind him. The twin girls, their eyes huge with tears, hung on to her arms, crying "Akka, take me with you!"

When the cart creaked forward her father had called out her name. He came up to the edge of the cart where she sat scrunched behind the hulking form of Kamala.

"Sowmya," he said and extended his hand.

Sowmya leaned across Kamala to touch him, but he stopped as suddenly, and the bullocks trotted forward and he kept receding, and Sowmya continued to hold her arm out until Kamala put it down with a touch. What was it that she saw in her father's eyes? Her mind circled and circled and came to rest without an answer. It seemed fear or regret at one time which was then replaced quickly by the fury she had seen arise at the very thought of her disobedience. Her thoughts made her anxious. If she were to run back home would he welcome her? Or would she be punished?

Sowmya held her head in her hands. She was afraid she might vomit.

A sprinkle of rain fell and she stood up with dismay, her heart aflutter. The crowd that had gathered in the courtyard had dispersed. How could she have become so lost? *So foolish!*

The sky opened up and poured as she ran. Outside the temple walls there were several shops selling flowers and garlands, sweets, beedis. The shop owners had let down burlap shields against the rain. The street was vacant; everyone had run for cover. Sowmya sought shelter beneath a large banyan tree, hoping for the force to ease a bit so she could hurry home. The rain swirled and undulated as it came down in sheets and she watched it with growing anxiety. She never planned to be so late. The rain had stirred up the earth and she smelled the fragrance of the first mingling of the two. The cool mist on her face was soothing and she waited for it to ease.

Somebody was smoking a beedi around her. Without turning she felt the man's movement behind her, the smell of the harsh tobacco, and she resolutely fixed her eyes on the rain, willing him to step back, hoping the rain would break so she could run home. The rain lashed on. The man pressed closer and she could smell his clothes, his breath, and suddenly he was brushing right against her. His hand slithered around her waist and slipped roughly inside her sari, advancing with insolence, and another hand closed around her breast. She let out a cry, broke free and ran into the rain. Her feet slipped and she skidded and hit the ground on her knees, her face getting splattered with mud. She heard someone shouting, maybe the man. She scrambled up and ran and ran without a glance backward, her heart thumping at her ribs, her eyes filled with tears of rage.

Kamala was at the vegetable cutter in the kitchen, slicing green plantains. How did she raise herself and come into the kitchen? She was bedridden when Sowmya left home only a few hours ago.

"Amma!"

Kamala's face was a hurricane.

"Where did you run off to? Who gave you permission? Prancing around the streets like a slut, *chee!*" She would have spit at her had she not been in the kitchen. She glared at her from head to toes. "Look at you, shoving everything out for the whole world to see!" Kamala's voice rumbled through her gritted teeth.

Sowmya looked down at herself. The mud-splattered sari clung heavily to her, and water streamed and pooled at her feet.

"Amma! I told you when I left—"

"For this long? *Three hours?*"

"I went to the temple—"

"Who gave you permission, who? I told you to go gallivanting? You will bring the whole village down on our heads! *Whore!*" Kamala shook her fist at her. "Your father has given you too much freedom. Wait till he hears about this. What shame! This will never do, we'll fix this, you need a lesson."

Sowmya pulled her sari tightly around her. This only made Kamala pick up the brass tumbler next to her and fling the water at Sowmya. Sowmya ducked. Water splashed into the hall outside the kitchen.

"What is wrong? Why are you shouting at me like this? I got caught in the rain—"

Kamala flung the tumbler. It caught Sowmya with perfect aim, its sharp rim cutting her just beneath the eyebrow.

On her way to the bathing room to change she paused at the cracked mirror that was hung on a nail on the wall. The gash at the left brow was weeping blood copiously. It mingled with the wet hair sticking to her face and dripped on her sari.

She looked down at the splotches of bright red and soft pink beginning to bloom on the pale sari at her chest. She thought of the rough and filthy hands that had groped her under the tree, the way she ducked when Kamala had flung the tumbler at her. You are nothing, *nothing.*

Sowmya grabbed the mirror off the nail and flung it blindly in the direction of the well in the terrace. It flew from her hand and slipped noiselessly straight down the dark tube. She ran in to the bathing room and threw up. Her stomach seemed to ride up her ribcage as she heaved several times but there was nothing much left to bring up. After a while she washed up and changed into dry clothes. What was Kamala going to tell her father? She couldn't gauge the extent of her crime but knew Natesan would be shamed. The vehemence of Kamala's fury proved its gravity.

Back in her room in the afternoon after her chores were done, Sowmya pulled her trunk out from under the wooden bench on which she slept. Rummaging through the saris her fingers found and closed over the contours of Mani's notebook. On the top right corner of the cover Mani had written his full name and his college address in Tiruchi.

Mani's friend Balakrishnan appeared to her with a face like that of Jesus in the pamphlets that the nuns would leave behind at her father's house in Ponmalar. He would have a sad and serious face, full of compassion, she was sure of it. He would take her as his wife to Ceylon, to the teardrop island that was so distant, a speck, its very name a foreign matter on her tongue. She shook her head, erasing any doubts.

The notebook smelled of glue and ink. *The desire of the moth for the star.*

Kamala walked into the room with a small tumbler of hot milk.

"Here drink this. Nobody wants you to get sick tomorrow with all this prancing around in the rain."

Sowmya drank it down, tasting something strange but too hungry to think about it.

• • •

The voices echoed as if from a well. When she tried to open her eyes they stuck together as if weights were placed on them.

Hands slipped under her armpits, raising her. Had her legs turned into sandbags? They would not move.

"What are you doing to me?" she wanted to say but what came out of her mouth was not any sound that she recognized. The words adhered to her tongue, which rolled thick and fat.

She felt dragged by her feet. Her struggling movements were met with firmly by the hands that gripped her limbs and squeezed painfully.

Kamala stood in one corner of the courtyard, her hands

clutching each other, as though she was massaging them. "Careful, careful! Don't hurt her!" she said.

Sowmya tried to signal to her but Kamala was not paying attention. *No. Please, don't, please don't.*

In the back terrace a sheet was spread. The barber, a thin man, waited holding a pair of scissors in one hand. *This was not supposed to happen to me, where is my father? He promised. Where is he?*

The barber's clothes smelled of sweat and tobacco when he crouched in front of her and raised his arm. His skinny fingers clutched her head gingerly. Screams came tearing out of her belly. She shook her head and immediately her head was held down roughly. Tears and mucous mixed with saliva in her mouth.

The barber muttered in helpless anguish, "Don't cry little mother, please hold still." Snip, snip, right below her earlobes.

She searched with rising horror for blood stains on her hair which fell like cut silk and piled up on the white sheet. It pulsed with the years of her mother's careful oiling and messages. She saw her mother's bosom in it, her aunt's knobby hands in it. The sound of razor scraping filled her brain and she smelled mango blossoms and blood.

"*Haieee!*" The barber cursed and jumped. Vomit went up her nose and she tasted blood. Someone splashed water on Sowmya's face.

When he was finished, the holds on her slackened. Someone poured a bucketful of water over her head. Sowmya slipped out of reach and ran across the courtyard, not caring that her sari was undone and trailing behind her. She ran into the store room, threw the bolt across the door.

● ● ●

When she awoke again a single bulb threw a weak orange light from a socket in the ceiling. The room smelled of pickles and jaggery, of earth and sprouts. She opened her eyes wide but it made no difference in her vision. Her head was tight and heavy with bruised colors, huge bulbous splotches of rotting purples and bloody reds. Something crawled up her leg. She jumped to shake off its prickly claws, its papery skin.

"Sowmya?" Kamala's muffled voice in the hall. "Open the door, let me talk to you."

She blocked that terrifying voice with her hands, folded her knees and pulled them tightly against her chest. She recalled now how she had slipped out of reach and run into this room after buckets of water were poured on her to cleanse the barber's polluted touch. *Please god I don't ever want to be pure again, ever.*

Sowmya leaned over and laid her head down on the cement floor, pressing her cheek against its cool hardness. She did not believe she could move, or breathe, or swallow, or blink ever again.

When she next awoke the moon was up at the window. She could no longer hold her urge to pee. She groped and felt her way to the door and heaved the bolt up.

"Sowmya, you are up. Please come here. Come here, let me talk to you. Things will be so much better now . . . have something to eat."

She ignored the whisper from the shape that was sitting up in the bed in the hall, and walked out into the corridor and out to the back terrace.

The air was sodden with mist and the smell of rotting garbage. Air swirled around her ears and neck. Her head felt light.

The bucket knocked around the wall a few times on its descent into the well, dropped into the water with a 'plunk' and went silent.

For a moment she stood there testing the slackness of the rope. She peered into the well. Nothing, not even the shimmer of water. This dark hole pulled at her like a vacuum, its force striking fearsomely at her chest. She was not going to be able to resist its power, it would pervade her being and blessedly erase all memory of grief.

A rooster crowed. The darkness liquefied, receded.

She pulled at the rope and drew water, bent down and poured it over her head. The razor cuts stung. Dipping the bucket into the well again and again she poured until the sting subsided, but could not cool herself even as she shivered. She pulled a towel from the line in the covered verandah, and then a sari, which was damp from the rain mist, and dressed.

"Heyyyiiia! Heyyy, heyyy! Ponni baby!"

She stood in the shadows. Murugan, the milkman's son,

was in the cowshed. He blew a sharp and long drawn out whistle. Cowbells jingled in response. In a few moments, Ponni came out, a white shape in the partial light, followed by the new calf. The boy slapped her flanks twice and then rubbed her down, talking to her. He separated the calf and tied it to a post. He then went back in and started to sweep the shed.

Ponni waited, swishing her tail, her udders swollen and proud, and her thighs rich and muscular and white in the semi darkness. Murugan came out and crouched down near her, and held the milk can firmly between his thighs. He patted her side. He stroked the udders, massaged them, and pulled at them firmly. The milk released and Murugan squeezed it into the can, *stirrump-stirrump*.

Sowmya ran inside. She allowed Kamala to apply coconut oil on the cuts on Sowmya's scalp and cover them with fresh turmeric paste.

The next day Kamala fell ill. It was not clear what was ailing her. She refused most of all that was cooked fresh for the day and lived on just a few things that she would allow touching her lips. She rarely left her bed, which was now the bench in the hall. At night she would sit up and stay motionless for an hour or so in her bed before falling back against the pillow and snoring instantly. Once after her bath, instead of going into the women's room to dress, Kamala had stood in the central courtyard, her sari circling her feet, a hand holding her naked breast. Sowmya quickly took her inside and helped her get dressed.

It was decided that Sowmya could not return to Ponmalar now. Hariharan drew up a letter asking Natesan permission to keep Sowmya for some more time, until his wife recovered. Now that Sowmya was properly tonsured she could enter the kitchen, cook.

The postman brought a response from Natesan. Sowmya saw her father's letter gleaming in a pool of sunlight at the doorstep where the mailman had flung it. How could he refuse Hariharan, so full of piety and sorrow? In his short letter, Natesan explained to her it was a simple request, a small thing. Be reasonable, he told her, you can come home soon. Her cousin Niru was visiting for the winter festival. Between the words she tried to see traces of something else, something she could not have described but would have recognized if she saw it. Maybe it was difficult to write guilt or regret. What she saw instead were sad and meager instructions. She imagined reaching out to her father and touching the fine bones beneath his thin shirt collar. How did she ever think her poor father could protect her from anything? How could anybody do that, when a force bigger than any of them could seize her as though her body were not her own? Nobody. Slowly her father's dear face, which had always been so clear in her memory, faded. The tip of his nose went first, and then the entire lower half of his face was gone. Sowmya rubbed her nail across his words, over and over, until the paper tore and the words disappeared.

— ● ● ● —

The next week the Hariharan couple was going to Sivankovil for a re-dedication of a temple. Hariharan was going to officiate. When they returned, in a couple of days, Hariharan would take her back home. Or she could continue to live with them here and be useful, her choice. He waited for her response.

Sowmya drew a pattern on the floor with her toe, and said nothing.

Upon awakening in the early hours of the morning of their departure, Sowmya lay on her mattress near Kamala's cot, and listened to the crackling noise from the wireless in the room above. When she had first arrived at this house Kamala had pointed to the room upstairs, which had belonged to Ramki. Hariharan slept there, she told Sowmya, ever since he returned form Ramki's funeral. Sowmya had followed her glance and saw Hariharan moving there like a shadow.

The wireless had belonged to Ramki and Hariharan often turned it on at dawn. The first time it happened Sowmya had jumped as though she had heard a ghost. She soon became used to that sound. Sometimes there would be short interludes of music. In that thin sliver of time between night and day she would lie in her bed and sense a connection to that young man who had perhaps listened to this same sound, which seemed to her then to contain some kind of jubilance in it. But today there was merely static coming out of it.

Kamala rose from her bed and went to the back terrace. Sowmya raised her hand to Kamala's cot, probed beneath the pillow, found the key bunch. Kamala did not linger very long at her bath, so there was no time to waste. It was difficult to see in the dark. Holding the keys tightly so they did not jingle, she removed one from the clasp, and returned the bunch to its place. She then brushed her teeth, washed her face and went into the kitchen and lit the stove.

She watched from the kitchen as Hariharan came down with a small trunk and a bedroll. He paced impatiently for his wife to get ready.

"Here," Kamala said, handing her the house key. "Lock all doors, don't forget to let Murugan in for the cow and then keep it locked." She carried a small bag and joined her husband.

As soon as the bullock cart carried away Hariharan and Kamala, Sowmya closed the door and dropped the bolt down securely. She took a gunny bag from the storeroom, pulled her tin trunk from under the bed in the women's room, turned it over and dumped the contents on the floor. She sorted through as though they all belonged to someone else, someone she no longer knew, a phantom. She twisted a sari and stuffed it into the bag. The letters went in, the notebook. The rest she threw back into the trunk, where they would remain, maybe get thrown out. A comb dropped to the ground. She turned it over in her hand. It seemed a long time since she had used one. The vendor had brought this to the door at Ponmalar. In the basket he also had mirrors, ribbons, tins of face powder, mirrored moneybags. From Singapore, he said, showing her the shiny plastic comb. She felt the heat of that afternoon sun on the front porch of her father's house, when she tested the comb on her hair. She saw herself there now, running inside to the courtyard where her aunt and mother would be busy with something. But the house was hollow, the rooms were gone. She threw the comb into her bag and rolled it up.

Inside Kamala's almirah the small cinch bag with money that Meenakshi had given her was empty. Sowmya's heart crashed to her stomach and she stood stunned for a few seconds. She then remembered how Kamala saved what Murugan brought after selling any excess milk, and she looked into that tin box next. It never had much in it, just a couple of coins. It too was wiped clean. She started rummaging the rest of the shelves, shoving the saris aside, the odd things that Kamala saved, empty cardboard boxes in which the saris came from the store, small betel-leaf bags from festivals. Something rolled to the floor. A jewelry box covered in dark blue velvet. It fitted in the palm of her hand. Probably empty, whatever that was in there cashed out long ago. She clicked it open. Seven tiny gold buttons. She clicked it shut, closed and locked the almirah with shaking hands. She then placed the key under Kamala's pillow.

She sat on the bench in the room and thought for a minute. She knew the Marwadi pawnshop on one of the temple streets. The man would surely recognize her. Kamala had sent her there once to pawn two brass lamps. The telegraph office scared her. She could not ask for help from anyone, it would raise suspicion. She practiced several times what she would say. Her heart raced but she needed to hurry, there was no time for fear. If she thought too much she may never be able to leave this house. She stood up. She had to rush out before courage failed her. Ponni, the cow. She needed to be milked. She could lock up and give the key to Banu across the street. What would be the reason? No, Banu would know immediately. She would hang the key on the hook where the mirror used to be and leave by the back door, cross over to the parallel street from there and leave the door unbolted for Murugan to come in and feed the cow.

Sowmya came out and stood in the small courtyard. Moss stained and mildewed, its crumbling wall hemmed in the courtyard on one side. A fine drizzle fell from the patch of sky above, across which ran iron bars--to keep birds from flying in. Ponmalar was far away, across, and over, and beyond her reach.

In the main hall, that was just an expansion of the courtyard, there were several framed pictures of gods and goddesses hanging on the wall, their faces benign with beatific smiles. In between were a few photographs of family members.

One in particular, almost half her height, took center stage on the wall display. Sowmya stood in front of this now. A smaller version of it lay wrapped in tissue paper in the bottom of a trunk back in Ponmalar. This picture was embossed in one corner with a gold stamp, *Selvan Studios, Thanjavur.* Inside the frame at the bottom was the obituary cut out from *The Hindu* dated July 22nd, 1928.

Ramki sat with one arm draped casually over the back of the chair, leaning back slightly. His legs crossed at the ankles, and he looked splendid, sad, and innocent. A row of seven tiny gold buttons went down his long silk shirt. A silk scarf, accordion pleated to show off a palm-wide border of embroidered gold, was draped stylishly around his shoulders. Diamond studs at his earlobes. It was a handsome face, feminine in its delicate lines. Generously shaped and full, his lips were slightly parted, allowing the faintest of a smile. Beneath a radiant forehead his eyes, clear and unfazed by their doom, looked back at her. Her own head appeared silhouetted on the glass right beneath Ramki's chest. Something with memory tumbled inside—the morning light framed by a doorway, the vendor calling from the street, and a foot that had dazzled her on that sad morning. She put her hand out and ran a finger gently down the side of Ramki's face and then touched it to her lips.

The owner of the Marwadi pawn shop wore a black cap and sat cross-legged on a thin white mattress, behind a desk. He took the buttons from Sowmya, weighed them in his palm. He listened to her story from across the desk, rolling the buttons in his hand. A present for the wedding, she said. Kamala wanted to cash these and give it to the bride. How much does he think he could give her?

The man held his chin, glanced at the gunny bag that she clutched. His eyes darted to the cut at her eyebrow, which was now throbbing. He placed the buttons back in the box, clicked it shut and threw it into a drawer. He opened a small safe next to him and counted out rupees, made them into two tight rolls.

"Keep them separated in two different places," he said handing them to her. "Tell amma I said that."

She nodded quickly, took the rolls from him, stuffed them into her bag, and then shot out the door.

She stopped at the telegraph office next to the train station. The man at the window took the message and started writing. She gave him her name.

"Sir?"

He did not look up.

"How long will it take for the message to reach?"

The man ignored her while he transcribed the message on to a form. He then stamped it.

"One anna." He wiggled his fingers through the window.

She gave him the money. He stamped some more papers, tore off a receipt and handed it to her.

"The party will get it at four o'clock."

It was mid morning. She hurried towards the train station.

"The train departs in ten minutes, platform two," the man said, handing Sowmya the ticket. "Hurry."

She looked up to where he pointed, at the bridge spanning a railway yard and descending into another platform.

Clutching her bag to her chest Sowmya ran up the steps and on to the overpass. A locomotive hissed steam as it entered the yard below. A loud clanging bell. She gathered the sari tightly around her and ran across the bridge. Red clay and stone buildings flashed past her, leaves shimmered on a cluster of trees. At the top of the stairs she paused to catch her breath, her face hot and sticky with sweat. Below her, parallel metal lines gleamed in the sunlight, curving here, merging and separating and diverging again, changing direction and stretching out and beyond. Iron wheels on metal tracks vibrated beneath her naked feet. She took a deep breath, tightened her fist around the cardboard edge of the ticket, and flew down the steps.

What she did not know was that within an hour after they left the Hariharan couple had to return home. A tree had fallen on the road leading out of Thanjavur making it impassable.

chapter 4

Mallika was returning from Thanjavur. The visit had gone badly. The income from a piece of property that had sustained her family was being stolen from her.

When her grandmother, Krishnaveni, was barely in her teens, a zamindar in the district had underwritten the expense of her dedication at the temple. Kindled not a little by Krishnaveni's slender waist, he had also deeded a nice parcel of land over to her. In return for the cultural services Krishnaveni would provide for the temple deity, the temple trustees had a house built for her on this land. She died as the head dancer at the temple at a ripe age, and this house and the land passed on to Krishnaveni's daughters. When Mallika's mother died, a disgruntled uncle contested the estate. Pointing out that women had neither ownership nor inheritance rights over land and property, he claimed all of it as the rightful heir. But that was resolved in Mallika's favor when the court ruled that the devadasis were exempt from Hindu personal laws. They could not only inherit property, it said, they could do with it as they willed.

Mallika was born in this house built on Nellyappan Street. She grew up watching visitors appear at the doorstep everyday to listen to her grandmother play the stringed instrument, veenai. Like the goddess Saraswathi herself, they said, leaving behinds gifts of appreciation. Frequently the zamindar would visit, with a retinue of servants bearing baskets of fruits from his orchard. He would stay until the early hours of the morning. When she woke up in her grandmother's bed Mallika would see him reclined against the pillows on a divan and looking as though he was floating inside a bubble of pure pleasure. Krishnaveni would have piled her hair, still damp from her bath, in a roll to the side just above her left ear. The zamindar's triple strand pearl necklace would glow against her grandmother's skin, as she sat in front of the instrument and slid her fingers over the frets and caressed music from it. Like this she would sing for him in the plaintive notes of the raga Thodi: *Grant me that sweet surrender, my Swami, without further delay...*

"Sing!" Krishnaveni would command, drawing Mallika onto her lap. But Mallika's heart had always belonged to dance. When she was five she threw such a tantrum demanding a set of her own ankle bells that Krishnaveni finally yielded. She would replicate the sound on her feet in time to her master's beats, under Krishnaveni's watchful eyes. Later, after she had mastered the fundamentals, she learnt from the most famous teacher of them all, Muthukumaran, who was also part of her extended family. From her mother she perfected the mime for *When will He arrive my friend, my Lord Tyagesa?* This was the world that

Mallika knew, from morning until night, surrounded like breath by the beauty of dance and music.

All that had changed when a lady doctor in Madras began demanding a ban not only on the dedication of young girls into the devadasi tradition, but on dance itself. "Our temples don't need these dancers," she argued. This system was merely contributing to the degradation of these young women's lives, she said, leading them into a life of prostitution. The devadasi's very sexuality, which endowed her with divine grace and good fortune, now embarrassed her countrymen. The activists' remedy was to kill the devadasi, wipe out her very existence, by taking dance out of the temple. The men of the devadasi community joined the chorus in the cities, expressing their shame in the lifestyle that turned their sisters and mothers into prostitutes. This transfer of property from mothers to daughters should stop, they demanded. Patrons and funds evaporated for the dancers at the temple.

There were opportunities in the city, Mallika's brother told her, and persuaded her to move with him to Madras. She did with reluctance, locking up her memories in the house on Nellyappan Street, and taking the train to Madras. That was several years ago.

The temple trustees had now seized this property, the house and the land. "Your people are no longer servicing the temple," she was told in a letter that arrived via registered mail, pointing to the civil action pending in the legislative council in Madras to completely ban dancing in the temples.

"We are not prostitutes," the temple dancers were reduced to plead in their petition to the government at Madras. "We are artists, our ways are different, sanctioned by our tradition. Our services are part of the liturgy for our Lord Nataraja. Maybe a few of us go astray out of desperation because our patrons have abandoned us. If one judge is caught thieving, would the whole profession become illegitimate?"

Mallika was fifty-five and she was so tired of pleading—for her livelihood, for justice, for her dance. What was a legitimate profession, secure in its place in the community, was now declared promiscuous. She felt like laughing at them one moment and spitting on them the next. She went to Thanjavur, filed a case against the temple trustees demanding her property back, and was returning home to Madras.

The first whistle sounded and brought her back from her reverie. She looked around her compartment: a ladies coupe with two berths facing each other and a small bathroom attached. The exit door opened directly onto the platform. It looked like she was going to have it all to her self.

The train hissed steam when the Brahmin widow suddenly scrambled into the compartment like a wounded animal. A deep cut near the girl's eyebrow was turning yellow from purple.

Mallika made room for her near the window. It was clear that this girl did not have a ticket and had climbed into the compartment because it was not crowded like the others. The girl turned her face away to the window where the cigarette boy tempted her with peanut candy from the platform.

Mallika watched her with only a mild curiosity. She had seen plenty of these widowed girls swinging from the rafters in their own sari, or floating face down at the bottom of their kitchen wells. A more mean-spirited people did not exist than those who occupied the lanes of the agraharam around the temple, with their fearsome purity and pollution laws for widows. The young women who ran away usually ended up badly. She wondered where this girl was going alone.

Suddenly the cigarette boy was jerked aside and the window framed the grotesque face of a man spewing intolerable curses. Before Mallika could fully understand what was going on, a bulky woman had climbed into the compartment, wheezing and whimpering.

"Sowmya, Sowmya," the woman called to the girl in a child-like voice, and managed to heave the young woman off the seat and was dragging her towards the exit door when Mallika stood up. She should do something, but what? The couple looked like her family.

The second whistle blew. The girl, Sowmya, cried, "Please, please!"

"Sowmya," the fat woman panted, "How could you leave us this way? Come, let's go home. Come."

The woman appeared demented, as though she was only half there. She now had the young woman pushed against the wall and was pulling the door to the platform with one free hand. Sowmya jerked her hand to free herself. In the tussle the girl's sari slipped off her head. Her scalp was covered with small scars and scabs.

Mallika could no longer stand it. She bounded up and threw her arms around the girl's middle and held on firmly, when at the same instant the train jerked forward. The fat woman stumbled and slipped on the steps, still holding on the Sowmya's hand. The girl screamed as she was also being pulled down the train steps. Mallika held tight and tried to free Sowmya's hand from the woman's fingers. The old woman let go, and fell on the platform in a heap. Sowmya was now trying to go down to help the woman up. Mallika pulled her inside the compartment and slammed the door shut. The train moved.

The women faced each other for a few seconds, panting. Sowmya started trembling as though with fever, and finally her knees buckled. Mallika grabbed her before she fell.

"Easy! Look, you're shaking like a leaf. Calm down. Come, sit."

Mallika led her back to the seat near the window. She felt light like a feather in her arms. The young woman shrank from the window seat, cowering even though the train had started moving.

"Sit amma, sit down child. When did you eat last?"

The train chugged out of the Thanjavur station. Morning sunlight crept over the paddy fields of the Kaveri delta, and small mountains appeared in the distance, then a farm of green groves and thatched roofs, a child peeing against the side of a cowshed. A strong breeze carried the smell of burning coal, gritty with bits that caught in the eye. The girl pulled back and rubbed her eyes.

Mallika opened her tiffin-carrier and offered her some idlis and lemon rice on a banana leaf. The girl ate hungrily, and drank down the buttermilk she was offered. Mallika let her eat. She had regular features that might break out beautifully with a smile, limbs lithe like the branches of a young neem tree. It was clear she had a family that had cared for her.

"What's your name? Where're you from?" Mallika asked later.

The girl's name was Sowmya, her native village was Ponmalar. The couple at the station were her in-laws, she said, before she pulled her legs up to her chest and curled up. She tucked a small gunnysack bag under her head. Mallika looked at the ruffled edge of a sari that peeked out, stained with soot and oil-grime that would never quite wash out.

The girl slept well into the afternoon. The father had sent her to help the ailing old woman for a few days during the girl's late husband's memorial service. That the girl's head-shaving was recently done by the in-laws was evident from the razor cuts. The older widows endured the practice stoically. But Mallika had once witnessed a teenager, like this girl in front of her, getting shaved. Three people had to hold her down and still the girl had escaped screaming, her head half shaved.

"So are you not going back to your father's house?" she asked when Sowmya finally woke up.

The young woman's mouth got tight and twisted. She rubbed her face hard and recovered. She might look as though a swift wind could blow her down, but there was the weight of teak in her nerves, Mallika thought.

"I have two sisters, twins. They need to be married and if anybody knows about this, it will all get very difficult for my father."

"This?"

"I cannot go back. I have shamed my father enough already. I don't know what he would do if he saw me." Sowmya shook her head. The sari slipped and lay around her shoulder. She made no attempt to pull it up over her head.

"I don't understand. How old are your sisters?"

"Three."

So in another seven, eight years the father would be looking for grooms within their small community.

"Widowhood is not a taint on character. You hair will grow back." Mallika said. She now wanted this girl to go back home.

Sowmya turned her face to the window and did not answer.

"Where are you going?" Mallika asked after a while.

Sowmya pulled a ticket out of her bag and showed it to Mallika.

"Tiruchi junction arrives at *midnight*, my dear!"

"A friend is meeting me."

Mallika waited and the story indeed came out. The friend, a roundabout relative, a student at St. Joseph College in Tiruchi, some khadi wearing Congress worker for sure, was going to meet her at the junction when the train stopped for five minutes. This boy, this Mani, was going to bring a friend with him——a Christian who was looking for a bride. The man was going to be the principal at the Anglican mission school in Jaffna, Ceylon. He needed to be married. That was the condition of his employment. Who was going to give a Christian convert their daughter to marry, even if he was born a Brahmin? Only the most desperate.

"I sent a telegram before coming to the station. He will be there."

Mallika held her tongue. And yes, all this would be enough to complicate her father's life, ruin her sisters' marriage prospects. But what kind of a relative is this, trying to ship her off to Ceylon like a sack of potatoes? Who is to thump this Christian man on the back and ask him a few questions if he were to slap this girl around? Or something worse?

"Lot of our people have gone there, to Ceylon," Mallika said. "They take the boat-mail from Danushkodi. They work the plantations, they never come back. I don't know about any school or school-teachers."

Sowmya was silent.

It was evening and the attendant came to take dinner orders. Mallika ordered for two. The overhead light had not come on yet, and they sat in the darkness that settled like smoke in the compartment. The driver was working the engine and the train screamed over the tracks like a demon.

"This tutor of yours. What if this tutor does not show up? The train stops only for a few minutes. What will you do in the middle of the night in the station, where will you go?"

"He will come."

In the dimming light Mallika saw the shine of confidence in the girl's eyes. The young man was sure to show up, earnest in his mission. Something fluttered like a small bird in Mallika's chest.

"Have you ever been to Madras? My house is in George Town."

Sowmya's eyes lit up.

"Is it near the sea?"

"You have never seen the sea? Well, as a matter of fact our house is just a few blocks from the beach. The sea breeze at sunrise and sunset will tear at your hair," Mallika said. "That is when I practice my dance in the terrace."

The overhead lights came on and chased out the night.

Mallika rose and opened her trunk, brought out a tin box. In it was a comb and other little tins and vials, cosmetics. She started combing her hair.

"Dance?" Sowmya asked.

"Yes, dance. My younger brother manages a drama company in Madras."

Mallika stopped combing and began to sing a verse:

. . . the faultless moon
kindles my ardent wants
this flower-scented night unendurable
Go tell him, my friend, his dear cherished face haunts . . .

Her face transformed into a young woman's, fingers shaping her tears, her longing, the love. Mallika mimed the meaning.

"You must hold your shoulders like this, see! So the arms form a beautiful symmetry with the rest of the body. Glance follows fingertips, body follows form. Like this!"

Sowmya moved her head, as if in agreement.

"Who taught you to dance this way?" She asked.

"I learnt dancing from my mother and my grandmother, and then my guru Muthukumaran Pillai. But now I am old. I do now what comes from my dreams! See, I am walking somewhere; I'm looking at a stream or the parrots on a tree or the peacocks in a field--the sculptures on temple carving, the sea shore. And these things occur to me, I cannot help myself, I have to dance this way." She paused. "You won't understand, you must think I am a mad woman."

Sowmya shook her head, No!

Mallika told her of dancing at the temple at Madurai in the hall of thousand and one pillars, the shops inside where they sold little clay carts; the one hundred and one steps carved into the hills of Pazhani where she did the dance of lamps for the Youthful God; the temple for the Virgin Goddess at the cape Kanyakumari, where the sun sets in a blood red sea.

"Have you seen it?" she asked knowing fully well Sowmya could not have traveled beyond the four corners of her courtyard. "Have you seen any of these places?"

Sowmya shook her head.

They had sat silently for a few minutes. "There was a devadasi at the temple on my wedding night. She arrived to do the arati," Sowmya said.

"When? Which temple was it?"

Sowmya told her, described the woman. She showed Mallika a move the dancer made.

"*Arre!* Very nice!" The girl had accurately captured a style. "That must have been Ratnam, that was her style. They used to live on our street, a few houses down and across. Large family, big house."

She had run into Ratnam once in the city and wished she hadn't. Amidst the censure of dance, an art critic in the city was bent on recovering and preserving the dance. His method was to separate the dance from the dancers. The critic, a Brahmin, even dressed up as a woman and gave a dance performance to prove somehow that the dance can be rescued from the lifestyle of the devadasis. Women like Ratnam, who had come to the city looking for a way to earn a living, got co-opted into the growing 'dance recovery' movement. But not all the devadasi women recovered, even if their dance did. The movement then became the 'dance purification' movement. Mallika swore she would teach no one. The wretched people who tore away at her day after day deserved nothing of her art, which needed no purification.

Her heart fluttered when she looked at Sowmya, taking a very small space on the seat next to the window. She imagined the girl, the shroud of a sari clinging to the horrid smoothness of the shaved head, getting down at the junction in the middle of the night and vanish into that darkness to marry a stranger. She wanted to tell this girl that marriage was not going to rescue her. She needed to do something for this girl, but what? What did she have to offer Sowmya?

After dinner, while they both got ready for bed, Mallika asked Sowmya if she had any money.

Sowmya showed her the two rolls of rupees.

Mallika sat down on her seat. "I told you about my brother's drama troupe. Sometimes I perform for them. I need someone to assist during make-up, running errands, things like that. If you want to come with me, I can hire you."

"Hire me?"

"Yes. I will pay you a percentage of whatever we make that night."

"Pay me with money?"

"I will pay you with coconuts. What do you think?" Mallika laughed then stopped when she saw the expression on the girl's face. "Yes, Sowmya. Money."

—— • • • ——

The young man, Mani, did show up as promised when the train stopped at close to midnight at the Tiruchi junction, where it halted for barely five minutes. They heard the banging and then his voice inquiring the stationmaster who answered him something that was not clear. Sowmya lay curled up on the seat, facing the wall, pulling her bag close to her chest. It did not take much to convince her that once Mani saw her it would be very difficult to resist his urging to get down. He also would not have looked kindly at Mallika, accusing her of all kinds of evil intentions.

Loud thumps on the door. After some hesitation, Mallika opened it a crack. He was young, thin, wearing glasses. Just as she had imagined him.

"What? This is the ladies' compartment."

"Did a girl get in here? About fifteen, this high."

He placed his hand at his chest when he said that, which she found endearing.

"A widow? Clean shaven head?"

"No, no, no! Long braid down to here."

So nobody knew yet about what had happened to this girl at her in-laws house. Mallika told him a tonsured Brahmin widow came in but a lady took the widow away. He looked at her as if she had slapped him. She searched for his friend behind him. There was no one. Probably backed out. Not everybody is stupid enough to do courageous acts.

"Let me in, I will check for myself," he said, trying to climb into the train.

"*Arrey!*" she blocked him. "I told you, this is a ladies' compartment, there are ladies in here sleeping," she said, and then shut the door and locked it.

"Sowmya!" he banged on the door. "Sowmya, Sowmya! Answer me if you're in there!"

Sowmya shot up from her seat. Mallika put a hand out, pressed a finger to her lips. The whistle blew.

"Sowmya!" Mani was banging on the window.

The train jerked forward once. Sowmya ran to the window and pushed her face against the window bars.

"Mani!"

Mani ran on the platform, holding on to the window bars. "Sowmya, what happened to you? Who did this to you? Sowmya, why? *Who is that woman with you?*"

"I don't know, I don't know why it happened!" Sowmya screamed, wrapping her hands around Mani's fingers.

Suddenly, he stopped, and withdrew his hands from the window. The platform had ended and the train headed into the dark night. Sowmya stared into the night, her heartbeat in her mouth.

chapter 5

It was the day before the opening of the *Madana Theater Group's* latest production. The troupe had gathered at the house in George Town for the final rehearsal. While they were finishing up in the terrace, Sowmya received the man from the Kalyani Mess, who arrived with two large brass containers strapped to the sides of a bicycle. One contained idlis, dumplings steamed to perfection, and the pongal, the savory rice dish cooked to creamy consistency and glistening with cracked black pepper roasted in ghee, separated in sections. There was hot sambar in the other.

She stirred the sugar and steamed milk into the kettle of fresh coffee and poured it carefully into two large thermos flasks. It was only nine in the morning and already sweat was streaming from every pore. With the loose end of her sari she blotted her head and face. Her hair had grown in where she could comb a parting in it after oiling it down. On a day like this she discovered the relief that a close crop provided. With a damp towel she wiped down the strips of banana leaves and stacked them. When she carried them all in a couple of trips to the second floor terrace, her arrival was greeted each time with cheer.

It was too hot to continue the practice in the sunlit terrace, which had begun at five that morning. This corner of the terrace had become the rehearsal stage for several weeks now, since the new program got settled. Mallika's brother Kitappa was the music director for the Madana Theater Group, which staged mythological operas. The company was known for its fabulously crafted stage settings. When he first began there in early 1930, Kitappa had persuaded Mallika into giving them a couple of dance items. That very first production was a huge success, and now tickets sold briskly when the flyers carried Mallika's name.

When Sowmya came up, Mallika and Kitappa were engaged in a small argument over tempo and choreography. A young woman named Neelam had joined them. She was related to Mallika and had arrived from the village only recently and lived with her aunt in Egmore. She would be singing for Mallika tomorrow, and the three of them huddled often over the program.

Somu, who played the flute, and Pillai, who played the mridangam, worked on contract for the drama company. Long memories connected them all from the time of Mallika's grandmother. Their common lineage traced back to the same narrow and familiar streets, with houses squished together, their tiled roofs and open porches always remembered in a timeless past. Like many others from the villages, they too had found their way to the city and had settled in proximity with each other. This colony of artists from the Thanjavur district was absorbed in the commercial heart of George Town, along with the Jain silk weavers and diamond merchants from Gujarat, the Portuguese and the British settlers, the Armenians, the Mussalmans, the goldsmiths and crafters of tin sheets, traders in mica and porcelain toilet fittings, furniture makers, and costume makers. Sowmya had seen only the high walls of the Fort St. George in the north end of Madras beach, from where the town spread out sprouting hundreds of temples, churches, and mosques, meat markets and flower bazaars, as well as houses of prostitution that serviced its barracks.

Sowmya put down the two carriers. She wiped her streaming face and head again, and looked at the performers to see if they were ready to eat. Some days the musicians lingered and continued to play long after the dance practice was over, with Pillai coaxing beats from his drum in syncopation with the notes that Somu drew from his flute. His one leg crossed over the other, Kitappa would bring his palms together and slap-count the beats, with an occasional cry of appreciation, *Sabhash*! Brilliant moments like these amazed Sowmya. Like her they too carried memory of destroyed lives, and yet how their work made them brim with cheer! She wanted that, to have that something that would possess her as she in turn possessed it.

Sowmya placed a scoop of pongal on a leaf, two idlis, and ladled some sambar over it all and took it to Mallika. It was then that she noticed the man seated next to her. Bald and frail looking, gray stubble covering half of his face, he was reading aloud a poem for Mallika. Sowmya had seen him before. He brought the poems he wrote to Mallika, and if she found them suitable she would have Kitappa set them to music for her.

"Give it to the poet," Mallika said with a movement of her head when Sowmya approached.

The man looked at Sowmya and immediately stood up. Making no move to take the food from her, he continued to recite:

. . .these bruised lips.
Who left these marks on your left breast . . .

Sowmya's eyes widened and she drew back. When he then made a move, she stuck her hand out holding the leaf to him, as if to block him. He paused and looked at her for a moment. His eyes twinkled.

"Thank you, thank you kindly." Still eyeing her, he accepted the food.

She quickly went back to her chore, her heart beating so fast she could hear it. She passed the rest of the food to everyone and then poured the coffee into brass tumblers, focusing hard on what she was doing to stop her hands from shaking. The small incident with the poet had created a sudden storm in her, of the smell of wet earth and beedi smoke, of a man's rough hands invading and groping her on a rain whipped afternoon when she had taken shelter under a tree.

After everyone had eaten she cleaned up and took everything back downstairs. Later when Sowmya was passing with the betel leaf box, her arms around the heavy casket that she pressed to her chest, the poet stopped her. He reached for the leaves. His fingers lingered inside the box and she felt as though his knuckles were grazing the front of her sari. She was afraid to drop her gaze down from his face. What if he misunderstood that as flirtatious? She looked unblinkingly into his small eyes, his beteljuice-stained lips that parted in a smile.

"You are not from these parts, are you? Hmmm? Where are you from, girl?"

Sowmya tried to swallow hard the burn spreading through her dry mouth.

From somewhere Mallika's hand zoomed in, firmly nudging his hand aside and dug in for a few leaves for herself.

"Who's the girl?"

"*Sondam,* Swami," Mallika said, and smiled at him.

Sondam. Kinfolk. Our own. The term made Sowmya's heart leap. She was suddenly pulled into a cool shade from the blistering sunlight. The power in that response made further questions cease.

"Oh ho!" The man nodded his head, still smiling at her.

Sowmya turned to look at Mallika. The way the older woman averted her chin without meeting her glance left her confused. Did she do something wrong? Did she draw this unwanted attention? The conversations in the terrace came to her in a garbled noise. Somu and Kitappa and all these people she thought she knew receded from her in a flash, and beyond that her parents, Ponmalar itself. *Her connection to the world so tenuous, it can vanish just like that, with a little lift of the chin.* She stood alone on that terrace, only feeling the heat that rose from below like the one true thing. With nervous fingers Sowmya fixed her sari around her bosom.

●　●　●

"Ours is such a business," Mallika told her that night at dinner. "What we do, our work—we are always out there. They look at us—we are an open field in men's gaze. You cannot let it frighten you or affect your work. Swami is an old lecherous man, but he's harmless."

Sowmya kept her head down, afraid to betray any emotion.

"I wasn't worried," she said.

"Good then. I thought I would tell you because you may not be used to our ways. The agraharam is a different kind of place."

Sowmya knew very well the fear, envy, and curiosity that devadasis evoked in the women in her neighborhood. It was enough to make them pull their sari closer and cover their neck, touch their wedding necklace. It was with such trepidation that the women invited the temple ladies to come bless their birth ceremonies and weddings. They were sacred beings, the beloved of the Dancer with

His Left Leg Aloft, even if they bankrupted their men who paid dearly for the dancers' attention. It was all too shameful to talk about so the women in the agraharam ground their fear and loathing into the chilies and coconut in the kitchen.

After they cleaned the kitchen and washed the floor clean, the women secured the kitchen doors. Mallika instructed Sowmya to turn off the light and went up to the open terrace to sleep. Sowmya walked to the front of the house.

The house Mallika rented was one of three identical ones inside a compound. The landlord was a Chettiar who traded in diamonds and wholesale teak furniture from Burma. He had built similar sets of rental properties all over the town.

A front porch spanned the width of the house. Mesh panels screened it and a trellis supported a scrappy vine of Queen of the Night, which now scented the porch. A tanpura, the string instrument designed and custom made for Kitappa, was leaned against a corner on its guard base, and a harmonium was at its side. A couple of rolled up mats leaned in another corner, ready to be unfurled for seating or sleeping when needed. This was a music studio for Kitappa where he received his visitors and composed his music. The polished cement floor was cool now. Two sets of doors opened from this porch, but the one on the far end was permanently locked.

Kitappa had been extremely disturbed by Sowmya's arrival. He accused Mallika of kidnapping and began to arrange for Sowmya's return right away.

"Child, give me the address," he had said, pen in hand, shooting hot glances at his sister.

Sowmya looked at Mallika and Mallika looked back at her in silence.

"Address, amma! Don't you know your own address?"

Even now she shuddered at the recall of her father's dark eyes, tight with the accusations that descended with a terrible weight on her chest. So Sowmya had mumbled an address to Kitappa, not her father's. Kitappa sent a letter. Twice. Nobody came to get her.

Sowmya pushed aside the curtain of glass beads that hung at the doorway and walked into the interior, a space divided by an archway, windows on every wall. These two rooms served the purpose of a hall, reception room, eating room, sleeping room, dressing room, and any other need that arose. Another set of doors opened into a terrace, a kitchen to a side of the terrace, and arranged against the rear wall, a well, bathing room, and a latrine. A staircase wound up above the kitchen to another terrace, where the practice for the opening day was held this morning.

The house's sharp contours were quite unlike anything Sowmya had called home until now. When she arrived here from the train station she felt the absence of the odor from the cow stall that permeated the darkened interior in the house in Ponmalar. She missed that smell. The street was removed from the house, so one could not peek out and watch the busy grid of teeming life that she knew was just outside the gate.

Sowmya switched off the lights in the front rooms, and finally sat down on the granite washing platform in the rear terrace. It was still holding the heat from the day. Banana trees curved against the dark sky. From beyond the back wall, a motor horn tooted. A little later a train swept past. Its rattle and then a long whistle faded into the distance, leaving an echo in her head.

Sowmya held her hand softly to her mouth. Her mother, aunt Meenakshi, her father, the twins—the very smell of home rose from her hand to her mouth and pooled in her throat like a bruise. If her father were to see her now he would not understand a home like this, run by a woman who mimed a poet's words, and got paid for it and kept account of it. Debauchery, her father would have called it, disgust curling his lips.

Sowmya turned in her seat. The man that morning had asked her where she was from. What village, who's your father? Perennial questions that would daunt her every time she met someone new. Mallika had claimed her as kin. Did she mean it? How long could she live like this in her house? Where would she go, how would she live? Nothing in her imagination could penetrate the fog that appeared as her future. As promised Mallika took out her drawstring bag and paid her a sum. Was her earning enough? She had no idea. Neelam took her share as the musician, tucked it into her own bag, and went home. Maybe if Sowmya also had some other skill, like Mallika and Neelam did . . .

Before she finished her thought, Sowmya got up and walked towards the stairs. The moon had risen high above and the sky was full of stars. She stopped just before she reached the steps. Something made her want to strike a pose that she had seen Mallika do many times. She was not sure what to do with her hand and she experimented, holding it first at her chest, palm up fingers fanned like a blossom, and then throwing it away from her. She repeated the gesture with her hand held another way, palm facing down. She would dance. The thought stunned her even as it made her giddy. That is what she would do. People would pay to come and watch her. She would really belong, be kin. No more questions about who her father was, the name of her village. Nobody asked Mallika any questions. But would Mallika accept her as a student, teach her?

Mallika used mudras, symbols, with her hands and fingers to speak the language of mime. Shiva's whirling matted locks, the crescent moon he wears in it, the river Ganga that flows down it, the garland of skulls, his four hands, the deer he holds, the flame on his palm, the rattle of life and death—Mallika's fingers and hands painted these sacred tales, over and over, over and over, each time plumbing the story a little deeper, revealing the mystery all the time. When Mallika danced to the verses of *Thy elegant foot raised in infinite mercy*, Sowmya found part of her rise up and walk away from her. She saw it whirling and whirling in a joyful frenzy. In those moments Ramki's death, which had smudged the edges of her life with charcoal, would recede from her. Her family, her mother and father, all of Ponmalar, vanished. She saw only herself in the shimmer of dance.

She started paying closer attention to the *jati*, the rhythmic patterns Mallika tapped out with her feet in response to Kitappa's calls. The swiftness and dexterity of it, its tempo and the melody, its tone and its insistence, *thai di-di-thai tha*! *thai di-di-thai tha*! The leaps and the twirls, the promenade, the pivot. She could not bear to watch silently. The soles of her feet twitched to the beat. It seemed that there was another being inside her who knew how to make those leaps, how to land with the grace of an antelope. She saw the music, she heard the dance.

In the privacy of the bathing room, she placed her feet in position and noiselessly stepped. Sowmya could already imagine a day when her feet would be ready to obey the beats emerging from Kitappa's block of wood in front of him. He struck it with a stick and commanded: *thaiya thai! thaiya thai!* Her feet would obey.

A little aghast at her own audacity she looked up at the window, set high on the bathing room wall. A branch laden with mango blossoms mocked her. *Widows don't dance, you foolish girl.*

Still, unable to bear it anymore, one rainy evening she asked Mallika for lessons.

Mallika was silent for what seemed like a very long moment. Would she reject her? Laugh at her foolishness to imagine that she could be a dancer?

Just when Sowmya was going to repeat her plea, Mallika said, "Why? Why dance?"

What should she say? I want to be like you, answer to no one? I want that thing, that thing in your dance that makes me choke with feelings I cannot even name? I want money in my string purse that I would tuck at my waist like you do? How did you get that way?

"I don't know why. I just want to dance. Like you."

Mallika looked up sharply and Sowmya geared herself for a rebuke.

"It might look glamorous, all the make-up, the shiny clothes. But it is hard work and takes—it requires thick blood to withstand the abuse. That pale thing that runs in Brahmin veins will never do."

The bitterness went straight to Sowmya's heart and she reeled for a moment as though Mallika had punched her.

Mallika put a hand on her shoulder and made Sowmya sit.

"Let me tell you something. There is no marriage in this profession. If cooking and housekeeping are what you desire, or if you want kids--do you want kids?"

"No!" Her eyes went round with shock and confusion, and Sowmya shook her head with vehemence. "No."

Mallika regarded her for a few moments. "Because if that's what you want ... and you are young, there is no reason why you shouldn't—but if that's what you want, just give up all this about dance right now. Find some other honest work to do."

Sowmya perspired, squirmed under this gaze.

"Stand," Mallika said.

She made Sowmya tuck the folds of her sari at the waist so she could see her feet and knees.

"Sit at half bend," she said and demonstrated.

Sowmya knew how to splay her feet and lower herself, until her knees bent at the same angle as Mallika's.

"Look up, not at your feet," Mallika lifted her face up by her chin, touched her shoulders, made them square.

She sat down next to Sowmya, scratched her head for a while. They sat like that for a long time while the rainwater dripped from the Queen of the Night vine.

The next evening, when Kitappa came home Mallika announced her plans.

Kitappa became furious. He called his sister a mad woman.

"Initiate this girl? Are you planning to get us both counting jail bars? You have already kidnapped this girl. If you start this initiating, and this and that, we're finished. We'll be arrested for running a whorehouse! Do you hear me, akka?"

Sowmya understood that with the new resolution at the Legislative Assembly, Mallika could be charged with getting a minor into prostitution simple by teaching her to dance. Dance was such a dangerous thing, yet no one was calling for the abolition of prostitution.

Mallika sat silently while her brother raged. After he was done she said, "You do whatever is necessary. Write to her people, write to the government, write to that doctor lady. Tell them all to come and claim this girl. She was going to be packed off to Ceylon by her people, like a sack of potatoes. All I have done is bring her home. Let them come and arrest me."

"So you will teach dance to a Brahmin girl." Kitappa looked her in the eye. "Tell me, what in the world is she going to do with it? Nobody is going to let her dance on stage, you can forget about that."

"You take care of writing to everyone, I will take care of teaching the girl."

Defeated, Kitappa turned to Sowmya.

"Child, don't let my elder sister put these crazy ideas into your head. Tell me, do you really want to dance? Do you?"

Kitappa was a jolly man. He had an open-mouthed laughter and kindness in his eyes. But he looked at her now with only annoyance. All she could think of was what it would be like to be a woman in a world of men. She wanted to set people in the state of elation Mallika's dance ignited in her, and get paid for it.

She nodded her head. "Yes, please."

Kitappa sighed.

● ● ●

"Listen. Just listen. Stop your thoughts, and just listen to me. The moment you start asking questions, you have stopped listening."

These were Mallika's first instructions.

Surrender to the dance. Listen.

Kitappa clicked on the wooden block.

"*Did-di-Thai!*" Kitappa called out. He sat cross-legged on the floor and struck a small wood plank with a stick to keep time.

Sowmya reflected the sounds back with her feet.

Thai Di-di-Thai *Thaa*!
Thai-Thai Di-di-Thai *Thaa*!
Thai-Thai-*Thai* Di-di-Thai *Thaa*!"

She repeated everything in double time, now triple time.

Sowmya's lessons began on Vijaya Dashami, the feast for the Goddess of Victory. To her surprise and delight, it was Kitappa, the musician with impeccable beat and rhythm pulsing in his blood, who was her instructor. She had been forgiven, she hoped.

The lessons were held as Kitappa's time permitted, and lasted as long as his mood did, an hour one day, three hours another day.

Sowmya crouched at half-bend, knees flexed, heels raised, resting on her toes, arms extended and level with shoulders, palms parallel and pointing down.

"Flex the knees more! The shoulder, don't let it sag!"

Mallika tipped her elbow with a finger. "Your muscles will strengthen in time, but posture should be held."

"Use the whole body, Sowmya! If you use the leg muscles alone, you will wear yourself out."

"Ok, from the top."

"TaKiTa Ta-Ka *Dhi-Mi,* TaKiTa Ta-Ka *Dhi-Mi*"

"Let's hear the feet speak! Let's go, let's go," Kitappa called out. "Accuracy is paramount, precision, precision!"

Sowmya used all the parts of her feet to tap out the sounds Kitappa called out. It made her recall the way Pillai used the parts of his hands and finger tips to produce texture to the sounds on his drum.

Sowmya learned to coordinate the shoulder movement with the chin movement, the chin movement with the eyes and the glance. She arched her brows, knitted them, and learned to make her whole upper body shimmer while her feet danced.

She learned to form the mudras symbols in her fingers, hold the pose and tap out the rhythm with her feet, and coordinate all these with precision. Kitappa kept pace, sometimes leading with his calls, sometimes following.

"Subtlety in facial expression," Mallika said. "It should arise slowly, fade and give way to something else to rise, leave space for a thought, poetry to form. This is what defines this art, the *abhinaya.* Take fury. Fury yes, but with compassion, this is what it's all about."

Sowmya danced. Desire. The celebration of the body, a gift, which is nothing if not love personified, bliss itself.

Bliss. It's only the body that can yield up its spirit in total bliss, in communion with itself. This is the dance.

chapter 6

The Raja of Bobbili was celebrating his son's wedding. At his personal request Mallika was giving one of her rare performances at the Amethyst Palace.

Mallika had a long generous face. Her cheeks would have been flat and sagged had they not been molded over a spectacular bone structure that made her face a wide canvas for all the emotions she brought into it. Here she was, a maiden with downcast eyes over those high cheeks, longing for her Paramour from the Seven Hills.

From the wings where she stood Sowmya saw melancholy in the way Mallika moved that day. The sight of the anti-dance protestors at the entrance wore her out. And now, dressed in her dance finery, she reminded Sowmya of the gold necklaces and silver waist-belts lying in pawnshop glass cases. Heaped in piles, their previous glory as ornaments lost, they seemed sad and diminished. Something terrible was certainly being lost in all these protests over dance and dancers. It was slipping through her fingers even as she watched Mallika dance, and urgency welled on her skin like pinpricks. She needed to hold on to this beauty before it got completely erased. She continued to clap long after the applause had died when Mallika finished her performance.

Later when Mallika was in the green room letting a photographer from an art journal take pictures, a man appeared at the door. Sowmya saw him shuffling behind a throng of people at the door waiting to see Mallika. He looked slightly abashed holding a bouquet, a man unaccustomed to waiting patiently at the back of anywhere. He was dressed in crisp, white clothes. His forehead shone like a mirror. About thirty, she figured, and pleasing to look at.

When he turned slightly and she got a better look, Sowmya recognized him as Satya, the owner of the *Madana Theater Group*. It had been bleeding cash when Satya bailed the company out of bankruptcy. Many of the leading artists were leaving the theater for the cinema production companies to work as actors and playback singers. He persuaded Kitappa to stay on as the director, brought artists in from the districts, hired musicians in the city. The company floundered a bit and had just barely begun to break even.

She worked her way to the door. He was startled when she touched his arm to draw his attention. She brought him to Mallika.

"Satya!" Mallika said as he approached. He gave her the bouquet and said something to her. They talked for a short while. Then as the fans started pressing into the room, he left.

She had quite forgotten about that incident until Kitappa mentioned his name a few days later. He was expecting Satya that morning, he said, when Sowmya began her dance practice in the back terrace. Satya had bought some recording equipment from an American who was going back to his country. He planned to set up a sound studio in Madras and produce playback for the talkies. He had wangled a job for Kitappa as well, a collaboration with the music director for the movie, *Rangoon Rani*. Kitappa was very excited and was anxiously waiting, and when Satya arrived they worked in the front porch for most of the morning.

Sowmya was working on a new movement to capture a certain line in a song, followed by the execution of a complex series of steps. She was missing the timing and the series just would not come together. It was a hot morning. She was streaming with sweat. The hair she had braided and pulled into a knot was coming undone as she did a double twist. When she unwound she ran straight into Satya, holding the symbol for lotus pointed at him. A stream of sweat trickled down her back. Satya stood rooted to the spot, holding aside the curtain of glass beads.

Her form collapsed. She placed her hands on her hips and looked at him.

"Who taught you to dance like that?"

Sowmya swiped her wrist across her forehead and shook it. Her dance lessons were kept quiet, not many people knew about it.

Kitappa came out, squeezing past Satya. He looked pained and uncomfortable.

"Our . . . niece," he said. "From back home."

"Unhmmm."

Sowmya gathered her hair and pulled it into a knot. Why can't he leave so she can get back to her practice? She smoothed the strands of hair and tucked them behind her ears, wiped her hot face on her sleeve.

"Come in, Satya!" Mallika called. She was sitting on the washing platform. "Sowmya, go get a chair, will you?"

Kitappa had already brought one and Satya sat down across form Mallika.

"Please," Satya said, signaling with his hand. "Continue."

Mallika smiled, but said nothing.

After a minute Satya asked, "How long has she been training?"

"She doesn't perform for the public," Kitappa said. "This is just, she was just . . ."

Satya turned around as if to see who was behind him.

"It's just me, there is no public. Please, please continue."

Sowmya's legs got very heavy, the cement floor hardened beneath her feet. This was precisely how the men must have arrived in the house in Nellyappan Street, at the legendary Krishnaveni's house. How easily Satya had walked in here, into their private space, and asked to see her dance? She did not think she could refuse, as if the dance belonged to others, to Satya. From the pit of her stomach she felt a "No!" rise. And yet, with a realization that shook her, her limbs wanted to dance for him, to this alluring power he possessed to command like a god. She wanted to watch every movement he made.

Satya leaned forward in his chair. "You have a protégé Mallika, worthy enough to follow your footsteps . . ."

How long had he been watching her dance?

"God's grace. She's gifted," Mallika said.

Satya smiled at Mallika. The tap near the well dripped water. When Satya looked at Sowmya, she could not lift her eyes and look him fully in the face.

"We can create great opportunities with such talent," he said without taking his eyes off her.

"Indeed."

"Arrange a debut."

"She should be so fortunate. But she does not wish to perform." Mallika said, and looked at Kitappa who was stone faced.

Satya leaned back and sat quietly.

"If this city sees her dance," he said, his voice now very soft, "if they see her, all this nonsense going on now? All that will stop. Look at the teacher she has. Your name draws crowds, even with the clowns at the gate. Such talent should not be hidden. It's God's gift, meant to be shared."

His voice was low, soothing. He would bring the world to her feet. Until now Sowmya had not dared to hope about performing on stage. But now she saw herself under the shiny lights, facing an audience. She felt a thrill.

"They never objected to our dance," Mallika said. "It is *us* they would like to simply do away with." She tossed a newspaper near him. There was an article that day about the anti-dance movement.

He gently shoved the paper aside. "Anti-dance. What is that? Don't pay attention to these people. It is not about the dance, it is not about you. Listen to me. It is about who gets the money, it always is. You know that, nothing new I need to tell you."

Satya, himself an attorney, had arranged for a friend in Thanjavur to file a suit against the trustees of the temple on behalf of Mallika, to claim her property back. The tradition of daughters inheriting all the property had angered the men of the dance community, and a political party had even taken that as one of its platforms—to outlaw the waiver of the Hindu inheritance law for devadasis. They even managed to argue that this discriminated against the women.

Satya drew a cigarette case from his shirt pocket – slim and golden. He flicked it open, drew a cigarette out and tapped it on the lid.

"I know the crowd at the Cosmopolitan Club," he said. "I know the important people in the city, I know their businesses. I plead their cases in court. I know council members. You take care of things," he waved his cigarette in the direction of Sowmya. "Your niece. Get her ready and leave the rest to me."

"Oh? Someone you know with a silver plate in her hand to invite Sowmya?"

Satya rose up. "Get her ready. The invitation will come."

chapter 7 1937

The night before her debut Sowmya sprang up from her bed, her throat dry. Parts of her costume were falling off as she danced, peeling off her limbs in strips and flying out and away even as she tried to grab at them. She stumbled over the folds that slipped from her waist, leaving her half naked as she tried to gather them up.

Sowmya stood up, the dream still vivid. It was a mistake to have designed the costume the way she had, it would not stand the rigor of dancing. She turned on the light and opened the almirah. The violet silk costume lay pressed and folded neatly. She ran her fingers over the seams checking that they were all double stitched. She pressed the garment against herself. The tailor had provided a solid waistband covered in mango colored silk, with wide tapes she could wind around twice. The sari pleats were stitched to the slim pyjamas. When she posed at half-bend with her knees flexed, feet flat on the ground and toes pointing away from each other, the pleats would unfold in a fan. The upper drape too was pleated and stitched in. There was nothing to slip or fall, nothing that was going to trip her up.

With a deep sigh she folded it back and put it away. She switched the light off and lay in her bed watching the moon go down, until the day of her debut brightened the eastern sky. It was the tenth day of October, 1937, the date emblazoned on the handbills announcing her maiden performance.

The early morning breeze was cool and tender in the back terrace. Sowmya brushed her teeth feeling jumpy, as though she was still in the dream. She dwelled on every feeling that emerged and washed over her. It had been months of arduous practice. She had stifled every question or argument that rose within her about Mallika's instructions. Instead she absorbed them all. Many times the practice broke down in tears (on her part) and in acrimony (Mallika's). Mallika expressed serious doubt that Sowmya would ever master the movements or live up to her expectation. She clicked her tongue in aggravation. She got into quarrels with her brother when Kitappa advised patience. This made Sowmya withdraw to a corner of the main room where she pulled out the bag she had arrived with from the train station. She would draw Mani's notebook out, somehow the touch of it bringing solace even if it was only in her imagination. She placed her finger beneath the words of the poem that Mani had read out to her in English on the last day he visited her in Ponmalar:

The desire of the moth for the star,
Of the night for the morrow,
The devotion to something afar
From the sphere of our sorrow...

Mani had a voice that flowed smooth like a stream over pebbles. After his visit everything would have shifted a bit and a dark hole would open up in her. In that corner of the room where she clutched his book, she felt that darkness burn a hole in her throat and knew it as mourning. Not for something lost but something never attained. One evening she looked up from the notebook to see Mallika standing at the doorway. She continued to look at Sowmya. "Come when you're ready," she said and climbed the stairs to the second floor terrace. When Sowmya followed her a bit later, Kitappa was impatient with annoyance but Mallika was calm. That day when when Mallika sang, *If you leave me now, O Rangasayee!* the anguish in the verse descended to Sowmya's feet and she knew exactly what she needed to show, and she knew how. She danced the yearning, she danced that bliss. She felt it all in a deep recess somewhere in her bones, in the pit of her stomach, or maybe it was between her shoulder blades. It was a burning heat that taught her exactly how to execute every movement, every flourish. The dance had finally possessed her. *"Sabbash!"* Kitappa clapped. Mallika beamed.

Sowmya splashed water over her face and pulled a towel off the line. The triumph that came after such despair still tasted sweet upon recall. She pressed the towel to her face to staunch the feelings that came so swiftly behind it. Mallika's beaming face, Mani's voice, the words of the poet, all converged in her head and brought forth a hot rush that filled her chest and throat. She knew it was not just Mani or his voice that she longed for, although it was that, but it was for that day when she swung up in the air with the forbidden flowers in her hair, the way she smelled her aunt Meenakshi right next to her in that house that her father had built. She wanted that day, that moment, returned to her.

Kitappa called to her from the front door. When she came out to the porch a man stood with a fruit basket wrapped in thin burlap. He handed it to her saying only that the boss had sent it.

She looked inside. Sapotas and guavas. A box containing pieces of candy wrapped in foil. A card that read *From Satyamurthy*. In a big lazy scrawl, the S enclosed the rest of Satya's full name within it. Such a feminine script for a man who acted like an emperor! A smile opened up inside. It was with a look of such imperious entitlement that he had stood frozen at the doorway when she was practicing. That day had stayed fresh in her memory. The agitation to ban temple dancers, the devadasis, was altogether in full swing in the city. Mallika had dismissed Satya's promise to arrange a debut as mere bravado. Then, when everyone had forgotten his promise, he had arrived with a contract from the Music Academy and an advance of two thousand rupees in an envelope. Mallika was speechless with surprise and pleasure. Satya came inside and sat back in his chair, lit a cigarette, and smiled at Sowmya. "Some fresh coffee, please," he had said. After that he would appear during practice. Arms flung across the top of the parapet walls, he would stand motionless, as though the music and the rhythm had settled on him like an invisible net, trapping him where he stood. She would look in his direction after an especially difficult execution of a movement and find him gone. Her feet would falter for just a moment. Later, she would find notes he had left behind, quick line drawings of her dancing, and she would be amazed at how accurately he had captured all the elements – the pose, the angle of the limbs, the hand gesture. She had saved all of them and would study them as though they were some clues to his heart and mind.

Sowmya unwrapped the foil off a piece of candy and put it in her mouth.

"Sowmya!" Mallika called from inside. "Come and light the lamp."

The candy melted into a smooth pool of bitter chocolate on her tongue. She immediately spit it out, wrinkling her nose at the taste. For no particular reason, she hid the card in her fist and ran inside with the basket.

Daylight had not yet entered the kitchen, which was never very bright to start with. Mallika was waiting for her. Already bathed, she had loosely knotted her dense damp hair, which was all gray now.

Sowmya poured fresh oil into the lamp and held a match to the wick. The flame hissed a bit as it caught on, shivered slightly and then settled down to a steady golden drop, setting the altar ablaze in its glow.

Only then she caught the glint of a silver tray on the floor, the shine of a zari border on the new sari, its color that of squash blossoms. And on top of it, like a shadow, was the set of ankle bells that were delivered a few days ago. Her heart lurched. Individually selected for their timbre, the tiny brass bells were stitched into four rows on a leather strip, lined with velvet where it would lie against her skin.

"I had my dedication ceremony when I was six," Mallika said. "Here, place your hands on the plate." She held up a brass plate containing a cup of oil, a few fresh turmeric roots.

Sowmya touched the plate.

"This is different, I don't have to tell you. You're a young woman, not a child. And this is not a dedication, it is your *betrothal*." Mallika placed a drop of oil at the parting of her hair. Weightless like twigs, the older woman's fingers shook. Sowmya wanted to hold that hand between her palms, tell her how much she loved and adored her. But one patronized Mallika that way only at one's peril.

Mallika took a turmeric root and drew it over Sowmya's cheeks and between her brows.

"The betrothal is to the art. The dance is the deity. It requires consciousness and purpose. This is what gives it beauty. Do you understand?"

Sowmya quickly nodded. These words were not new. She must have heard Mallika repeat them a thousand times, in various versions. What was always behind the words was her fear that Sowmya might introduce an improper movement here or there that would renew the ire on the devadasis. It was a spectator event after all, and their bodies were always exposed to improper gaze. This was the reason the "dance purification" movement was stripping the tradition of any erotic interpretation while emphasizing its sanctity. This, it was insisted, is the only thing that would save the dance from the dancers. Mallika thought of it as nonsense but she was also a realist.

Mallika picked up the sari and the ankle bells, and gave them to Sowmya.

Sowmya touched the bells to her forehead, to her eyelids. She was being entrusted with something immense and it filled her with self-doubt, grief.

"Do you understand, Sowmya?"

"Hanh?"

"Everything I know, my memories even, they are all in your now. The rest will come from that heat in you. Dance to that heat. Fear will reduce you to water on stage. Fake confidence. Don't make eye contact with the audience, look slightly above their heads. Smile."

Sowmya nodded. Her eyes floated in shiny wet glass.

"It is your dance that will cleanse your audience, remove their sorrows, redeem. Remember this when you see those jackals at the gate," Mallika said, reminding them both of the pickets, the anti-dance protestors who would be waiting for them tonight at the entrance to the auditorium.

Sowmya's fingers grazed the colored silk Mallika had presented to her. Wholeness, joy, beauty, all of these in the recall of that texture, in the smell of the weaver's starch. She fought memories of saris tumbling like water that pressed into her chest. Today was not a day to mourn anything; it was a day of celebration. Going down on her knees, she touched Mallika's feet with her forehead. Mallika raised her up and drew her into an embrace. Sowmya held on. Mallika had given her dance, and through it, belonging.

"Dance well. God bless."

After Mallika left the room, Sowmya remained in front of the altar. Smoke from the agarbathi mingled with the burning oil. Tonight her hair would be braided and decorated with hair ornaments, circled with flower garlands. She would line her eyes with kohl and dot the middle of her brow with red kumkum paste. She would dress in silks. All adornments removed from her after Ramki's death ten years ago would be returned to her. Would she know her place in this life of color, how to breathe in it? She had permitted the sheen, this exuberance of dance, into her life, breaking all prohibitions. How was this going to cost her?

• • •

Sowmya's performance was arranged under the auspices of the recently founded Music Academy and was held at the Raja Krithivas Hall on Thambuchetty Street. A hired car took Sowmya and the rest of the troupe the short distance from Mallika's house.

A group of about seven or eight people stood at the gate. Women from the Ladies Temperance Society hung placards around their neck, like garlands, as they walked to and fro. A man in the long robes of the Christian missionaries, bounded up to the car. "Go home, go home," he said. Other than this it was a quiet affair, a few young men waving large placards with some writing.

"Outlaw the dirty business of the devadasi! Our temples don't need their services!" Kitappa read the placards aloud for his sister.

But for her hands, which she held over her lap clutched tightly, Mallika sat without expression. Sowmya reached and held her hand. More faces converged near the windows. They patted the glass, leaving sweaty fingerprints. Even though never more than a dozen people turned out for these protests, this constant display of self-righteous anger was disconcerting. Sowmya fought the urge to get down from the car and lock eyes with a woman who peered at her and ask her what she wants. A gatekeeper held back the crowd of people and let the driver enter the compound.

Sowmya carried the suitcase that contained her costumes and walked into the building. It was not an auditorium but a large hall, airy and lit by the evening light from several windows. Workers were setting out chairs in rows for about a hundred people, all invitees.

Standing at the door to the hall she had a clear view of the stage, a raised platform, which was being set up by the lighting crew. Satya had brought these special equipments from his studio and was working with the men. He wore a blue shirt and had rolled up his shirtsleeves to his elbow. His watch, which he wore loose and gliding on his wrist, glinted in the light. She heard Kitappa stop and greet someone behind her, and the rest of the troupe was filing in and passing her. Satya suddenly turned his head, and upon seeing her he jerked his chin up slightly as a greeting, *hello there!* His smile went through her like a shot. For an instant she felt she had crossed some invisible border and was in a strange landscape, where she was someone else, someone who could put her hand out and touch the triangle of warm skin at the open collar of this man's chest, the whorl of hair that grew there. Her mouth went loose and soft.

Sowmya thought she would thank him for the fruits, but her shoulders and chest grew hot at the very thought, and it was impossible to see him, all of him, as if she were caught in a bright glare of light. Neelam, Mallika's niece and one of the singers, was beside her now and she gently nudged Sowmya with a finger at the waist. Sowmya smiled vaguely in Satya's direction, catching the edges of him, and then quickly walked across the hall and into the back room where she could get dressed and wait for the performance to start.

The room was small and dimly lit. Sowmya put her suitcase down on the floor, her heart still beating in her throat.

"What happened to you? Why didn't you say hello?" Neelam said, following her in.

"I don't know."

"Very dangerous when you don't know what you know, darling." Neelam's cheeks dimpled.

She was going to sing for Sowmya tonight. She had left a husband back in their village, she once told Sowmya, because she could no longer endure the small life he wanted to lead. The young man would come up once every few months, Neelam's plump and sweet boy in tow, to persuade her to return to him. But Neelam was trying to become a radio artist. Stay *here*, she would plead with her husband, while planting a hundred kisses on her little boy who squirmed and giggled with overflowing happiness and love. But the two always went back.

Neelam began to change into a crimson silk sari, ran a comb through her hair, which was already neat, tidied her make-up, which was already impeccable. "Have you seen Satya's wife?" she said, looking into a small hand mirror.

Sowmya spread a white sheet on the floor. She pulled out her make-up box from the suitcase, the costumes and jewelry, and laid them all out in the order in which she would get dressed. It was when she had gone to collect these from Naidu's shop that she had run into Satya's wife, Yamini. The now familiar black Chevrolet that Satya drove was parked at the curb. She got down from the rickshaw expecting to see him. Just as she was about to enter the shop the door opened. A thin, tall woman with striking eyebrows like wings emerged in the sunlight, in a swish of silk and flashing gold. She was a few years older to Sowmya but she immediately knew when the woman got into the waiting car and drove away. In that glimpse of Satya's personal life, that was so suddenly revealed to her as she stood on the sidewalk, Sowmya saw him tainted by his wife's wealth. Confused by her thoughts, Sowmya had clutched her fake jewelry and reached home with an angry headache. Being reminded of that now, she was afraid that headache was going to grip her again. She shook her head as if to chase it away.

"No?" Neelam checked her face one more time and turned to leave. She paused at the door, holding it open.

"Once," Sowmya said, turning towards Neelam. "I saw her at the market."

"She'll be here today," Neelam grinned. "Dance well." She left, closing the door behind her.

Sowmya sat back on her heels. The image of Satya from a few minutes ago, his smile, was still causing her heart to tumble. Did he smile that way when he looked at his wife, held her, touched her? No, denitely not, not like that.

It took her over an hour to make her hair and apply make-up. She had attached the hair ornaments, the sun and the crescent, with tiny braids at either side of her parting. She wove a hair switch into her braid to lengthen it so it fell to her hip and trimmed the end with velvet tassels. Finally, she stepped into the dance costume in the color scheme of sky-blue and mango. It shimmered in the cottony dying light that was converging inside the room.

Sowmya switched on the single light bulb that hung from the ceiling and waited.

The stage would now be decorated, Neelam would be lighting the lamps at the altar. Tentative notes emerged from the instruments getting tuned. The tanpura pumped notes into the air, infusing it with its drone. A cold fluid collected in Sowmya's belly and flowed into her veins, making it difficult to take a deep breath.

She tied on her new ankle bells and took a few steps. Perfect. They fit with comfort. She looked into the mirror someone had placed against the wall, the silvering all broken down. She shaped the sandalwood dot at her brows and tried a smile at her image. It felt as though the effort would crack her face. She stepped outside the room and stood at the wings.

The musicians sat on the dais under the hot lights that shone overhead. She thought she smelled the pomade in Kitappa's shining hair, and its familiar fragrance soothed her twisting stomach. Neelam hummed the scales, warming up her voice. Mallika sat upright next to her, with no trace of the terror that was in her eyes earlier in the car. Sitting sideways to the audience and facing the dancer, Pillai had turned his instrument on its side and was tuning it by tapping a piece of wood with a small stone, tightening the skin over the drum, testing the sound, *Thum-thum, Thum-thum*. Somu ran his slender fingers over the flute like a caress. Sowmya had been practicing with them daily now for several weeks. The sight of all of them together on the unfamiliar dais was not enough to ease her panic. She swallowed hard.

Voices rose in an excited drone from behind the heavy velvet curtains. A good turn out. All these people had walked through those same gates that they had a while ago, right past the picket signs and slogans, and had come to see Sowmya dance. She took a deep breath and fiddled with the pleats that draped over her bust.

Neelam lifted her voice in a high note and sang praise to the Single Tusked One. The huge velvet curtains drew apart. Mallika looked in Sowmya's direction and tilted her chin just a bit, *ready?* In that flash of movement Sowmya saw that it was going to be all right. Even if her lungs were heavy with breath and she could not take another one, even if her feet felt like lead glued to the floor, it was going to be all right. The music invited her on to the stage, into the space made sacred by Neelam's invocation. Her heart beating in her stomach, she made her way to the musicians' corner and performed the dancer's obeisance, touched the earth and then her eyelids, seeking permission to dance. She took her position at center stage.

Then Kitappa clicked the tiny cymbals tied to his thumb and fingers and, in his robust voice, called Sowmya to dance:

Thaam di-Tham *Thai* tat-Thai
Thaam di-Tham, *Thai* tat-Thai

And so she began, her very blood rising up in response to the call. Mallika's voice, the silvery tone of the cymbals, the majestic beats from the mridangam that never failed to make her want to move, and the lilt of the flute and the violin, all merged and flowed into the beats that Kitappa called out.

Beginning with flashing eyes, Sowmya moved to the rhythmic beats, from her head and neck down to the arms, shoulders, legs, calf and finally the feet, pacing them carefully. The music filled her and carried her until she became the sound. The beat picked up and she embraced the movements, balanced herself and extended her arms, folding and unfolding them in geometrical shapes.

Thaam di-Tham dari kita Thai tat-Thai,
Tham di-tham, kita taka Thai tat-thai,
Thaam di-Tham dari kita Thai tat-Thai.

It was a warm up, inviting the audience to the pleasure and the beauty of the gestures, the forms and shapes of the dance. It ended with a flourish of steps:

Thai diditai tha! Thai diditai tha! Kitataka, kitataka,
kitataka talang-thom tha!

The finish! Her lungs eased, her pulse synchronized with the music and the beat. The weight and cold left her. *Look above their heads, don't make eye contact.*

She stood center stage again. Something from her depth stepped out and became the nayika, the storyteller and the story all at once. She felt powerful, took possession of the stage. With each step she took, each pose she struck, one moment built upon the other. She mouthed the lyrics. She was the shimmering bird one moment, its plume fully unfolded and strutting, and next she was the Youthful God of the Seven Hills riding the peacock. Her face held in a bashful slant, she was the maiden, signaling her longing, recounting the dream when He promised marriage, *would you fail me now?* The verse repeated and each time she told another facet of the story, plumbing the meaning, the mystery, completing the series with a flourish of steps.

Before she approached the main and central piece of the dance, she danced two other minor pieces, made mostly of gestures and miming that did not tax her strength too much, that calmed and controlled her breath. She was warming up for the main piece, the varnam, color.

Varnam was the jewel in the teacher's crown, the culmination of all the student's training expressed in the colors of the nine emotions. Bringing rhythm and melody together in a rising arc, where the verse and its meaning receded to a mere excuse, it tested the dancer's mettle, the accuracy of her footwork, its precision and speed, all of it synchronized to a fine detail in the resolution of each vignette. This was the dance critic's test, what would make or break her in the reviews that would appear tomorrow.

Neelam sang:

Do not desert me now, on this intoxicating night!
Lethal love arrows, like pouring rain.

Your sweet lips, the Divine Face.
Lord of Lords, the Presence, Unfathomable,
embrace me. Now!

Sowmya surrendered to the longing. She did not notice that her costume, damp with sweat, was sticking to her legs, or that a bell from her anklets had torn off and flung out on the floor. She only saw the sound, only heard the dance: the leap she would make, the pause for a fraction of the beat before landing with the elegance of the antelope. There was nothing else in her vision. She summoned to her face all that was needed to communicate the agony, the bliss, the sacred story, the mystical moment. *It will cleanse your audience, redeem!* Her feet, weightless, flew over the ground.

Kita-thaka-dharikitathom! Kita-thaka-dharikitathom!
Kita-thaka-dharikitathom!

The house lights dimmed but just before total darkness descended, in an instant like a blink, she caught a familiar face out there among the audience. And then she heard something like thunder. It was applause! Her feet would ache tomorrow but now she felt exalted.

The lights came up. Sowmya pinned her eyes to the spot where she saw the face before. He looked thinner than she remembered but she would have recognized him anywhere. Just as suddenly she lost him when a crowd of people stood up and started to move. She wondered if she had imagined him, conjured him up with just the force of her desire to see him again, but then she saw him inching against the wall walking towards the door. Why did Mani not wait to see her after coming to watch her performance?

Someone held her elbow and led her to the side of the stage near the orchestra. She now saw clearly Satya's wife, Yamini, standing up next to Satya. Her end drape, rich and heavy with zari, clung to her thin hips. When she smiled it would be brilliant, Sowmya knew, and when she laughed it would ring with the nonchalance of privilege. None of Satya's clues had revealed all this.

"You killed, amma!" Kitappa grinned with happiness. "Vanquished them!" Mallika's hand was on her back, kneading her shoulders. Had Sowmya tried to speak she would have wept.

A woman slowly rose now from the audience in the front row and was escorted to the stage. With short hair like straw, she was a white woman in a dark long dress, stockings, and black shoes. Another burst of applause as the old woman was garlanded. Sowmya only knew they called her Mrs. B. She spoke for a short time and turned several times in the direction where Sowmya sat crushed between Mallika and Neelam, surrounded by the musicians. She smiled at Sowmya and nodded and then continued to speak into the microphone in English. Sowmya followed with great difficulty and with a little success. She mentioned the classic traditions, the need to return purity to Indian art. "Thus," she said, "we will strengthen India's nationhood, through dance."

Neelam's restless knees pressed against Sowmya's back, and she felt Kitappa's breath behind her.

Everyone was clapping and it seemed the applause was for Satya and Yamini. He never looked in Sowmya's direction nor did he, later when the garlanding and tributes were over, appear in the back room with congratulations. Surrounded by people, many of whom she did not know, Sowmya kept glancing at the doorway. Her eyes hurt at his absence.

"You should have picked an eggplant purple for the costume," Mallika said in the car that Satya had arranged for them, as they set off towards home. "You needed a color with some weight. The violet got washed out in the light."

Sowmya leaned back in the seat. The humid night pressed on her face.

"Are you listening to me, Sowmya? Pace yourself, you cannot put all this energy in each item! What was that English lady saying? What did she say about the dance?"

"She said *ooh*, and then she said *aah*," Kitappa said. "When white people do that everything we do suddenly becomes *art*, it's gold. Why else do you think Satya arranged for the English lady to come and garland you, akka? He knows exactly how to wring money out of the big people in this city. They need that *chaap!*" He said, punching the air with his fist. "The *English* stamp of approval."

"Foreigners will always be our masters."

It had started to sprinkle rain and puddles of rainwater spotted the street. The crowd had thinned out and people were walking home in a slow, sporadic way. The car passed a knot of people holding posters over their heads as shelter from the rain. Sowmya turned and looked at them through the rear window. A thin young man was riding a bicycle and she looked closely at his face with a beating heart. Mani must be long gone now.

She turned around and sat back in her seat. It seemed not so long ago that Mani had kindled her imagination, made her see that something that lay beyond the interminable stretch of hot, sunlit hours that had filled her days in her father's house. She had been sure she would find it if she could just get past that never changing horizon, if only she could fly over and beyond it. She was in that place now, and what was happening right here at her doorstep was all too real, and there was no magic in it. *Swadeshi*, buy domestic. They made bonfires of foreign cloth from Manchester on the streets, but all she saw was the owner of the small piece-goods shop that she passed by every day, head in his hands, watching his entire life going up in flames.

She had made a few feeble attempts to find Mani in the city, always with dreadful certainty that he was in jail somewhere. It had become her practice to get every journal and newspaper available and search for him among the anonymity of heavily censored and meager news items.

She scanned stories of Congress party activities and arrests, communal riots and worker strikes, derailment of trains, anything that would provide a clue to his whereabouts. Gandhi had issued a call to all young men to leave their colleges and dedicate their lives to the national movement. Once she saw one S.Mani was arrested at a *hartal*, a workers' strike in a coffee plantation in Karar. She was sure it was him. Then the war news, soldiers returning from Italy, from Singapore and Burma, had erased his tracks.

What, or who, since she could not imagine him at a dance performance, brought him to see her dance? He must have been furious when she did not get down from the train at the junction, knowing very well that Mallika had been lying to him. When she sent the telegram to the address he had written on her notebook, she never doubted for a moment that he would meet her. So thin that he seemed frail, he had carried the weight of love and anguish and had come to meet her. How badly she had mangled this gift he'd given her, for her own selfish reasons? And now, out of nowhere just like that he had appeared before her. Why did she expect he would have stayed or would wish to come up to speak to her?

Following the debut there were angry letters to the editor in *The Indian Standard*. Bristling with outraged sensibility, the letters condemned the dance and the dancers for contributing to the degradation of the social fiber, the corruption of national character. Mallika banned the *Standard* from the house.

Through the Music Academy's support Sowmya performed at several more venues. Satya arranged for a few performances in the auditoriums where he was on the board or through people from whom he had chits to collect. The money Sowmya made covered the expense of costumes, the accompanists, and paid the rent.

Amidst the harsh disparagement of the dance tradition, a few reviews appeared that spoke with a quiet clarity. "A true protégé for Mallika," one journal said after a performance, giving a thoughtful critique. Sowmya brought the journal home and read it out to Mallika, but their measly praise only angered her.

"Where do they think this dance comes from?" Mallika said.

Rejection of the body Sowmya understood very well. She kept all writings about dance and against dance from Mallika's eyes.

To avoid the picketing at the front gate, the performance hall's secretary would hold a small door open for them that would lead into a back alley, his expression slightly abashed. It wore out Mallika, a little more every time.

"Like thieves," Mallika said. "We leave like thieves."

chapter 8 1938

The summer monsoon had failed to arrive. Sowmya looked up at the ceiling fan that merely stirred down curls of hot air. She pinched off a small amount of the moist paste of the marudani leaves, rolled it between her fingers, and pressed it into a border along the edge of Mallika's foot. It was the only cooling thing to do. When the paste dried in a few hours and was rinsed off it would leave a beautiful coral stained pattern.

"Look, your hand will get all stained this way, and the pattern will not show," Mallika said.

Ignoring her, Sowmya lifted Mallika's foot with one hand, and dabbed a small amount of the paste on her nails. The foot was slight and small in her hand. The old stain form months ago on the toenails had completely grown out but for a sliver of crescent at the tip.

Mallika did not know of the latest cancellation, and Sowmya did not have the heart to tell her yet. The secretary of the theater company, Ragini Sabha, came by last week to announce his helplessness. The sponsor had backed out, he explained. The opposition to staging the dance was coming from some powerful members. The man's awkwardness was genuine. "We go way back," he had said, remembering Krishnaveni who had lived on the same street as his grandfather. Mallika listened in silence.

Now Madras Fine Arts had asked for a return of the advance. Earlier that morning they had sent a letter through a messenger, who was instructed to wait for a response.

Mallika had always believed in settling her accompanists' bills right after each performance. "We all have bellies to fill." Now she found it difficult to look them in the eye when they came to visit, and was filled with shame when they left without mentioning what was due. Their loyalty for old time's sake would last only so long, soon they would desert her.

Sowmya patted a circle at the center of the sole. Mallika's toes curled.

"Enough, girl! What do I need to doll up for? Here, give it to me, I will put it on you," she reached for the dish.

When Sowmya drew the paste away from her and lifted the other foot, Mallika surrendered and leaned back on the chair. Sowmya carefully worked the paste into a pattern.

"There is a small *javali*," Mallika said leaning forward to look at Sowmya. "A short, sweet love song of a dance. My grandmother taught me this."

Sowmya paused and looked up.

"Radha accuses Krishna. 'You are flirting with the milkmaids' she says, 'and you ignore me.'" She mimed. With eyes like daggers, the young woman slays the handsome Krishna with deadly scorn. Heaving with desire, yet she sulks. "She scolds the Blue-skinned God," Mallika said, signaling the cloud-capped sky, the peacock feather in his cap, the flute-player, stealer of hearts.

Sowmya sat back on her heels. Timeless emotions captured in Mallika's aging face made them new.

"So what does Krishna do? He offers to massage Radha's foot. Radha then instructs him on how to do it right!" Mallika chortled at this pluckiness. "You can add this as a small piece towards the end for the program next month. A sweetener, a surprise—"

"Program got canceled." Sowmya stood up, wiped her hands on a wet towel, and picked up the marudani dish.

Mallika sat up.

"The secretary came this morning. We returned the advance. What was left of it." Sowmya folded a pillow and tucked it under Mallika's feet so the paste didn't smear before it dried.

The terrace was sunlit and smelled of white heat. She rinsed her hands. They had stained a bright orange already, these were *excellent* leaves. She threw handfuls of water over her face, which was slick with sweat. But even that did not offer relief in the heavy, still air that had even silenced the crows.

The bright shimmer that she had thought was dance, a life source, had become clouded, become something much more complicated. The pickets at the gate did not frighten

Sowmya anymore, but it was destroying Mallika. She had lost the case to retrieve her property back in the village. More than anything, it hurt when her own cousin bought the auctioned property. Sowmya's eyes prickled at the unfairness of it all.

Satya appeared regularly at the house, as though these visits would somehow erase his guilt in this whole venture that was turning painful and ugly. The truth was when Satya came, even in his arrogance, a stance that came to him so naturally, it felt as though all things were possible. But the sight of him only infuriated Mallika.

"Send the man home to his wife," she would say between gritted teeth when he left. "He looks stricken. We are all done with that kind of thing here, somebody tell him."

Sowmya wondered if the message was a warning for her. This must have been how they came to the doorstep at Mallika's house on Nellyappan Street. Her dance, and no less her youth, drew admirers. Mallika fell in love. "Give up your dance," the man said, she once told Sowmya. A wholesale trader of peanut oil, he had a wife and three children in Salem, and yet he came bearing gifts. He would marry her, he said, make her his wife, give her respectability—and steal her soul. What else could Mallika do but refuse?

"Dance has to please you first, Sowmya," she said. "If you dance for him," gesturing with a tilt of her head, "what happens when he leaves?"

Sowmya would tease her then, making a joke of her fears. But later when Satya left their house in George Town, a cold stone would settle in her stomach. She imagined his long legs clad in white garments striding up the stairs to their bedroom, his head bending over her, except it wasn't Sowmya; it was Yamini's face that was on the pillow. Yet his weight was on Sowmya's hips, his breath on her eyelids. The protest from her heart would make Sowmya toss in her bed. She struggled with the burning and the melting, the quivering force that shook her as her fingers brought her to that sweet death. The erotic verses she mimed for her dance mocked her in her solitude.

"Let's go to the beach," she called from the terrace. Sunlight had dimmed from white-hot to yellow gold. "At least we can catch some sea breeze and cool off."

When Neelam came to visit a little later, the three of them set off with Kitappa towards the beach.

The fisher folks' catamarans became visible as they approached the sea, and they smelled the salt and dead fish from the nets spread out to dry in the sun. White-crested waves rolled in, air-soft and bubbly. Sowmya hitched her sari up to her knees and waded into the water. A big surf crashed close sending her scrambling backwards.

"Wafers, sir? Fresh and hot, madam." A man approached, scurrying impossibly in this heat, two large tins slung over his shoulders.

They crunched on the thin, crispy rice wafers dotted with cumin and cracked black pepper, and made their way towards the lighthouse in the north, away from the crowd. Kitappa and Neelam walked up front and Sowmya followed beside Mallika.

"Have you seen the poster?" Neelam asked, her voice picked at by the breeze.

"For The Thief of Blue Mountain?"

"Satya had designed the poster himself."

Satya had set up a studio in Mylapore, where his wife owned some land, and was producing a film. No need to go to Bombay anymore for sound recording. Neelam was on the staff at Madras Broadcasting Company, and was recording two songs for the film. An actress would lip-synch the song. Talkies had made everything possible.

When they arrived home at dark, Satya's Chevrolet was parked at the top of the narrow lane leading to the house. A cigarette tip glowed inside.

Satya got out as they approached. He was dressed in neatly pressed white veshti, which he always wore long and flowing, the zari edge sweeping the floor at his feet, and a loose open collared white shirt. His hair was combed neatly to a shine. He smiled directly at Sowmya and made the stars rise up bright. He accepted with ease the invitation to eat with them.

The power went out just as they sat down for dinner. Kitappa carried in a hurricane lamp in and lit it. Sowmya and Neelam brought the dishes from the kitchen to the front room and they ate in the moonlight that flooded the windows and doorways.

Later, after the women cleaned up, Sowmya closed up the kitchen door and plopped down next to Mallika on the sofa and rested her head on her shoulder. She was glad for the power outage. In its darkness she could observe Satya closely without being watched.

A young woman from Bombay, Devaki Bai, would lip-synch Neelam's song in the film, Satya was saying. He had arranged for her to come down for a screen test.

Shooting and *screen test*. These were words so remote from the silent shadow images Sowmya had seen on a silver screen so long ago in Ponmalar. *The Seizure of Draupadi's Robes* at the tent cinema. A projector ran noisily. Lights streamed out of it and raised shadows on a luminous screen. A man appeared before the screen and started narrating the story. He read the text out from the screen, taking on different personas, using a squeaky voice for the women characters. Every time there was a reel change, a troupe came in to sing. It came as a surprise to recall now that it was a silent film. It had seemed so full of sound and action.

"How much will you pay her?" Sowmya asked Satya.

"We haven't negotiated yet," Satya said.

"A Hindi-speaking woman from Bombay, cannot even speak Tamil properly," Neelam said, clicking her tongue in disapproval. "You can't find someone to hire locally?"

"Find a Tamil speaking talented actress for me! Someone who can dance. They are all afraid of the cinema.

Devaki Bai was famous even before she came to cinema," Satya said. "She's experienced. She is very popular in Marathi dramas. She sings. And she will dance."

"Here in Madras, they don't take risks. They stay with what they know," Kitappa said. "They know drama, a sure thing."

"There is more money in cinema."

"Drama or cinema, a woman always makes less than a man, a *lot* less," Neelam said. "Even the most talented ones."

"Dance for the cinema?" Mallika bristled. She waved a reed fan uselessly over her perspiring face. "What kind of talent do you need for that?"

Satya looked at the tip of his cigarette, tapping at the ash. Kitappa rose to raise the wick in the lamp, his face illuminated in the glow.

"How much would you pay *me*?" Sowmya asked, watching the way he played with the cigarette.

Satya turned and looked at her. "For you?" His voice was mellow, warm honey in the semi-darkness. He tapped at the tip of his cigarette again. "You can—"

"Sowmya! If you go into the cinema——" Mallika turned and looked at her. "Why would you want to do that? That's all for those foreigners and their, their--debauchery. It's *not* our way. You will lose your authority, you will—"

"Authority? Tell me. How much advance did we get this month? How many bookings?" Satya asked. He knew every engagement they got.

Still, it was a cruel question. Sowmya's face grew hot.

Mallika looked at Kitappa for an answer. He looked at the dusty designs on the floor. The Chettiar's agent had paid a visit on Saturday, a gentle man. How is everything, he had asked. Six months' rent was in arrears. He may not be so gentle the next time.

Tenderness surrounded Sowmya's heart for the way Mallika was hurting. But it would not compare to the humiliation they would suffer when they have to vacate the house. The Chettiar was not going to be patient forever. If dancing for the cinema would pay the rent, why not? Mallika was so charged with her own demons that she would not see reason.

Suddenly the light bulb above came alive with dim yellow light. The fan creaked overhead.

Satya slapped a hand over his forehead.

"I almost forgot what I came to tell you!" he said. "I have arranged for a dance for the earthquake fund. We will get Gandhiji himself to preside over Sowmya's performance. Even Doctor M will finally be silenced. Let's see the pickets then!" He turned to Sowmya. "It is also great exposure for you…"

The earthquake had occurred in Bihar four years ago, in the winter, destroying life and homes. As if that was not enough, floods followed and malaria had become rampant. Gandhi had declared it all as punishment for the practice of untouchability, the tainting of people forever by the menial work they did. He urged every Indian to clean his own latrine.

"Satya, what we know is our dance," Mallika said with forced patience. "What do we know about making speeches? We have had enough social reform. You seem to think we live in your personal orchards in Mylapore. It's all right for your Brahmin women to march on the streets, roll bandages, satyagraha for Gandhi, this, that. We *work* for our living."

"Well, we can get her into those orchards." Satya looked at Sowmya. "Simple enough," he smiled.

Sowmya looked at the odd patterns of russet stain on her palm in the silence that followed.

"How simple? Tell me," Mallika's voice was soft but Sowmya heard her fierce breathing next to her.

"Mallika! What I meant was—"

"Akka!" Kitappa said, rising up. "It was a joke, take it easy. Satya, be careful please, these things—"

"Mallika. You have completely misunderstood—"

"Shhh! Everybody calm down, please—" Sowmya touched Mallika's arm.

Kitappa put out the hurricane lamp. The room smelled of kerosene.

"I'd like to see the studios," Sowmya said.

Satya looked a little stunned from Mallika's assault and it did not seem like he heard her. Sowmya watched the single stream of sweat that ran down from his impeccable hairline, a small pulse beat at his temple. He would make her shine like a star, she knew this.

"Some day, when it is convenient," she said.

Satya stood up. He offered to drive Neelam home and they left together. A second later he appeared back at the door. "I'll send the car around tomorrow," he said and left again.

Their voices in conversation could be heard as Satya and Neelam walked out of the compound and up the lane towards the car, the sound diminishing and finally the night became silent again.

"A man of many talents," Mallika said.

Sowmya exchanged looks with Kitappa. She got down on the floor and kneeled close to Mallika. She took the older woman's hand in hers, and Mallika did not jerk her hand away this time.

"Look! How nicely the stain has set!" Sowmya stroked Mallika's open palm.

"You must stop judging him like this," Kitappa said. "Your anger is misplaced. He's only trying to help, that's all he does."

Mallika looked at her brother. In that heartbeat of time Sowmya saw the shame of overdue rent, the protests and slogans out there in the city and the humiliation of cancellations, all these forces that seized bits and pieces of their lives, recede. In the way the siblings looked at each other, life was once merely ordinary, sweet.

"It's going to be alright," Kitappa told his sister, nodding. "The world will not end if Sowmya danced for the cinema."

Mallika looked down at Sowmya's hands, picked up

her hand, turned it over and examined her palm. "Good. These were excellent leaves."

Sowmya switched off the lights, locked up the doors, and stood in the still moonlight that lit up the terrace like it was day. She wondered about the studio. She could not begin to imagine what it would be like or how they made movies but she was sure she wanted to be part of it, part of Satya's dream.

When Sowmya finally climbed the stairs to her bed, Mallika and Kittappa were both snoring, keeping up a steady chorus.

She had brought with her the leftover marudani paste in its leaf pack. She sat down on her mattress and began to shape the paste into small caps on each of her left fingers. Carefully arranging her pillow, without smearing the damp and soft paste, she stretched out. The moon grinned overhead.

The bachelor who sublet one of the rooms in the house next door played his gramophone. The hit song from the film *Chakku Bai* played:

The song I hear in the wind
Oh how it stokes my dreams!

chapter 9

Satya's Chevrolet arrived at nine in the morning. Sow-mya had made a loose braid of her damp hair to dry, and dressed carefully but casually. She certainly did not want to send any wrong signals to anybody, particularly the married ones. She tried to get Mallika to go with her as a buffer.

"Come with me."

Mallika shook her head, *No*. But she followed her movements with a wounded expression as Sowmya walked between the two front rooms, getting ready, as if her visit to the film studio was an act of betrayal against Mallika. She succeeded in getting Sowmya to feel vaguely guilty.

The black car waited at the usual place, at the top of the lane. The driver, a skinny fellow named Lazarus, opened the door for her. She recalled Yamini stepping down from this very car once in a swish of silk and gold, and vanishing into Naidu's shop. The car very likely belonged to her. Her father had made his wealth as a contractor for the Indian Railways and had built a house in the orchards of Mylapore. Sowmya entered the car feeling like an intruder.

The driver had lit an *agarbathi* and stuck it to the dashboard on a holder. It had burnt down to a stub and its fragrance blended with that of the hot leather.

The car negotiated the narrow lanes thronging with pedestrians, vendors, carts, and animals. Once he turned into the Beach Road, however, the car sailed along, the sliver of shimmering ocean at her window. Sowmya relaxed into the comfort of the cushioned seats and the smooth motion of the automobile. The colleges, Lady Wellington and the Presidency, several other buildings, some built in a style to capture some bygone grandeur, some just plain and painted white or cream and their faces impersonal, melded into the landscape of bright hot light and tarred pavement.

The Ice House passed by. The man who built it must have had some kind of vision. He had built it two stories high, with circular verandahs and large paladin windows -- baleful eyes watching the sea forever. Sunlight flashed around its window frames. It had warehoused ice that came from America at one time, but now a woman ran a boarding house there for young Brahmin girls, all widows. At night, these windows glowed a sad orange and sent a small shiver down her spine when she passed them.

The car turned right into Lloyd's Road, which was canopied green with banyans and pipal. Within a few minutes Sowmya saw the gates with a small hand-painted sign in black and white at the entrance—*Madras Cinetone Studios*. She had somehow expected to see a large building on a busy street, like the *Vel Studios* on Mount Road where her promotional pictures were taken. Instead the car entered what seemed like a coconut grove. It dipped and bobbed over a dirt path that led from the gate. Curving around the periphery of this property, the driver finally brought it to a stop near a shed of corrugated tin topped by a thatched roof. A small table and three chairs were set up on a patch of grass in front of the shed. It seemed quite unbelievable that cinema was made, captured in tin cans, *here*.

The sandy earth was cool with shade when she stepped down from the car. A slim young man hurried up to her, dressed in white pyjamas and a long peacock-blue tunic. His hair hung to his shoulders in glossy waves.

"Namaskaram," he said, and struck a pose with his hands pressed together. "Please come. Satya-sir is waiting inside."

"Sowmya! Come, come, come in!" Satya emerged from the shed. "This is Kumar, I was just telling him to expect you. He's the choreographer."

"Choreographer," she repeated.

"I saw your debut at the Krithivas Hall," Kumar said, two small diamonds twinkling at his ear lobes. "That final piece in *Mohanam . . .*" Kumar pressed his right palm over his heart, shook his head, rapturous. A mother of pearl ring glowed on his fifth finger.

Kumar and his appearance delighted her. She didn't know what to say, she smiled and bowed her head in acknowledgment.

"Yes," Satya broke in, giving Kumar a look, which the younger man ignored. "Yes, yes, yes, right. We can all see how much you adore Miss Sowmya, Kumar. But there is something I need to show her, if you don't mind. Sowmya,

come in, come inside the studio. Kumar, get me when
Prakash gets here."

Satya picked up a chair and followed her inside the shed.

It was hot inside and smelled moist, of roots. A bright
patch of light fell from the open doorway. A table in the
center divided the room.

When her eyes adjusted to the dim light she saw that at
the far end of the shed was a beautifully decorated room.
Intrigued, she drew closer. It was not a room at all but a
set. Set up with several painted screens, it was constructed
to look like the interior of a mansion.

There were several painted flowerpots on painted ped-
estals. Voluminous draperies were tied back over painted
windows. Outside the window was a park, a bridge over a
small brook. In the distance was a hill on which a house
or a temple, she was not sure, stood. Its walls covered with
vines. There were woods beyond in the perspective. Her
eyes searched for something in that painted horizon, in
those mythical woods.

She turned to see a young boy setting up a screen a few
feet from the table. He placed a gramophone on the table.
A projector had been wheeled in to the center.

Satya dropped a disc on the gramophone and cranked
it up. He signaled to Sowmya to sit down on the chair
he had brought in. The projector lit up the screen with
blinding light and whirred noisily.

A white woman appeared on the screen. Her skirt, a
gauzy material in black striped with gold zari, billowed

all around her legs, as though a wind was blowing. The camera panned the woman's sturdy calves, and the bells she wore around her ankles, stitched in the stringy North Indian style. A wide belt gripped her bare waist. Her short and close fitted bodice was edged with pearl tassels, and she waved a sheer drape. A silk turban capped her hair, from which strands of beads hung. A peacock feather stuck out of it, and waved to and fro as she danced.

She held her face up like a flower; she lifted her chin and looked at the camera from beneath her half-opened eyelids. She smiled vaguely, as though she was either in a trance or being pious. She stooped down to pick up a plate with a lamp and some flowers in it. Carrying the plate on her left hand, she strewed flowers with the other.

Now a man, also white, in a tunic and dressed like a prince joined her. He shadowed the woman's movements.

The gramophone suddenly began to play. Expecting to hear some European melody Sowmya sat up when she heard Kitappa's voice. She looked at Satya with surprise but he pointed to the film silently, *watch*. Then a woman's voice joined in. The white couple continued to dance to the Tamil song. Sowmya tried to ignore the mismatch of the melody and the movements of the silver images as they finished.

The film ran out and the projector sprayed white blinking light on the screen. The gramophone contin-ued to crank out the song and then the song too ended.

Satya shut down the projector. The record swished in the gramophone.

"Ruth St. Denis and Ted Shawn, dancers from America," Satya said as he lifted the needle off the gramophone. "Two years ago they toured Bombay and Calcutta, and here. She was not a big hit here in Madras when she came, but they loved her in Bombay. Somebody called her the avatar of Shiva in the *Times of India*."

"Shiva's avatar!"

"She calls it an Indian temple dance."

Sowmya looked at him for a moment. "I see."

"I know," Satya said, nodding. "I don't know what song that they danced to originally, the record that went with it is missing. Many dances are like that in Europe, no lyrics. The dancer expresses the feelings that are in the music." He came near her and leaned on the table. "I just want you to have an idea of what it looks like in film."

She imagined the dance again, the billowing skirt, the peacock feather, and a turban! Her expression of solitude was a passive portrayal, with very slight facial animation. The man seemed to be there only to highlight her dance. It made her nervous and excited.

"I just want you to see what is possible with film. You see what they are doing," Satya pointed to the blank screen. "You see how the camera catches it all differently? That is the beauty."

Sowmya thought of the camera panning the ankles, the calves, the bare waist, the woman's face.

"You want me to dance like *that?*"

"No! No, no, no. I don't want you to dance like that or in any other way. I just want you to see the possibility . . ."

Her mind raced with the brilliantly lit pictures. She nodded. She remembered Mallika in the front room, sullen, silent.

"This is not *our* way."

"You sound like Mallika," Satya said, annoyance darkening his face. "She will of course hate it. She cannot accept anything new—"

"Not true."

Satya clicked his tongue dismissively.

"She's fearless when she dances," Sowmya continued. "She has developed so many new moves. This city has been just *so* hard on her . . . "

"I know all that! You think I don't know that? Every single thing I do, trying to get a *sabha* to open up here, over there—everything I do, I do for *that,* what she has. What she—"

"I am sorry," she said, seeing him upset. "I shouldn't have said that, I am sorry. Please don't be so angry. Just . . . just don't call this," she pointed to the screen, "a temple dance in front of her."

They sat silently.

"I have to make her comfortable about this. The costume, the dancing, I don't know … well, that's impossible. Let me see, let me see."

"You are her *student,* not her possession." A deep groove

formed right above his left brow. She wanted to reach up and stroke it, smooth his annoyance away.

"Same thing," she smiled to mollify him. What Mallika had given her was precious, and she did indeed own that part of what Sowmya had. She did not have to explain any of this to him or anyone else. She only needed to make her dancing work for his cinema.

"What I'm thinking is this," Satya squeezed his chin. "Kumar can copy this dance sequence, he can copy anything. He just has to see it once. He can work with you. If you *want* to work with him," he added quickly. "Whatever you want."

Sowmya dabbed at her face with a kerchief. How was she going to meet all of this energy with just her dance?

"I am thinking a group dance. I already have a male lead, a singer. The hero—" Satya looked at his watch, frowned. "Prakash should be here, any minute now."

"The hero?"

"No, the screen writer."

"Isn't he the one, he wrote the lyrics—"

"For *Rangoon Typhoon,* yes," he nodded. That song that Kitappa set to music was lip-synched by a handsome actor in Satya's film. It became an instant hit. The film however flopped. Satya lost heavily. He had quickly moved on to this next film.

She looked at the projector that stood silent, the film of the woman dancing that it contained. She rose, went around the projector and stood facing it. The film played in her mind.

Satya's wrist watch flashed when he moved his arm. His attention distracted her, so she focused on the watch, the way she would focus on Mallika's face to steady her mind. She lifted and tucked her sari folds at her waist. She began to think of the woman by her name, Ruth. She raised her hands, extended them overhead as Ruth did, and brought them down in a wavy motion. She twirled on her toes, trying to feel the movement. She imagined herself in that skirt that looked like it was made of a piece of rain-cloud, the way it moved with the dancer's movement. A smile floated on her face, prayerful. Shiva's avatar.

Satya crossed his arms and his shirtsleeve formed a V around his rounded and smooth elbows. In the humid room lit only by the light from the open door she realized she wanted to keep looking at him, and for a very long time. The dancing figure of Ruth St. Denis evaporated. She plucked at her sari folds, smoothed them down, and fixed the drape over her blouse.

Satya scratched his chin, ran his hand down his throat, stubbly already with beard. She watched him, waiting.

"Mallika'll hate it," he said.

Sowmya sighed, leaned against the table. She tried to heave herself up but it was a little higher than what she had judged. Satya made a move toward her as if to help, and she was afraid he was going to hoist her up like a child. She steadied herself and perched on the table. In the heat of the room she smelled the starch on his clothes, his sweat. She looked down at her bare feet, dangling above the floor.

She swung them slightly. She felt giddy with a lightness around her shoulders. She wanted to laugh, as though there was something wonderful and shiny out there in the world, a fragile thing.

"What is your film about?" she asked, looking at her swinging feet.

"Well, that's what this meeting with Prakash is about. I had discussed a rough idea with him. Let's just say it's about freedom. It will be that, if I get the permit when I finish the film."

"Freedom? You mean *Swarajya*?"

"Well yes, but not like that. More personal kind of freedom," he said. He sounded reluctant, like a boy shy about talking of some secret passion. She wanted to reach out and ruffle his smooth hair.

"Isn't he in the Justice party?"

"Are you asking me how can we be friends?"

The Brahmins are incapable of the concept of democracy, Prakash had written in a Justice editorial, and the removal of Brahmin supremacy in the legislative council is paramount. Satya's father-in-law, Sundaram Aiyar, a Brahmin, was contesting in the election. She read these things in the journals she brought home and sometimes Kitappa would talk about it with her.

"We have known each other since we were so high," Satya held his hand at waist level. "I have eaten in his grandmother's kitchen. Politics is politics, you cannot take it personally. In an election, Brahmins will win every time.

It's difficult to fight tradition and perception. So they talk about exploitation, but what they want are quotas, reservation of seats for non-Brahmins. Power, everybody wants that."

He was standing very close to her now, and she smelled cigarette on his breath. It was not the smell of the tobacco that Kitappa chewed, but of money. He had a slim silver cigarette case. She has watched him as he selected one from the neatly arraigned row of white paper cylinders. When she was alone she would mimic his ways by holding the imaginary cigarette between her fingers, crinkle her eyes and suck at the tip like he did. These gestures of his were alluring, so full of power and determination they seemed to her.

She realized he had just asked her a question. He smiled at her, "Hello?"

Confused and embarrassed, caught with her lustful thoughts, she looked away from his face which, like the sun, drew her and repulsed her at the same time with some blinding radiance.

With a small movement Satya placed his hands on either side of her on the table, cradling her. His face hovered close, his heat in her hair and on her cheek, his breath in her ear. Irresistibly seeking a caress, she tilted her face, brushing against the roughness of beard, urgent moist lips opening, the taste of his mouth, his teeth, tongue——

"Prakash-sir is here."

The servant boy was at the open door, silhouetted against the bright light outside. Satya dropped his hands and straightened up. Sowmya jumped down from the table.

"Fine," Satya's voice croaked.

The boy stood rooted to the spot for a moment and then left.

"Sowmya—"

She did not want him to apologize. She wished he would say nothing. His breath was still flowing down to her curling toes, pooling in a stain.

"Did I make you uncomfortable?"

She was quiet.

"Sowmya, I am sorry if—"

She hid her face in her hands, finding it impossible to look at him.

"What? *no?*"

She heard his smile, and smiled back through her fingers. He said her name softly, *her name in his mouth*. Voices came from outside the shed.

She quickly turned and walked out the open doorway, into the bright sunlight. The servant boy was talking to the man who had arrived and they both watched her. Her face was flaming hot, surely they must all know?

Satya walked out behind her. He made an elaborate gesture of lifting up his wrist to the light and looking at his watch. "Prakash, this is a record. Only late by two hours."

His friend laughed without apology. Dark sunglasses shaded his eyes. A thin and tidy mustache expanded over full, deep purple lips. His thick, curly hair glistened with pomade. He had parted it in the center.

Satya snapped his fingers at the young boy, raised three fingers. "Coffee, fresh, hot. *Jaldi*, man. And get something for yourself at the canteen."

"How's the family?" Prakash asked. She couldn't tell, from the luminous glasses, whether she was being watched or not. She heard Satya respond formally with returned courtesy.

The coffee came in small, silver tumblers, each nestled in a silver bowl.

"So what's the story, professor?" Satya turned to Prakash.

"Miss Sowmya has agreed?" Prakash asked as he opened a small leather valise he carried and pulled out a bound notebook.

"Working, working on it," Satya said and turned to look at her.

Her body shamelessly responded from her center to his look. To hide her discomfort she raised her tumbler to her lips, and the coffee spilled on the front of her sari.

"Oh, oh," Prakash stood up, and attempted to brush the coffee off her sari. She quickly moved away, shocked at the brash gesture, pretending nothing had occurred.

She walked over to the garden tap to rinse with water. She took her time to walk around the garden before returning to the meeting. She heard Prakash laugh lightly and she felt exposed, as though he thought of her as a dancing girl.

When Prakash rose and took leave he made an exaggerated bow toward her. She did not respond.

"What does he mean by a new role? I thought it was only the dance. I am not sure about the dance at all."

Satya was silent, fixing the pages in front of him.

"Whatever you want to do, it's fine. Think about the program for the Earthquake Fund," he said when she was ready to leave. He followed her to the car, shut the door for her and leaned on the window. "The government is coming down hard on every demonstration, every public speech or publication. They need to energize the movement. That is what your dance must do."

When the car moved she looked up. The driver's eyes quickly darted away from the rearview mirror.

When Sowmya returned home from the studio, she went directly to the trunk in which she had stored Mani's notebook. She flipped it to the pages of Bharathi's poems that were copied out in his tidy script. She flipped the pages, thumbed so many times the letters were smudged with fingerprints.

Bharathi's prolific writing was consumed with fervor. He extolled, cajoled, scolded and lamented a nation to its liberation. She searched through this outpouring. The ideas were immense, of a nation in bondage to an alien power, a call to break the chains. She went into the back terrace and looked up at the clouds. How do you capture the sky in a bottle? That is how the task before her seemed, to express a grieving nation in dance.

In the evening, Lazarus arrived with the projector and gramophone. He set it up and turned the projector on, wound the gramophone, dropped the disc in. He showed her how to stop, resume, and then turn it off.

"I can come and get it in the morning, madam," he said and then left.

Sowmya lifted the needle off the disc and the music stopped. Now Ruth danced in silence. She watched the movements that seemed random at first, the dreamy expression, a smile that was not quite a smile. Gradually shape and rhythm appeared in the movements, a grace in the dancer's . Sowmya sat down and watched the shimmering light in silence. She no longer noticed Ruth's hair, the turban, the bare waist or arms, but only the expressive hands, the movement. When the man, Ted, appeared, their movements reflected each other's and became two pieces of a unit.

Sowmya ran it again, and again. Finally she turned the projector off and sat for a while in the silence of the evening that was falling outside the door. A bird called plaintively in the dying light. Quickly her vision flooded with images of her own dance, the movements across the stage, its age-old grammar pre-stamped with meaning which was efficiently conveyed through symbols and stylized emotions. Bharathi raged at the cowardice of his people, submitting to a foreign master, selling out a nation.

Sowmya walked into the compound and stood in the still evening light. She hummed a tune softly, and took a few steps on the earth. One of the songs settled in her mind and she tested the images of the ancient story, translating Bharathi's emotion in the movements of her limbs. Mani knew in his center the fire that was in these words. If he were here she would have lit her own fire from it.

She thought of the dancer's dress, so free and weightless. She went inside, pulled off her sari and dressed in a long skirt and a blouse. She imitated Ruth's movements, her pattern, drowning the remembered rhythm beats of her own, the dance postures that had now become natural to her. She waved her arms, bent sideways at her waist. She twirled. Free of the sari, she felt different. She was not sure if she liked it, the bareness seemed cumbersome.

Hopeless. I hate it, this is nothing, it is a nothing dance! It is empty. I am imitating this woman imitating me, and it is not even me!

"What are you doing?" Mallika stood at the doorway.

"Umh! Come here, watch this." Sowmya picked up her sari and quickly draped it back on.

Mallika sat down and looked at the projector with suspicion. The film rolled, the dance finished. Sowmya turned the projector off, and moved it away to a corner.

"She's American. She's called a prophet, an *avatar* of Shiva."

"Hmmm."

"People pay a lot of money to see her Indian temple dance."

"It is a north Indian style of dancing," Mallika said. "They call it a lamp dance."

Sowmya was surprised at the calmness with which she took this in.

"She has changed it somewhat," Mallika said.

"I have some ideas for the dance for the National Fund. I am going to add a new number."

"Like this?" Mallika pointed to the silent projector.

Sowmya brought the poem she had selected and read it out to Mallika. Mallika listened quietly but Sowmya knew that ideas were filling her head.

"What do you think?"

Mallika moved her head in little nods. "Work it out and see."

The next morning, Sowmya asked Kitappa to look through the notebook as well. He agreed with her selection. They went in to the front porch and Kitappa pulled out his harmonium. He sat down on a mat and placed the notebook in front of him, punched a few keys, pumping the instrument with his other hand. He played with the raga, testing the notes for a few minutes.

"We can do this," he moved his head side to side, "Yes. Child, fetch me that blue notebook, please," he said, pointing to a small shelf against the porch's wall. A fat notebook, it was bound in blue canvas. It contained every song he had ever composed or set music for. This book went with him wherever he went, he was never without it.

Sowmya clasped her hand together with glee and jumped up to fetch the book.

Kitappa sang a verse to the tune he composed, made some notations, picked up the verse again. This went on for about half an hour. Sowmya waited patiently and would sing for him a verse when he asked. Then when Kitappa was finally done they sang it together. Mallika watched from inside.

Kitappa set the song to dance rhythm, inserted a few *jati*, a little pleasing decoration of series of beats.

Sowmya stood up, demonstrated.

"Do the verse in moderate speed. Set the last two lines to repeat in double time." Mallika was at the door, holding the beaded curtain aside. She tapped out the beats on her palm, breaking down the syllables in demonstration.

Together they worked on the beat, making it come out right. Sowmya mimed variations: the toddler waking up to a new dawn; the sacred rivers, majesty of the mountain ranges; the young girl frolicking at the river, a sunbeam on the water; a maiden dancing in the moon-lit night; the worship of the ancestors; a wedding and a love-making; freedom.

Then Sowmya held up her hand. "Brother, just your voice. Just sing it, please."

Kitappa muffled the harmonium. His pure and un-blemished voice rang out.

Her eyes still closed, Sowmya said, "Now the mridan-gam. Alone."

After a few seconds of silence Kitappa's fingers stroked the sides of the instrument and it spoke to her. She saw the spinning of the wheel, a lone flag fluttering in the wind. She saw the entire dance shine behind her lids, and it was new and she suddenly understood what Ruth St. Denis was doing. She had invested the song with a brand new feeling, patriotism. To make it concrete in her dance she would express a little bravado, a little piety, and some kind of joy or affection.

"It has to be that kind of a thing, as if you are the child and the mother at the same time," Mallika said.

Sowmya found a man named Farid at Amarjothi Tailors, at the corner of East Mada Street, who agreed to make the tricolor flag for her. She found him some silky and slippery material that would unfurl as required. He kept the project inside his house and worked on it at night. She would meet him at his shop after his work was done, and he would take her to his house and show her how he would piece the parts of the spinning wheel together in the center and embroider around it. She was pleased.

On the day of the dance the lawn at the congress office was covered with white sheets. The program started in the late afternoon with a welcoming ceremony and several speeches. So the stage was set up and ready when Sowmya arrived with the musicians. The lawn was now dotted with people who had gathered among the long shadows. Satya introduced Sowmya.

Sowmya began the program in the traditional way, with an invocation to Ganapathi. Nervous about how it would be received, she had planned the new item for the final piece just before a short and sharp concluding hymn.

When the time came for the dance the stage lights dimmed. Somu played a dirge like beat on the mridangam. The flute came on, and then Kitappa and Neelam's voice rose in unison.

This land of a thousand years,
shaped by a thousand thoughts . . .
my mother's playground,
where she learnt her first sounds,
and danced in this moonlit night,
frolicked in these rivers,
made sweet music with my father,
this land of my mother.

Sowmya raised the standard and pulled the string. The flag dropped down, and she leaped around the stage to the beat of the refrain, the flag unfurling:

Would I not adore it in my heart
and cry out in joy
Vande Mataram! Vande Mataram!

Even before the dance came to its conclusion, people rose to their feet, cheeks wet. Sowmya found her eyes filling over with tears when she finally stood waving the flag.

When she went inside to change and remove her make-up a messenger came in and gave her a slip of paper. The manager of Saraswathi Sabha wanted to meet her. He was waiting with Satya when she came out of the room. The man greeted her shamefacedly and she returned his greeting. He wanted her to perform the next evening at the sabha.

She looked at Satya.

"All the funds go for the relief effort," he said.

She thanked the man.

The next day a journal carried a report of the event and an announcement of a repeat performance scheduled for the evening. There was a photograph of Sowmya receiving a garland from a congress leader.

The next evening the sabha was packed. This time when she went back to her green room, a young constable was waiting for her. With a shy smile he told her to come with him. When she came out to the front of the auditorium she saw three more constables and Satya was talking to them. He quickly walked up to her.

"Don't worry, I will meet you at the station."

"Police station?"

"They are charging you with subversion. These people will take you down to the station and finger-print you. Don't say anything, don't admit to anything. I will meet you there, but I first have to go see some people."

The constable who met her swung his baton and cleared a pathway through the crowd, waiting for her at the gate when she came out. A fight had broken out earlier, protesting the arrest, when word had first spread through the crowd. It was put down swiftly by the police. She climbed into the van, still in confusion over what exactly was happening.

At the station in Santhome a clerk rolled Sowmya's fingers and thumbs, one by one, on an inkpad and pressed them on a form. She was charged with violating public order and peace, and was banned from using the flag during her performances. She looked at the flag that Farid had worked on for several weeks. It was rolled up and thrown into a metal bin with other confiscated items.

She was pointed to a bench. She sat down and waited. A man was brought in, charged with vagrancy and thrown in a cell. She became nervous after an hour and there was no sign of Satya. The constable who brought her strolled by, watching her. She felt naked in the costume she was wearing, an orange skirt with glitter, a white blouse, and just a yard long sari of green chiffon draped across her shoulder. He returned after a few minutes and told her she may have to be moved to a cell for the night. As he was telling her this she heard a motorbike. Satya. She was grateful that he had thought to bring a cotton shawl to throw around herself. He carried a letter and asked to see the sub-inspector of police. In a half hour he came out, paid bail, and had her released.

Once outside, Satya pointed her to the motorbike and asked her to get on. She hesitated; she had never rode one before. He kick-started the bike, threw a leg over it and asked her to climb on behind him, "Come on, come on."

She sat sidesaddle on the pinion and gripped his shoulder. It felt solid under the shirt fabric. The motorcycle wheeled around and soon they were roaring out on Santhome High Road towards Marina Beach. Her hair ruffled in the wind. She wrapped the cotton shawl around her to keep it from getting windblown. The barely contained power of the machine was beneath her, carrying her away. She smiled into the wind. It had been a strange night.

Satya suddenly veered towards the curb when they arrived at the Marina Beach and pulled up, cutting the engine.

"Come on, let's go cool off a bit before I take you home. This is big, what has just happened."

He helped her down to the wide promenade which, pleasantly crowded earlier, was deserted now. A bright full moon grinned up above, but the violet light from the mercury lamps turned the colors of her outfit into strange shades. The breeze pressed the sari to her limbs and she felt light, as though floating. Satya's shirt had turned a brilliant white and she pulled at her sari, which was fluttering towards him.

When they had walked about a mile, small gardens began to appear against the granite culvert, bright red cannas bordering patches of lawn, hedges of bougainvillea. They entered the beach, which was littered with remnants of moonlight picnics, and walked towards the water. Near the shore she saw a man and a woman nestled in the shadows of the catamarans. As they passed she got a better view of the woman, who seemed about fifty, her hair undone and loosely falling over her shoulder, staring out at the sea. The man was sleeping beside her. Sowmya caught, in the corner of her sight, the gleam of the woman's diamond nose stud.

The tide was high. Waves crested and heaved in the moonlight, shimmered silver against the dark, and smashed themselves against the shore. She matched Satya step for step, keeping up with his long strides effortlessly, and their undulating motion was like breathing.

He pulled out a large handkerchief and laid it down for her to sit on. He dropped down beside her, stretched his legs out and leaned back on his elbows.

He took out his cigarette case, flicked it open and took a cigarette out. When he lit it the flame kept going out. " Here, cup this lighter for me, will you?"

She drew close and cupped her hand around the flame, and in the sudden flare of the lighter she saw the way he sucked in his cheeks, his fingers, touching hers to steady them, smooth and beautifully shaped, with clean white nail beds, and in the shadows, the shape of his arms rounded and solid. He drew deeply, and the tip glowed. She reached over and held the cigarette. He looked at her with a bit of amusement and let her have it. Clutching the cigarette, between thumb and finger, she took it to her lips and tentatively puffed on it.

"Take a small whiff, like this."

He showed her how and handed it back to her.

She pulled on the cigarette and went into a coughing fit.

"Easy," he said.

She drew again, smoother now, and then handed it back to him.

"Keep it, keep it, this is a celebration. You have pulled off something quite big. Watch what happens in the next few days." He lit another one, turning towards the side of the catamaran to protect the flame.

"What did you tell them at the station?"

"Don't worry about it, it's over. You just watch the headlines tomorrow." He grinned at her. Her heart flipped watching his happiness, something she had had a part in causing. He seemed proud of her and she realized the full depth of what she had done with so little awareness.

They smoked silently for a few moments, the roar of the waves constant in the breeze.

Satya buried the butt in the sand. He laced his hands behind his head and slid back on the sand and reclined. He had never seen so many stars in the sky, he said, every single one of them brilliant.

She probed Satya about his marriage, standing at the very edge, terrified of what lay in its center. Quite willingly he started to say something as though he had anticipated her questions. As quickly the words vaporized from his lips before he uttered them and he gazed at the stars silently for some time. A year after they were married he had got himself tested, he said. Yamini had wept when he told her it was possible she may not conceive. While it had descended on him as an unexpected shock, Yamini bore a heavier burden. Her barrenness would be held against her as a crime, no matter the cause.

Yamini. Her neck delicate and exposed as she bent down, concealing her pleasure when she gave herself to him. This burden gradually growing like a prickly vine binding him to her, piercing the skin. To free himself now would be to tear flesh. It was a marriage like that, he told Sowmya, it was not without affection. Sowmya believed him.

Sowmya stretched back on the sand and listened to him some more. A sprinkle like rain, barely perceptible, fell. The stars were still shining. She allowed the starlight to sink into her, percolate through every pore, taking into her the night air, and the man, who if he reached over, could fold her in his arms. She saw now how he must have looked as a youth. Not his physical form but what must have been in his eyes when his mother had called to him, *Come to me, my golden child,* from her bed, dying from hemorrhage and fever in her polluted state after a still-birth, her young son standing at the doorway in the light that fell from the open courtyard. Taken away abruptly Satya never saw her alive again. She knew what that kind of memory could do. He grew up on the favors shown to him, from one relative to another. She saw his eyes lit up with images from the silver screen at the Gaiety, the swashbuckling hero, the masked man who rescues the beautiful woman. He would enact them in the light of the hurricane lamp, the shadows looming over the wall. He married the daughter of his mentor, he owed him much, and dutifully prepared for the Bar. But his dreams he kept. *Sowmya, always there are ways of getting things done.* He remained untouched by the means he employed to get them, all appropriation being rightful when the goal was so clearly for beauty. She wanted some of that energy, that kind of a desire so formidable that it made everything appear attainable. Sowmya turned and laid a hand on his chest.

The weight of her hand right below his neck, the faint perfume of her jasmine hair-oil, all mingling in the saltiness he would taste in her lips. She waited, her skin erupting with a thousand sparkles. Instead, he leaned into her and brushed the hair off her face, again and again, the motion infinitely more comforting than what she saw in the piercing brilliance in his eyes that had revealed so much.

Raindrops fell.

chapter 10

A fine sprinkle started when Sowmya and Satya walked from the shore towards the road. Satya knew the night manager at the hotel, where only Europeans stayed. A man, he said, who could be counted on to be discreet.

"Don't look at me like that, I am not in the practice of visiting hotels. I just know D'Silva from college."

By the time his motorbike headed towards Mount Road the sprinkle had turned heavy, although still not rain. She leaned into him, rested the tip of her forehead, then her cheek, on his back. *So this is how it feels to claim this man's broad shoulder, all of this.* Yamini's sari swished, bellowing up over Sowmya's face, checking her breath.

The doorman at the hotel saluted smartly and opened the door as soon as he saw Satya. The gleam in his eyes when they passed made Sowmya pull the shawl that she had thrown over her head further down on her face as she went through the door. Was she concealing only her face?

The lobby's carpet, red and plush, yielded under her feet as though she was walking on a bed of petals. Where the carpet ended there was marble floor that ran up the grand staircase, which was held up by marble columns, urns and statuaries. Small palms grew in brass urns, sets of sofas upholstered in dark material, and rosewood tables were in view. The fans above whirred in a noiseless white blur. She turned and walked away from the desk while Satya spoke to the manager. Outside the tall windows, the sprinkle had turned into a gusty rain that swung in gray sheets.

Within a few minutes, Satya was escorting her down a lobby lit by the orange glow of wall sconces. It was not complicated at all, Satya said. How many such arrangements must the manager do for the guests of this plush hotel? She did not look at Satya's face too closely.

She walked with her face concealed in her shawl. They stopped in front of a wooden door with a brass knob. Satya opened it with the key the manager had given and they stepped into a small room. In the little light that fell from two tall windows she saw the outline of furniture, a bed, a chair and table. Water and wind raged outside. The dark shapes of the trees hidden behind the sheets of rain made her feel, for a moment, as though she had been here before. The door closed behind her with the metallic click of the bolt and she turned. Satya stood where he was and smiled at her. She shivered as he walked towards her.

"Cold?"

His shirt smelled of rain and perspiration. She had thought she would be nervous, that her legs would shake. But she felt quite calm even if her body acted like all its nerves were exposed, burning where Satya's hands touched her. She let him lead her to the chair near the window. He removed the shawl from around her shoulder and she stood in the glittering dance costume, in the colors of the flag.

He gently sat her down on the chair and sat beside her on the floor. Rain mist swept in from the window.

"Sowmya."

His hair stood up in clumps of curls. She ran her fingers through them making them curl up more, playing with it. "Hmm?"

With a finger he reached up and wiped the water droplets at her cheek. She turned her head and kissed his palm. Wanting more she threw her arm around his neck and pulled herself closer. They tumbled, and next moment she was straddling him on the floor, kissing his mouth.

She thought she would never forget those first moments but all she remembered later was a buzz of urgent disconnected movements, his shoulders clipping her cheek, his urgent hands pushing and pulling at her, the top of her kneecaps rising. She looked up at the ceiling panel, at its smooth and flat surface uninterrupted by rafters or roof tiles. His head bumped near her chin, his tongue was drawing circles over her, dissolving her into a molten state. She clenched her eyes shut and grabbed at her sari that was nearby but he gripped her hand, stopping her.

"Open your eyes, look at me," he said.

She looked. The weight of him pinning her down made her stomach contract as though it would disappear inside her. His eyes moved closer and closer until they were unfocused orbs of light penetrating her. Her back arced, and she gasped at the initial sharp twinges of entry, the swelling that filled her, the grunts, the collapse. After a while, Satya lifted himself off her and looked at her watching him. He roughly slipped a hand beneath her knee and gripped it. He kissed her mouth, both her cheeks, her ear lobe, and moved on her until he pressed his lips to where her hair parted. She went to the brink of a throbbing edge, the eye of a hurricane, swirling out into enormous raging circles that started to spin tighter and tighter and *tighter* as he sucked her breath out and made her come out singing, coming, singing. She rippled like a river and flowed.

She awoke from deep sleep with her eyes wide open. She shoved the sheet aside and realized her hand had gone numb under Satya's weight. Gently but steadily she pushed until his weight shifted and rolled off her. Her hand tingled now with the pinpricks of rushing blood.

The room was full of his breathing. The cut-out of the cotton vest glowed white in the night light against his smooth warm skin. She placed her hand on his stomach. He had developed a small paunch, a slight rounding of the belly. Solid, healthful, she found it pleasing and a comfort. She rested her head on it, a dreadful kind of peace coiling inside her. Satya raised his hand slightly and tousled her hair and she found herself stirring to his touch. But within seconds she heard him snoring again.

She kicked off the sheet and rose from the bed and stepped onto the floor that was damp from the rain splash. She gathered her clothes and dressed. The damp blouse

was hard to get on. Outside, the storm had stopped, leaving a thickly layered silence. The moon shone brightly
through broken clouds. She turned away from the window and looked at Satya. She tried to see him in the house
in George Town, lying beside her in an afternoon siesta in
the darkness behind shuttered windows, the sound of the
market from over the back wall. It made her think of a
family, a baby. Already the pangs of separation from this
man, who was somebody else's husband, beat like a pulse
in her heart.

Satya moved, his arms flinging this way and that and
then he shot up from the bed. "Sowmya!" he cried out.

He threw his legs to the floor and sat up at the edge of
the bed and then he saw her at the window. He rubbed
sleep off his eyes. She watched him warily and with tenderness when he looked at her and patted his lap. This
gesture of summoning her settled heavily in her limbs.
What claims does he imagine he has on me now? She didn't
know from where that thought came.

Her shadow fell on his shoulders and chest as she approached and he looked at her with sleepy distractedness,
like a child awake. Inside the circle of his arms, she knelt
down on the floor and nestled herself between his legs,
within its now familiar shapes. Cupping his face in her
hands she kissed him, loving the taste of his warm mouth,
his rough stubble against her lips and cheeks, the feel of his
shoulders in her arms. She loved it all and held on tight.

"What happens now?"

He kissed her. "More of what happened before?" he mumbled between kisses.

"Satya."

He dropped down to the floor and pulled her to his lap.

"I don't know. The manager is my friend. There may be some talk but it will die down. But Mallika might ban me from the house." He leaned towards her. "What will you do then?"

She pushed his face away gently.

Later he told her about his meeting with Prakash, the screen script for the woman writer's novel.

"This novelist, isn't she the one who was in a protest march—"

"Hmm-hmm," he nodded. "It was Ramani's liquor shop in Mowbray's Road. They ramshackled the shop, smashed all of the poor chap's bottles. He used to reserve a bottle of Jamaican rum for me under the counter. He closed down the shop, it bankrupted him."

"I read her story in *Kalaimagal,* called *Another Chance.* It's like these are two different people, the woman and the writer."

"Why's that?"

"Look. Here she is, leaving her house, her husband, and goes off on these protest marches, making speeches. And then she comes home and writes these stories of women, with a husband, a home, and security?"

"Your point is?"

Sowmya looked at him.

"Nobody will read her, no one will publish her, if she writes her truth," Satya said. "Take Mallika. Why do you think she keeps harping on the *nayika's* love in dance always being so pure, so *divine?* The public is not interested in seeing a woman's raw desire, it's too unsettling. Or her frustration, which is deadly."

"Deadly?"

"Deadly. Living with a frustrated woman is deadly, ask anyone."

"Not their frustration, they don't want to see that," Sowmya said. "Sorrow yes, anger no. Flirting, teasing, yes, yes, yes."

Satya laughed. "Yes." His teeth gleamed between parted lips. She leaned over and kissed him.

"What do you think?" Satya asked.

"Of the script?" Sowmy made a dismissive sound. "How much do you have to pay the Mudaliar back?" He had taken a loan from Prakash's father for his last film, which had been a failure although Kitappa's songs had become hits.

"In black or white?"

"What? How much does it cost to produce a film like that, the one in your *dream?*"

Satya laughed. He had told her about an Italian film he saw, the beauty and simplicity of it, this was how he would like to tell his stories. He had the scenes, he said, the setting, even the facial expression, and the lighting. He had all these in his head.

"I make the kind of films that will pay for the one in my dream."

Kitappa stood silently when Satya brought her home in the first light of the morning. But Mallika's silence was fraught with wounds. At first she had simply refused to speak. When the silence broke she was brutal. Don't become the merely possessed. Love *withers*, she said, men *leave*.

"What then? Where is your safety?"

"I am happy when I am with him. When I am with him, I feel I can do anything."

Mallika looked at her for a moment.

"Yes, I know how it feels. But they are borrowed feelings."

Sowmya refused to go back to the hotel, she did not like the way it made her feel. Satya bought a small bungalow on the banks of the Adyar river. It had a thatched roof, no electricity. It seemed only appropriate to her that their meetings occurred in stealth and in darkness. The flickering flames from oil lamps threw up grotesque shapes that shook while they made love. Witnesses.

The day after Sowmya's arrest there was a protest march up North Beach Road. A man climbed up the Fort St. George and hoisted a flag with the *charkha,* the spinning wheel as a symbol of homespun cloth. The police followed him up, arrested him, and confiscated the flag. Letters to the newspapers protesting Sowmya's arrest poured in and rose to a fevered pitch. Within a few days the government withdrew the ban on public display of the flag and returned the flag to Sowmya.

chapter 11 1942

It was the day before Pongal, the celebration of the new harvest, products of which were filling the market. Sowmya took the list Mallika made – rice, sugarcane, ginger shoots, jaggery, fruits and flowers, saris and shirts for gifts for the maid, the milkman--and set off towards the Kotwal market. She enjoyed these trips where she could walk unnoticed. Here she could be lost in the hustle and bustle of the market, just another woman shopping, a housewife with her bags, going home to prepare a meal for her family, send her husband off to work with his tiffin box, put the baby down for a nap . . .

After the publicity over the flag dance, her first film, *Ocean Waves,* was released on Divali day, winter of 1938. It ran for a record hundred days. The anti-dance picketing no longer deterred the organizers. Their secretaries arrived at the house, advance in hand. They wanted her to come and dance in Salem, at Madurai, in Chidambaram. After *Heaven's Gate,* in which Satya had her dancing on a moonbeam, she was invited to give a performance at the Travancore Palace. Women from Brahmin families in Madras were learning to dance and to sing, and this made dance and song respectable. Her rescue by Mallika was revealed by a cinema magazine, which highlighted the fact that she

was a Brahmin. Half the city was outraged, the other half
hailed it with glee. Billboards appeared at Harry's Corner
with pictures of her dancing. She made a documentary
with Kumar, *The Dances of South India.* When she went
anywhere now she drew a crowd. The women would come
up as though they knew her and would feel her sari between their fingers, wanting one just like it. Soon after
Swarnalatha came out, a blouse designed for her for the
film, a blue velvet with a zari paisley appliqué on the right
sleeve, became fashionable.

Sowmya traversed the narrow paths that divided the
vendors' stalls into grids. Shoppers and stray animals were
everywhere. "Amma, amma? Make my first sale, amma,"
vendors called out to her, waving a fresh fruit or a bunch
of green coriander.

She walked past all of them until she reached a stall that
was doing brisk business. Attracted by the pile of banana
blossoms the man had, she picked one up. It rested dense
and fresh in her hand, with good color. Her mouth wa-
tered thinking of what Mallika could do with it. While
she considered it the back of her neck prickled with the
feeling of being watched and she turned to look.

The young woman stood a little away from the crowd,
pressed against the stall that was across from the street.
The swiftness with which she averted her face made Sowmya look at her more closely. She peered through the
crowd of heads, and then stood tiptoe to look above them.
Who else would pleat and pin her sari with a brooch quite

that way, edge the blouse with English lace? Niru! It had to be Niru, the cherubic face, the smooth skin . . .

The last time Niru came to Ponmalar it was for a wedding, just two years after Ramki's death. Niru's aunt, her mother's young sister, was getting married. Ponmalar was a convenient overnight stop before setting out for the festivities in the morning. The sari Niru was going to wear was still fresh and vivid in Sowmya's mind. She could feel its beauty in her fingers even now, the sheer silk from Banares, embroidered in silver. And the blouse! From France, Aunt Anu had said. Not even in her imagination had Sowmya known such things existed, delicate net-like material, designed with roses.

"Give it to me," Aunt Anu put her hand out.

Sowmya pressed it to her cheek, feeling the softness.

"It's getting late, Sowmya!" Aunt Anu jerked it away, brushing the blouse with her hand as though she could wipe away all traces of Sowmya's unlucky touch. The memory rose with furious lucidity.

The shopkeeper said something. Sowmya ignored him and worked her way out of the pressing bodies, still holding the blossom. The woman shaded her eyes from the white daylight with her hand, and watched Sowmya walking toward her. The sari folds shifted when she lifted her hand and revealed her pregnancy.

"Niru?"

Sowmya closed her fingers over Niru's hand, which nestled into hers, plump and soft. They stood silently that way, Niru's hand in hers.

"How are you?" Sowmya pushed a strand of hair that had fallen across the younger woman's face. What she really wanted to ask was *why didn't you come and see me, why didn't you try to find me, do you still love me.*

A man turned from the stall, carrying a basket full of vegetables.

"Take it to the car," Niru said. The man hesitated, looked at Sowmya. "Go," Niru ordered, "I am coming."

After he left she turned to Sowmya. "I am not even allowed to come outside until I pop this baby out. This was an escape because the cook took sick and somebody had to go to the market. Look," she took a piece of paper out of her bag and wrote down an address. "It's my bangle ceremony next week. Come—will you come? I have a lot of things to tell you. We have to talk."

And then she was gone. Without a backward glance she vanished into the swirl of festival shoppers.

Sowmya looked at the slip of paper that Niru had stuffed into her hand. Judge Shivan, the Orchard. She knew the place in Mylapore. It was a small colony of old money and illustrious lives, separated from the humble lives of the agraharam, but not by much. The manner in which people were shown their place over there was swift and direct. Satya's father-in-law had built a house there. Even the thought of entering the area terrified her.

She clutched the address tightly. But she had to see Niru. She was visiting at Ponmalar when Mani must have arrived with the news of the failed meeting at Tiruchi. She was quite sure Mani would have caught the very next train out of Tiruchi to go see Natesan. What kind of a storm swept over father's eyes when he heard about her treachery?

She returned from the market her head heavy with these thoughts.

Mallika's nose-ring twitched when Sowmya showed her the address.

"It's Niru's bangle ceremony! How can I not go?"

Mallika tied the cluster of tender turmeric shoots around the pongal pot's neck and applied a wash of lime around the rounded bottom. Sowmya unpacked the bags from the market.

"Isn't it fate? After so many years of silence, of nothing, why now?"

"Ah, yes." Mallika said. "Fate."

Kitappa was more impressed when she showed the address to him at breakfast. "Big people," he said, tilting his head side to side in approval. "You should go. Don't mind my sister," he said, grinning at Mallika. "She has a special relationship with the ladies over there, in Mylapore. They want her to teach them dance, and she does not want them to learn. If you are afraid they'll turn their nose up at you, take Mallika with you. She'll fix them, phata-phut! You are *famous,* who doesn't know Miss Sowmya?"

Is that why Niru invited her, because she was famous?

"Hire a Victoria carriage. Wear a good sari, big border. Let them see her and burn," he said, turning to Mallika.

Mallika placed a scoop of hot pongal on Kitappa's leaf, another one on Sowmya's.

"Yes, hire one, why don't you?" Mallika said. "Go and see your family."

"*Your* family! And what are we, borrowed?" Kitappa chortled.

Sowmya picked up a morsel from her leaf and looked at Mallika. "I will. Maybe I *will* hire a carriage tomorrow."

"Do it. Who's stopping you?"

chapter 12

Sowmya stepped away from the mirror. Knife-folded pleats fell straight and true. She hoped the brand new color, coral with a high contrast black border, a novelty, was not too bright. She shaped the red dot to a teardrop between her brows, and then placed a pinhead size of sandalwood paste at the base, hoping to smooth out the traces of a restless night.

Excited voices of children rose outside the window. The Victoria carriage had arrived promptly on time. The children were feeding grass to the horse.

"Should be back before twelve," she told Mallika.

"Take your time, what's the hurry?"

Sowmya sighed and left.

After clip-clopping along Luz Church Road, canopied with banyans and tamarinds, the carriage entered the vicinity of the Orchards. Red and purple bougainvillea frothed over compound walls. Sweeping and curving gracefully, these Madras style bungalows had balconies that projected from the second floor. She imagined the women in the interior, the arch of an eyebrow that could singe.

She looked down at the brilliant piece of silk draped over her arm, and knew now that she had dressed all wrong. The color was fine for the stage but too loud here in the daylight. The new velvet tassels that trimmed the end of her braid were gaudy with cheap tinsel and beads. She undid her braid and tore them out with shaking fingers, flung them down on the dark and dirty carriage floor. Perspiration beaded over her upper lips, collected in rivulets down her legs. She had dressed like a slut.

The carriage came to a stop at the top of a sandy lane. At the front of a house was a huge white kolam drawn with rice paint in the shape of a lotus wheel, edged festively with rust colored paint. A canopy was raised on bamboo poles over the gate. Young banana trees were staked to them, heavy with purple blossoms, and coconuts that hung like breasts.

Sowmya leaned back on the seat. The slip of paper that Niru had given her was now a crumpled, sweaty mess.

"Amma? This is the house?" The carriage man turned around. Was that sarcasm in his smile? It was clear she did not belong here.

She wiped her brows and did not answer him. If she did, she would have instructed him to turn the carriage around and go home as fast as possible. At the same time, a kind of excitement bubbled in her, as though she wanted to test a bright new object.

"My cousin," she told the man, pointing with her chin. "It's her bangle ceremony."

"A feast then!" He smiled kindly. He was not a young man, probably had a wife and kids of his own waiting for him at home, maybe even old parents, a family. The whole world revolved around marriage and childbirth.

She sat up and tamed her braid by looping it into a respectable bun, fixed the pleats of her sari. She was a dancer, she knew how to make an entrance. Aunt Anu would be surprised at her transformation, would welcome her, fold her in embrace. *We are of one blood, aren't we, Niru and I?*

"Go inside," she said.

She made the carriage stop before it reached the portico and stepped down on to the gravel.

A small crowd of children had gathered. Evidently they had been told to expect her because a child shouted and ran inside with the news. "Sowmya! Flag-dance Sowmya!"

A little girl twisted her skirt in her fingers and examined Sowmya. People gathered at the gate and looked in through the railing. Faces appeared above the compound walls. She heard her name come at her from different directions.

The coachman suddenly took charge. "Scat!" he hissed at the children. "Keep your sticky hands away, let the lady pass."

"Sowmie! You came!" Niru was at the portico, blooming with happiness.

Several women trailed behind her, as though they were afraid they would lose Niru, she may be abducted. They swiped shy sidelong glances at Sowmya. When Sowmya clasped her palms together in greeting, they looked at her as though they did not understand her gesture. She dropped her hands and waited for Niru to approach.

She took the silver tray from the carriage man, a present she had bought at Naidu's shop, and turned towards Niru. Aunt Anu hurried up from the portico.

Sowmya looked at the bright parting in her aunt's dark hair, a dot of kumkum at the hairline. How gracefully she had aged from the time she saw her ten years ago. It made her want to see her mother, to see the trace of the years on her beautiful face. She smiled at her aunt.

Without even raising her eyes toward Sowmya, Aunt Anu held on to Niru's elbow, muttered something to her between gritted teeth. She took the gift from her daughter's hand, and immediately handed it over to someone else, as though getting rid of contamination.

"I told you to come early! We are just getting started." Niru gently pulled her arm away from her mother and linked her arm with Sowmya's, as though they were still little girls.

Niru led Sowmya to the center of a hall where several silk dhurries had been spread on the cool mosaic floor. "Sit," Niru said, pointing to the women who were already seated on them. They shifted their bodies slightly to let her pass, when Sowmya hesitated at the edges. Several heads turned to take a look.

Niru walked over to a chair that was decorated with garlands, a soft pillow on the seat, and sat down. Two women came forward and swirled turmeric-tinted water in a silver plate in front of her. Sowmya saw Yamini at the back of the room against a bank of windows. This was unexpected, but she should have known. In the Orchard everyone was connected.

Yamini straightened up when she saw her. Sowmya's cheeks flared hot. She dropped her gaze to the floor and sat down. She remembered with shame the wedding, a year ago, where she was invited to dance in the evening. She had gone alone since Mallika and Kitappa both were busy. She had selected a song on Madana, the love god. When she was demonstrating his five love arrows that strike her at the chest, mouth, eyes and head making her ill from the pangs of love, a man in the front row bounded up, caught her by her braid and swung his arm up to hit her. Someone stopped him before it came down on her, but the force had felled her to the floor. The whole crew cleared the place immediately, surrounding Sowmya with their bodies while they bounded out the door. It was only later, as they caught a rikshaw to take them home, that she was informed that the man was Yamini's father, a guest at the wedding.

Sowmya was gripped with fear that something like that was going to happen now. These women in front of her might rise as one and attack her. She turned towards the front door ready to bolt, when she heard Niru call her. Someone handed Sowmya a silver platter with two small bowls containing sandalwood paste in one and kumkum in the other. Nobody else seemed to have noticed the husband stealer in their midst.

Sowmya approached Niru. Pregnancy had cast its shadow in Niru's eyes, in her wilted cheeks. She dipped two fingers into the sandalwood paste and dabbed Niru's throat and cheeks, and dotted the middle of her brow with kumkum. She picked up Niru's hand, which was stacked with bangles to her elbow already, and slipped a couple of glass bangles from a basket nearby over her wrists. Sowmya smiled when Niru looked up at her. The jasmine that she had pinned across her braid, cinema style, swung forward as she bent towards Niru. She had tucked the sari pleats low at her hips, and she knew well how slender her waist must seem and how radiant the skin. She imagined the words that went up and down and across the crowd of women behind her. *Would you just look at the way she's dressed!* Back in the villages a devadasi came to bless such ceremonies. Her touch endowed fertility, and the husband's continued attention. But Sowmya was merely an *entertainer*, a cinema woman, a widow pretending to be like them just because she was wearing silk and flowers, and taking a man to her bed every night. She was merely a whore and had no place at all in this gathering. Sowmya then picked a couple of bangles from the basket and slipped them over her own wrists.

When the ceremonies were over Niru went into the interior of the house to change. Lunch would follow. The hall emptied as the rest of the women trailed behind her inside towards the kitchen to prepare for the feast.

The decorated chair stood vacant and the rugs had shifted, and stray flowers here and there from the women's hair. Sowmya stood with uncertainty. A maid sat on her haunches and was sweeping one side of the hall. When she drew the broom in wide arcs across the floor, new bangles twinkled on her wrist.

Niru's voice came from the interior in response to someone. Aunt Anu's voice rose. "It *matters* Niru!—this shameless creature—"

The voices suddenly hushed, whispering fiercely.

Should she leave now, before Niru returns? So foolishly she had been lured by the pleasures of a family celebration, believing she could be part of this glimpse of the ordinary life, that the glitter of her successes would somehow restore her in her aunt's eyes.

But Niru had become the only conduit to that part of her life that had broken in two. She may never see her again and if she left now how was she going to find out what happened in Ponmalar? She had left Mani the terrible burden of explaining her actions to her parents and Aunt Meenakshi.

Niru emerged from the interior, followed by a man, an assistant to the cook, holding two rolls of banana leaves. Niru's eyes were pink and teary. The woman who was sweeping now unrolled a dhurrie and placed two low wooden platforms in front of it. The man briskly placed the banana leaves on them and went inside.

The woman stood up. "Girl is new, not from around here," she said, looking at her but addressing Niru. "Where is she from?"

"Are you finished? It's getting late, go take a break. Go eat."

The woman became sullen and left.

"Sowmie, we'll sit here and eat. Come now, I am starving." Niru sat down and signaled to Sowmya.

She looked at the two places set for her and Niru. An excited swell of women's voices rose from the interior, someone was singing a devotional song. *Where are you from, who is your father?*

Niru called to her again. Sowmya sat down at the place next to Niru.

They went upstairs after lunch, where there was a hall identical to the one below. Niru reclined on the sofa, rested her arms over her belly and stroked the new glass bangles. The thinness of this precarious joy she must feel for her unborn baby must frighten her a little. Sowmya reached over and gently touched Niru's belly.

"I saw the *Ocean Waves*. Twice. Not your dance performances though, they wouldn't let me," Niru said. Her husband had taken her to see the film. "I was so afraid you would not come today, that you might be afraid or something. I always think of you as a soft thing, a pussycat! Now look at you!" She laughed.

Perhaps it was just curiosity that made her invite Sowmya, to know the sordid details of what she thought Sowmya's life must be.

"Yes, look at me," Sowmya said, laughing with her. "You have something to tell me, Niru."

Niru took a deep breath.

It was Deepavali, 1932. She had come to Ponmalar hoping to be with Sowmya who was expected back from Thanjavur very soon. She found Aunt Janaki pale and weak and bedridden. She had lost the pregnancy and had hemorrhaged so much it was frightening Niru's uncle.

Janaki had difficulty holding her pregnancies, had lost two before she had the twins, and that had been a difficult delivery. How cruel had she been to her mother just before she left for Thanjavur.

"And then Mani arrived, at daybreak, even before the milkman had come. He was a wreck, as though he had come though some famine, so thin and dark, his eyes sunk into his face. Your father stopped him at the door. Mani asked for Aunt Meenakshi. When she came out she was so alarmed to see him. "Mani! Why are you *here?*" Nobody understood, we thought she was afraid of your father's anger at Mani. "What did you do with Sowmya?" she said. The earth shattered after that. Bit by bit the rest of the story came out. "Your telegram, the Ceylon plan, the Christian man. He said he saw you, that they had … That he saw you in the train.""

They sat in silence for a few seconds, the moment of recognition playing out between them.

"There was chaos. Oh, my uncle was abusing everybody, all kinds of names," Niru giggled a little nervously. "He might have hit Aunt Meena, or Mani, anyone, he was so full of rage. If your mother had not got in the middle, one of them would have surely had it. She stood between them. 'You never should have sent the child away in the first place,' she said. Look what happened."

"My mother? She said that?"

"Yes, she said that. Oh I don't know where she got the strength from because she could barely *stand*. But she went on, her voice barely a whisper, her face going so pale and finally she started wheezing, she couldn't catch her breath. We had to make her lie down. It was a hard thing to watch my uncle like that, Sowmie."

Niru was put on a train to Calcutta the next morning. Word came from Thanjavur about Sowmya with a dasi on the train. After that the Natesan family did not exist anymore, as far as Niru's own family was concerned. A daughter who had run away from home is as good as eloped. She had tainted not just the family but the entire clan. Niru was forbidden to talk about Sowmya and she never saw any of them at any family gatherings or festivities, ever. "Someone would pass through and bring us news about your family. The last we heard was that Uncle Natesan had sold the house and moved the family to Bombay. I hadn't told anybody here that you were coming, that's why all this . . . My mother didn't know, you see. She would have thrown a fit if she knew. All these people, who have seen you in the cinema, don't even know you are related to me. I had to meet you, tell you what has happened to your family. Everyone has been horrible to you, I am so sorry. I will be leaving for

England very soon after the baby and this was my one chance to see you."

Sowmya held Niru's hands and kissed them.

The anger and hatred her father must feel for the way she had behaved must surely be enormous. She did not have the courage to even contemplate it fully. Everybody they ever knew had turned their backs on them because of her.

"But who would ever have believed?" Niru was saying, as though musing to herself. "A Brahmin girl in a dasi's house! Here in the city nobody much cares, it happens. I wanted you to know, I was hoping . . . It took courage. How did you do it?"

Sowmya looked at Niru for a moment, her plump arms and sweet face. She compared them to her own limbs, lean and long and darkened by the sun.

"Terror makes you brave, Niru. You have nothing to lose. What else did Mani say?"

Niru thought for a while. "I don't remember, really. Now of course everyone knows about how Mallika had kidnapped you."

Sowmya's eyes widened with shock. "That's what they think?"

Niru shrugged. "Isn't that what happened?

"No! Mallika *saved* me."

Niru gave a short laugh and stopped when she saw Sowmya's expression. It would be useless to explain.

After a while Sowmya asked Niru once again if she had seen Mani, perhaps he might know where her family lived.

"I once saw him briefly at some political rally at my college, he was speaking. The police came and broke it up. It's not just the political thing, that of course was always there, but he's . . . well, I don't know. He may be in jail, they are throwing all students and young people into jail now, as troublemakers. My father says there will be chaos if Gandhiji starts his fast again."

The afternoon heat had pooled inside the carriage when Sowmya got in. The streets around the temple tank were deserted. In another hour, when these shops re-opened for business, cartwheels and rikshaws would creak over them. They would fill with people freshly groomed for the evening, their oiled hair braided with flowers. As the daylight dimmed the single electric bulbs in the shops, suspended on wires, would come on making everything glisten. When she first came here with Mallika, soon after her arrival, these streets had electrified and terrified her with their energy. Now she was one of its prime customers. Just before the New Year in April, when the advance payment for the new documentary came in, Naidu had carefully selected the three diamonds from his stock. "Small, but they have *fire*," he had said. His thanksgiving for all the business she had brought him. They glistened now on Sowmya's nose.

The gilt on the velvet tassel she had ripped out of her braid shone on the dirty floor of the carriage. She picked it up, smoothed it, and wiped it clean. All the things that she thought would bring her joy, her dance, her achievements, her fame, were mere bubbles, fragile and beautiful but ultimately worthless. *Who are your people? Where do you come from, who is your father, what village?* These were the *only* things that mattered. It made her want to think of a husband, a child. The child would anchor her, so she would not dissolve and float away into incoherence.

When the carriage turned the corner a slight breeze blew in from the waters of the Kapali temple's lily tank. Steps led down from the streets on all four sides to the water, a rectangular sheet of green glass. A purple sari ballooned up in the sun as two women held it between them to dry. At the base a man was taking a dip; a woman was finger-combing the tangles of her damp hair. Across the tank the temple towers rose above the waters, the entire epic of Lord Shiva and his divine play sculpted on its walls in minute and colorful detail.

As the carriage passed, little brilliant dips in the water caught the sunlight and dazzled. Waves of brown and green silk. Beneath, at the slippery bottom where life floated, toes would sink into soft earth. Sowmya was a girl, still in skirts. Water bobbed up under her skirt, spread and floated it softy like some strange flower. She smelled fish and leaves and clay, and felt the shape and weight of a hand on her shoulder.

It was time for the afternoon service and someone was ringing the temple bell.

Sowmya leaned back on the seat, cupped her cheek in her hands. It smelled of cut vegetables.

— ● ● ● —

The late afternoon light shimmered through the trees when Sowmya got down from the carriage. She stood for a moment, stilled by a feeling of strangeness as though it could have been the dawn's early light rather than the dying evening one that was gathering itself. Quite suddenly it would withdraw and let darkness fall. The Queen of the Night clinging to the trellis in the front verandah was full of tight buds that would bloom soon and perfume the night with its fragrance.

Sowmya turned and walked into a quiet house. Mallika was somewhere inside and had not heard her come in. She sat down at a low bench near the window and then lay down on it. Light from the open half of the windows cast a glare. She flung an arm over her eyes to block it and slept.

When she awoke, she sat up vividly alert, as though someone had taken her by the shoulders and shaken her. Outside the window the light was still fading, so she could not have slept for more than ten minutes, but she seemed to have wandered somehow among the rafters, into swaying sheets of gray rain. The prospect of evening gloom to come filled her with intense melancholy. She stood up, shaking it off from her shoulders. She hurried to the back terrace, pumped water into a pail and splashed her face with it.

"Girl, you slept like the dead!"

Mallika was leaning on the door to the back terrace, fingering the garland the flower girl had delivered just a while ago. "And who wouldn't, gallivanting in the mid day sun like this? A splitting headache is what you'd get."

Sowmya pulled a towel off the line and pressed it to her face.

"The feast was a little too rich?" Mallika tilted her head to the right. "Your aunt, cousin, niece, everyone, all doing well?"

"Big mistake, going like a maharani. They thought I was too grand to sit and eat in the same room with them." Sowmya stuck her hand out to take the garland from Mallika. "I had a special *seat!* Away from the usual crowd, in the front room with Niru."

Mallika held on to the garland, forcing Sowmya to look at her.

"They didn't let you in to the interior, did they? You're tweaking their noses. It frightens them, don't you see? Frightened people can be the most vicious." Mallika spoke from a very deep, dark place.

Sowmya took the garland inside. She cut the garland into three pieces, and handed one to Mallika. Lit the lamp at the altar and placed the second one at the base. She then undid her braid, shaking it loose.

"Get married then, have a bangle ceremony" Mallika said in an outburst. "Be ordinary, isn't that what you want? Go then, go clean up the filth in our work like that doctor woman, what's her name, says! Give us *respectability*. Get married, give up your dance."

Sowmya combed her hair, smoothing it away from her face. Parting it into three sections in the back, she braided it quickly. From a drawer she brought out a box printed with tiny orange powder puffs, and powdered her face. She twisted strands of hair at her ears on her fingers and released them. Curls popped out and framed her face.

"I have risked both our lives to dance. Why do you think I am so weak?"

"We are all weak in front of that heat in our belly, that is the divine plan."

She turned and faced Mallika.

"I love him. What can I do? Tell me what I should do?"

"Does he pleasure you? Are you his equal? Or do you see a baby that you want him to put into your lap?"

"Why are you so cruel?" Heat spread across her eyes.

Satya's motorbike pulled up near the trellis in the front verandah.

Sowmya pinned the fresh jasmine garland to her braid and looked out the window. Satya had unclipped his trouser legs, and was straightening up. He stood for a moment rubbing his neck, as though thinking.

Just a trace was left of the evening light, but in that absence his unconscious beauty lit up the place for her.

Sowmya quickly went into the adjoining room and closed the doors to change. She opened the almirah, reached in and fingered a sari, a silk with heavy embroidery, a gift from the Selvan Brothers who tailored the entire costume designs for one of her films. She recalled the flash of Yamini's heavy silk, the weight of prestige and status embroidered into its drape. She heard Satya greeting Mallika in the front room.

She chose a piece of chiffon that had come from England. Light as air it had flame colored butterfly-like petals on a cream background. It made her think of a city square in some foreign land. At the completion of *Swarnalatha* she was asked to select whatever she wanted from the wardrobe, as a bonus, and this was the only thing she had wanted. She knew very well how it made her look, the way her breasts lifted the sheer silk. She pulled it out from the stack and quickly dressed.

When she came out Satya was slipping his sandals off at the doorway.

She leaned against the doorjamb. "Come in, Satya," she said.

He stopped and stood without moving when he saw her. From the look in his eyes she understood that Yamini had told him all about the morning events.

"*Arre!* How long are you going to stand there?" She pulled her thin gold necklace at her neck and placed it over the chiffon. Mallika's glance bore into her. "Coffee?" she asked.

He shook his head, came in and sat down.

"What possessed you?"

Did his calmness mask anger? She couldn't tell. She dabbed at the perspiration that gathered in a fine mist over her upper lip with a kerchief. The glass bangles from the ceremony tinkled.

"I needed new bangles."

He looked at them, nodded. "Nice bangles."

"I am sorry . . . your wife—'

"*I* am sorry, I feel responsible. When I heard—

"No need for apologies. All this is very inconvenient for everyone, a constant reminder."

"Hell with the whole lot! Why didn't you tell me?"

Sowmya thought of the women at the portico, holding onto Niru, their eyes full of fear and disgust and awe. She would never see those women again but at the same time she wanted them to see her. She wanted them to see her like this, her eyes bright with *kohl,* her splendor, and this man who was looking at her right this moment as though he would, indeed, die for her.

She felt the love in her arc out and touch him in the evening gloom that engulfed them. It was a brilliant light like the sparkles at Deepavali, when the wire would get hot in her fingers, yet she would hold on mesmerized by the violent play of heat and fire until it burned itself out and lay inert in her hand, leaving an impression of its beauty still burning behind her eyes. That would be their love.

"Could we go for a walk?" she asked him. "This time of day always makes this room so dingy, stuffy . . . could we please?"

part two

chapter 13 1944

Jawaharlal Nehru was rushing towards the policeman who was swinging the pole at the crowd. "You have no right," Nehru said, his voice becoming squeaky with rage. "You have no right to make a lathi charge." Mani pulled Nehru by his sleeve, trying to get him out from under the swing of the policeman's pole. The train whistle blew loud and long. But all trains were cancelled that day, how could there be a train coming through? He pulled and pulled at Nehru's shirt and felt the material give. The sleeve came off in his hand and he was clutching the awful density of Nehru's arm through the thin fabric.

Mani rubbed his face with both hands several times quickly, shaking his head to clear the dream. He stared with disbelief at the night that was passing furiously outside. How could he have been so irresponsible and dozed off like this?

The train rattled through a tunnel. As it emerged, the engineer blew two whistles in quick succession.

His seat was a window-side bench, meant for two passengers, into which a third man had squeezed in and was now snoring at Mani's shoulder. Mani eased his shoulder away from the man's and lifted his hand to the faint light inside the compartment. It was impossible to read the dial on his wristwatch.

The passing night was marked only by dull flares of light coming up occasionally. He drew the wool muffler tightly around his neck and was thankful now for its coarse scratchy feel which had chafed in the station at Bombay, but was now a comfort against the night-chill of February. However the trousers and shoes that he had borrowed from Gopal trapped a body that was used to the loose flow of the kurta-pyjama and open sandals. "Anyone wearing home-spun cloth, khaddar, was arrested at the Poona Station and summarily thrown in jail," was the word that went around. European clothes were safer, raised less suspicion.

Mani stood up and raised his wrists above his head. He pulled on them in turn to stretch. Jammed against each other on the wooden benches, and amidst trunks and baskets and bed-rolls, passengers had shaped their bodies against each other in their sleep. Among the shapes in the darkness he could not locate either of his men.

He shuffled past the sleeping passengers' knees to his right, through the aisle, stepping carefully around sleeping children, and made his way towards the bathrooms at the end of the corridor. The two men were huddled in the dark space of the vestibule, smoking cigarettes. Avoiding eye contact, he looked at his watch again in the dim electric light that glowed above. In another twenty minutes they would arrive at Poona Station.

He opened the exit door slightly and stood in the wind that blasted into the carriage, blowing his hair, pressing his glasses to his face. With a tremendous rush the train passed through fields that were merely a shapeless mass. He imagined miles of them flushed green with winter rain once daylight broke. Already in the distance the ghats appeared like the bodies of prone elephants. The horizon above this had paled, signaling approaching daybreak.

Another whistle blew, an elongated one. A station was approaching. The train only slowed down at these small stations in the hills but rarely stopped. As the train cut its speed, Mani opened the train door wider and stood at the doorway, holding the railing. He shivered slightly and it was not only due to the cold. He watched the slow approach of the tiled roof of a station. Steam or smoke or mist, something floated opaque in the dim light of the small station. The white uniformed station-master waved the train on with his green flag. Chugging past the station, the train hooted again and hissed a fresh burst of steam. In the shadows against the station walls figures huddled in blankets. A soldier patrolled, a rifle slung across his shoulders. A boy, balancing a large wicker tray laden with cigarettes, candy, betel nuts, jogged parallel to the train calling to him, *"Sir, cigarette!"*

The soldier turned and looked at Mani as the train hurtled out of the station.

"Two minutes," Mani had been told. "You have two minutes to gather up and get out. Then foot it to the Agha Khan Palace while it is still dark."

So the plan, as the messenger had explained it, was to leave the train at a little station before it reached Poona, a small dairy village where it stopped very briefly.

The police were on high alert and soldiers patrolled every station from Bombay to Poona. The prospect of a national uprising if Gandhiji died while imprisoned was enough to safeguard his health. The Congress party had become ragged and broken. Most of the leaders had been jailed, and the organization was falling apart. Riots were rampant in many parts of the city and a curfew had been imposed. The cause of riots was not always clear. Often it was simply an excuse to plunder.

Mani had set out from his room above a teashop in Parel just as the streetlights were coming on. As he approached the Victoria terminus, he passed a woman being interrogated by a police officer. Her eyes were wide with fear or tears, and they shone in the dimming light. She clutched a small bag in her hand and talked to the officer. A youth and a younger woman stood behind her, their faces intense. Light gleamed off the glasses of the boy as Mani walked behind the policeman. A truncheon swung casually from his hand behind him. They wielded it without discrimination. Nehru's mother was hospitalized last week with head injuries after a demonstration. Mani swallowed the wrath that rose to his throat, slipped by the small group unnoticed, and reached the corner around the traffic circle near the station.

Once they reached the terminus, the men that Mani was leading had mingled and dispersed among the crowd on the platform, and only after the first whistle blew did they all climb into the third class compartment. He knew them by the signals they had exchanged.

Mani checked his watch again. This station better come up right now before daylight completely broke. The engine driver picked up speed again. A thick dark stream of smoke emerged and traveled towards the compartment. Mani's eyes teared from the gritty soot.

His friend had mailed him a press clipping from London. The Secretary of State for India, Mr. Amery, had described a country in revolt in his report to the British parliament. Gandhi's Quit India movement had caught fire. Mani closed his lips around "arch saboteur," Amery's description of the gaunt figure with the wire framed glasses curving over those huge ears, the man whose life the British Government was guarding now.

He felt the movement of passengers behind him eager to get off when the train stopped briefly here. The smell of burning coal and the urinal at the end of the corridor, mingled with the odor of panic that had lodged within the creases of his clothes.

Hissing steam, the train approached the rural station

at the village. The dirt platform was crowded with milk-men waiting to board the early morning train to Poona, their expectant faces turned toward the approaching train. Since it was only a brief stop there was bound to be a great scramble. This was good. Three men emerging from a single carriage needed the cover. Mani jumped to the platform, even before the train came to a halt, and immediately walked towards the back wall of the station and stood behind the line of jostling passengers and vendors. He stood silently as his men walked past him towards the exit, which would lead them down some stairs and into the breaking dawn. He then moved without hurry and reached the stairs.

"*Swaraj paayje?*"

Before he could sense the direction from which the voice mocked him in Marathi, a hand fell between his shoulders and shoved him. Hurtling down the stairs, he managed to break the fall at the bottom by grasping onto the banister. His face slammed into the wall as his arms were grabbed behind him. He felt what must have been a rifle on his buttocks. His cheek was pressed against the rough plaster and he tasted blood in his mouth. He thought he could feel a loose tooth.

● ● ●

When they came to get him he was not sure how long he had been in the cell. Two, maybe three days had passed, or perhaps it had just been overnight. Someone must have come in and bandaged the cut on his head with a piece of cotton and some gauze, but he could not remember anything like that.

He touched the bandage, stiff with blood. His head felt as though it was water-logged and throbbed with the smallest movement, and so he crouched on the concrete floor and held his head between his knees.

He did not see his companions in the cells that he passed as the constable led him towards the office in the front. At the counter, he collected his belongings. His wallet was empty, no surprise there. The Indian clerk's response when he asked for his wristwatch was to jerk his thumb towards the door. Mani looked at the shiny dark eyes, the lips pursed with belligerence. Stepping back from the counter he held his fist up, *"Jai Hind."*

The constable who brought him out shoved him towards the door, "Go. Get out."

He hitched a ride from a lorry driver who was hauling steel pipes back to Bombay. It was early morning and the city was stirring when the lorry pulled into the outskirts. The driver woke him up at a tea stall and brought him a glass of tea, and a sticky sweet jelebi before letting him off at the intersection of the trunk road. Mani could not remember when he had had a meal before that.

When he arrived at the KEM College hostel he found that his friend, whose room it was, had disappeared. Not a trace of the papers, journals, and notebooks that usually littered the desk. He looked with disbelief at the old ink stains on its bare faded surface, now covered with a fine dust.

This boy, his friend, edited a journal called *August 9* from this room. Mani ran copies of the journal in a cyclostat machine that he kept in an office in Andheri, and distributed batches of them in different localities. He moved the machine from place to place to avoid detection. He had brought it here to the hostel room for safekeeping during his absence from the city. It was gone.

In the almirah he found a shirt and a clean pyjama. Mani took off his own shirt, rank with sweat and grime and blood stain, rolled it up and wiped his neck and chest with it. He stepped out of the pants and the shoes and checked the blisters at the back of both his ankles. He pulled on the pyjama and the shirt.

The dressing that was wrapped around his head disgusted him and he needed to do something about that. His left shoulder hurt when he moved it more than two inches from his side. His heart lurched when he thought of his friend who had disappeared. He had to find him. He needed a place to bathe, some food and money.

He sat down on the bare cot and looked at the shirt that he had flung down on the floor. The white shirt was freshly laundered and creased when Gopal had given the set of clothes to him. The engineering company that Gopal worked for had a dress code. But that was not the only reason Gopal took such particular care in the way he dressed—the creasing on his trousers just so, the shoes polished to a high shine, his hair glossed and parted and combed flat. How he loved the stiff collar and tie, the boots and hat, he loved them all, the little sahib! Who else, but to Gopal, would he have gone to in order to borrow these European clothes?

Mani picked up the shirt and the pants from the floor, shook them out, smoothed them down, and folded them. He looked at the pair of dirt encrusted leather shoes. If he had a rag he would have cleaned them. He carefully placed the folded clothes on top of Gopal's shoes.

"This is foolish! We cannot all be *farmers*!" Gopal had sneered, back when they were both at St. Joseph in Tiruchi. In response to Gandhi's call Mani had decided to drop out of college and join the movement. Gopal went on to build a career as a civil engineer at Lawton & Bowles in Colaba.

Roommates, they disagreed over almost everything. They belonged to adjacent villages in the Thanjavur district. Over the years they had managed to keep in touch with each other, all through Mani's jail time and all through his wanderings. Gopal was willing to give him small amounts of money from time to time, but did not want to know how it was being spent. He pretended that these were loans and Mani went along.

Mani managed to find the hostel attendant at the staff quarters and got some soap and a pail of water to wash. When he finished, the man brought him some cotton and gauze from the college's first-aid office. Within seconds, while he wondered what to do with them, a young Anglo-Indian nurse had followed the man into the room with a kidney-shaped enamel tray in her hands. Wordlessly and expertly she cut the soiled bandage open with scissors, cleaned the wound, a gash above his left ear, painted tincture of iodine over the scraping on his left cheek. She applied a fresh dressing on the wound.

"What's you name, sister?" he said.

"Come and see me tomorrow, so we can check if it is healing properly," she told him. "And don't pick at the scab." Her canvas shoes padded softly as she disappeared down the hostel corridor.

At Lawton & Bowles, he waited for Gopal to come out and meet him downstairs in the reception room. He walked up and down the tiled verandah that wrapped around the front of the building, lined with potted palms. The uniformed watchman would look up at him occasionally but mostly they ignored each other.

The verandah that he was sauntering in snaked past an office, its huge shuttered doors opening into the verandah. He walked past the open doors through which he saw a table piled frighteningly high with dusty ledgers and files, pressed down by their own weight. The clerk was poring over some papers, and there was the sound of a clacking typewriter. A large fan swiveled overhead. He went past this office several times without really paying attention and yet mechanically taking in every detail.

On one of his turns at the open doorway, he came to an abrupt stop. The typist sat at the far wall. Light fell on the desk from a window behind her but put her face and shoulders in the shadow. She typed expertly, glancing at a notebook on the table from time to time. When she looked up in his direction for a moment, the resemblance was remarkable— Sowmya's oval face, her eyes, the slightly prominent forehead—and unmistakable. Features that were so familiar to him before they became familiar to the entire city, the entire *world* it seemed sometime.

The girl had looped and tied her braids with ribbons at her ears. She could be no more than sixteen. Abruptly she stopped typing and leaned back in her chair. She looked right back at him from across the room. She did not look like Sowmya anymore.

"Mani?" Gopal's voice startled him from behind.

Gopal had stepped out into the verandah and was now scowling at him, bristling with impatience.

Mani quickly glanced back at the girl as if to check that she had not vanished, then turned and walked over to Gopal, handed him the package of clothes that he had wrapped as neatly as possible in sheets of newspaper.

"Sorry, they are slightly—"

"It's all right." Gopal stared at his bandaged head. "When did you get back?"

Mani told him.

"There is a *war* going on, this is madness . . ."

"Yes, between the fascists and the imperialists."

"All *right!*" Gopal hissed, trying to silence Mani. "All right."

"Anyway, enough Indian blood is being spilled all over Europe and Asia. For democracy, for freedom, all that good stuff."

When Gopal turned to go, Mani asked for a note with his signature. "There is someone I need to see in that office," he said, pointing with his thumb over his shoulder.

"Who? You don't have any business here."

"Someone I know. Please."

With a sigh, Gopal signed the note.

With the note in hand, Mani approached the watchman and said, "Accounts."

The watchman looked at the note, looked at Mani's face with some suspicion, then he escorted Mani into the office.

The clerk at the desk looked up questioningly at the watchman as he approached note in hand. Mani flashed him a smile and kept walking straight up to the girl.

He had acted impulsively and now that he was face-to-face with her, he realized he had no idea what to say. The girl had resumed typing and ignored him.

"You're from Ponmalar, right?"

He looked into the pair of eyes that gazed directly at him as though in challenge. He wondered if she recognized him. Perhaps she lived in one of the flats right near where he lived, and she had seen him and knew who he was, his connection to everything that had happened. He might have even run into Natesan on the crowded streets, and they could have passed each other unrecognized.

But the twins were children when it had all happened. Quite likely they had forgotten him, and he wondered if this girl even remembered her sister being sent away to Thanjavur. Perhaps Sowmya had faded out of their lives in Ponmalar, expunged from the village's history. He searched the girl's face to see if he could tell any of this. She was calmly examining the bandage around his head.

"You are bleeding," she said.

"You're Natesan Aiyar's daughter, aren't you?"

The clerk who was at the desk now approached him at his elbow, looking a little annoyed. "Is there something you want, can I help you?"

"You don't know me, but I am related to your aunt, related by—"

"I know who you are," she said, and to the man in Marathi, "It's OK, Raoji, he's my cousin. I will be just a minute."

He was taken aback. He had expected an angry rejection, his name banned in the house. He had not expected this casual and immediate acknowledgment. She had claimed kinship that did not exist. He took comfort in that, even though he knew it was for Rao's benefit.

"How is everyone doing at home?" he said.

Her lips curled slightly at the corners in an unpleasant way, as if in a smirk.

"Why don't you come and see for yourself?"

Was it an invitation, or a challenge? He took her address down on his notebook. Just as he had thought, it was just a couple of blocks from where he lived.

"Jaya or Uma?" He pointed at her with his thumb, recalling the twins' names.

"Jaya," she said.

He slipped the notebook back in his pocket. Memory of the twins flashed, running across the courtyard, flinging their thin arms around his legs. So Natesan Aiyar had moved his family to Bombay. He thought of the house in Ponmalar with sadness, its brightly lit central space that drew him in from the street. Migration from Madras provinces to Bombay was rapid now. Many from his own village were selling off the small plots of land they inherited, which barely yielded enough to pay the revenue collector, and moved north in search of employment. They arrived to cramped spaces, which they shared with several families. Mani thought of the night when he came home to find out that Sowmya was being sent to Thanjavur. His own life had always been so meager, so reckless, he had nothing that he could offer Sowmya at that moment. It was a long time before he had the courage to name his feelings for her and when he did, the shame and the arrogance of his offer of Balakrishnan struck him like a blinding light. It became impossible to regard himself as anything but a coward. He could not gather enough self-worth around himself to go see her when he was in Madras, when he saw a poster announcing her dance. He went to see her but slinked away before it was over. He could neither forgive Natesan nor himself for failing miserably as men who could protect their own. Who gave them all the right to play with Sowmya's life this way? It blotted out the easy and fond relationship he once had with the older man.

He had for some time now put the whole Natesan family away from his mind. In the quietness of a night train somewhere in the middle of the country, or while hiding out interminably in some safe house, the ways in which he had failed them would torment him and he finally had to stop thinking of them.

$$\bullet \quad \bullet \quad \bullet$$

Several weeks passed before his work took him again into town. At around quitting time Mani waited at the gates of Lawton & Bowles, hoping to see Jaya as she came out. Workers emerged, riding out on their bicycles, walking in clusters. He wondered if he had missed her when Jaya appeared carrying an aluminum flask and a tiffin box in a mesh bag. The perky braids and ribbons were replaced by a single braid today and she looked a little thinner. The unflinching glance, with which she had met his questions, had been replaced by lassitude.

She was wiping her face and neck with the end of her sari when he stepped up to her. She stopped. She accepted quickly with a nod when he suggested some tea. He mentally counted the change in his pocket. Just enough for tea and train fare.

He brought their glasses of tea to where she sat, on a culvert in a sandy spot, just a little outside the crowded shack of the Irani tea-stall. The buildings of Colaba rose behind her. Jaya raised the glass to her lips and blew on it lightly before sipping. Her earrings were replaced with tiny wooden stems to keep holes from closing. A small pulse beat at the dimple in her neck. She seemed transparent to him just then, as though he could see the tiny network of blood vessels brightly flowing through her. Held all together so delicately by her skin, they would fall quick with just a touch.

"How old are you?"

"Sixteen, last month."

She drained the tea quickly and handed her empty glass to the boy who approached them with a hamper to collect. Mani wiped his lips with his handkerchief, paid, and they walked out towards the station.

"Did you mean it when you said I could come home?"

"My aunt Meenakshi will want to see you. But my father may not let you inside the house."

He laughed out loud. "Much obliged for that information. And still you are talking to me, inviting me home?"

She walked silently for a moment. "You are the reason why my sister ran away."

He stopped in his tracks.

"I have to catch the train, I cannot be late," she said, turning. "My mother needs help at home to take care of my aunt."

"What happened to her?"

"She was struck down with it a few months ago. Her speech is affected."

"What happened to her?"

"We don't know. The doctor says it's emotional, something else, we don't know. She has stopped eating properly. The doctor keeps telling us to get tonics and medicine but she refuses to take them, she listens to no one." She made a sound of hopelessness.

Mani wondered where the money was coming from for the doctor, the medicine.

"My uncle is helping out when he can. But it's been difficult," Jaya said, as if reading his mind.

The compartment was packed tightly and they stood facing each other. Her face stayed pinched, and he refrained from making further conversation. As the train finally passed the mills and tenements and reached the environs of Dadar, he noticed the lines around her mouth begin to relax. They walked at a steady pace out of the station, as the commuter crowd flowed past them rapidly.

"It began when they started to throw cow dung at Aunt Meenakshi," she told him after they had walked a little while. "People we had known all our lives, on the very streets that we lived on, turned on us. My aunt eventually stopped going out altogether, like a prisoner in our own house. The family priest, the same priest who has been in our family from the time of my grandparents, refused to perform the annual memorial service for my grandfather.

It hurt him very much, like he had failed his duty, which of course he has."

"All this happened after Sowmya left?"

"Yes, she is directly responsible for everything my father has lost."

Mani held his tongue.

"About eight or nine months after all this happened, two or three people came to our home and demanded that my father should perform a funeral and purification ceremony for my sister. He would have had to mortgage our house for the expense. He refused. Everywhere he went, this became a refrain. If the rains failed, if babies were stillborn, it was all because of his refusal. This went on for a while and then one night five men descended on our doorstep, banging on the door. Soon after that he sold the house, cashed out whatever he could, and brought us here to Bombay. Uma and I were just six."

The girls had to gather information through Janaki and Meenakshi in bits and pieces when Natesan was not around. He had forbidden them to talk about the past, in particular any mention of Sowmya's name. But then he would start reminiscing about the house and the life, as though a piece of time had been frozen by magic, laid out in shades of green and gold for him.

Mani listened in silence turning occasionally to look at the girl's face to see how she was doing. The bits of information that she received, in secret hushed tones, or that were revealed rudely in Natesan's outbursts, had embedded themselves in her own mind and created a monster out of Sowmya. She was the cause of all their misery. But before all that there was Mani.

"My father talks all the time about his house on the Kaveri. It is getting worse every day, all the time this is what he wants to talk about," Jaya said. "He speaks of it like it was a palace."

Mani recalled the lemon trees that Natesan had planted in the side yard of the house.

"It *was* a palace."

"I would hate it," she said. "I hate everything about that place my father glorifies. I don't ever want to go back there."

"You *remember* the house, the village?"

"Vaguely. But I know enough. Look," she said pointing with her chin. Around them a few cars honked, carts and bicycles, the clanging bells from trams. "You're one in a crowd. Nobody has time to stick their nose in where it doesn't belong, to come banging on your door."

They walked for a while, stepping nimbly through the vendors who had set up shops in the narrow lane.

"We lived with my uncle Subbu and his family when we came," Jaya continued.

"*South India Mess* Subbu?"

"Is there another?" She giggled. The sound made him happy. He smiled at her.

For the single Brahmin men who arrived in the city, the Mess was where they could find food that smelled of home. And it was cheap, he had eaten there himself. Subbu and his wife ran the place, which was not much more than a shack he had put up in front of his house, where the customers bought meal tickets by the week or month. He now owned a teashop in addition and did catering.

"My uncle has three children, his wife was suffering from asthma. So there were five of us living with them. This is how we grew up, until my uncle bought his own flat and moved a couple of years ago."

A man her uncle knew, a customer, got admission for the girls at a typing school, she told him. When they turned fifteen he also got them jobs as stenographers where he worked.

"My father was adamant about his daughters not working, but Uncle Subbu reasoned with him. Finally he had to let us, what else could he do? He tutors a bit, which brings in some money. My mother and aunt cooked for other people, for feasts on special occasions, but now— with this sickness—that has stopped. My mother is very weak, she cannot do it alone."

"Where does Uma work?"

Jaya walked silently for a while. "She doesn't live with us now."

They were on a footpath now that was too narrow to be walking abreast. He fell behind Jaya. Her sandals were worn thin, heels that were cracked and dusty, and the edge of her petticoat that flicked up as she walked was soiled with street grime. She turned to see if he was still following her.

"I don't know if this is a good idea," he said.

"You're afraid of my father?"

"Yes."

"He has reasons to be angry, don't you think?"

Across the street a poster for *A Doll's Wedding* was pasted on a wall, tattered and smeared and crowded over by other posters. He had walked into a dark theater once to see it and then walked out within ten minutes, unable to withstand her image so big and beautiful on the screen, splashed in posters at every corner of Bombay. Through it all, Sowmya smiled at them relentlessly. He looked at Jaya, at the worn and frayed neckline of her blouse, and rumpled voile sari. She must pass this lush smile in the poster everyday.

"Where is the building that you live in?" he asked.

She looked at him without answering for a moment and then pointed to a narrow lane. She then turned and walked away without waiting for him to follow her. He watched her until she turned the corner to enter the lane, not looking back even once.

Meenakshi's illness scratched at his heart, he needed to see her. It had been too long.

The narrow lane on which the family lived had three-story buildings on both sides, with small balconies that almost touched. He glanced up at one and saw a woman standing at the railings of one, her gaze cold with gritty curiosity. He wondered about the anonymity that Jaya found in this city.

● ● ●

A month later, with a few inquiries, he found the building they lived in and entered it. A baby's cry echoed in the dark stairwell. He thought he could hear Meenakshi's voice and realized it was only his yearning to see them. From behind the doors of a flat, a male voice sang a film song about the mansions of love someone would build, one of silver, one of gold.

Natesan must have observed Mani from the window as he was walking up. He was at the door when it opened as though waiting for him.

He was dressed in a drab smoke-stained veshti that hung limply from his waist, and a cotton vest. His hair, gray and thin, hung to his shoulders. For no reason at all Mani thought of the swing in the central hall in Ponmalar, the mid-morning light that would fall from the open sky. Bathed and dressed in sparkling fresh clothes Natesan would be reading, and would rise to greet him when Mani walked in, *Mani master!* Such a long, long time ago.

The older man's lips withdrew into the folds of his mouth, leaving a thin, grim line. The warmth that had gathered in the crevices of Mani's chest dissipated.

Jaya poked her head through. Natesan merely moved his shoulder slightly to let her pass and then stood blocking the entry, his stance full of rancor.

"Mani!" Jaya said.

"He's been beaten up!" Natesan said, directing his voice

somewhere behind him, to the women in the flat. He was staring at Mani's scars, which had healed but some scabs remained. "The police after you?"

Mani did not mind the question. After all there were riots everywhere, the police were brutal, and nobody wanted trouble. Pictures of Gandhi were removed from the walls of some of the homes. Still, a slow rise made him want to pluck this man away from his path. He looked past Natesan at the one room and the corridor in the back, where a line of laundry hung. He noticed a bed had been made in that corner.

"I fell down," Mani said. "I slipped on the stairs at the station."

"Appa, please let him come in."

"Did you invite him? Why did you bring him here, have you lost your senses?" Natesan turned his glittering eyes on Mani. "You! Is there anything you forgot? There's something else you need to fix in this family?"

"Mani is here! Mani!" Jaya had moved away to the back of the room towards the person lying in the bed, speaking loudly as if to the deaf.

"Get out!" Natesan was now pushing at his chest with a hand, his voice shaky, roiling with emotion. "Get out, out! I don't know why—" his hand holding Mani's shirt trembled, and he lost his footing slightly.

"Appa! Let Aunt Meenakshi—"

"No!" He barked at her. Then turning back to him, "Out! Get out!"

"Let him in! Please!"

Janaki's voice came from behind Natesan.

Natesan whirled around as though she had slapped him.

Janaki's dark eyes remembered everything. Meeting hers seemed like such a terrible invasion and Mani lowered his gaze.

"Let it *be*," she said to Natesan. "Please let him in." She pulled her sari over her shoulder.

Mani folded his hand in a silent greeting to her. Janaki had always given the impression of weight. It was the way she moved with deliberation. Although she stood before him now a frail woman, her arms bare and thin, bony feet that splayed below the sari, that aura of the commander still remained in her.

Jaya signaled to him. Mani walked past Natesan and over to the corner of the bed.

Several bottles of medicine were arranged on the windowsill by her side. A small slip of paper with writing, a schedule, was pasted on the wall. The cotton blanket made a pitiful bump as it draped over Meenakshi. Her eyes were so deep in their socket he was not sure if she was awake at first, and then saw her shiny eyes. Did she recognize him? Not yet.

Meenakshi raised an arm. He clasped the hand and sat down on the bed beside her.

"It's me, Mani."

Meenakshi's eyes widened slightly and then she closed them. Her lips began to quiver. Her hand in his clasp trembled, as though she was cold, and he enclosed it with both his hands and rubbed it. Slowly the other arm rose, a fist, the thumb out. Who? Where? Mani looked at the thumb that shook weakly. Why, she was asking him why. She let her arm drop.

"Meenakshi, do you see who's come to see you?" Janaki said from behind him.

Again Meenakshi made the same gesture, the hand trembling with the effort. *What did you do, why did you lose her like that, where were you, how did it all happen, why, why, why?* As though there had been no interval, it was as if they were standing in the same place on the street when Natesan had ordered him to leave. "Do something, Mani, *do something for the girl,*" she had whispered. They had embarked on a journey of rescue, he and Meenakshi. And he had bungled it.

He turned and looked at Jaya. She offered him nothing. She pressed a hand over Meenakshi's forehead, stroking her cheek over and over with the back of her other hand.

Meenakshi's hand shook like a trapped bird in his clasp. He squeezed it gently to keep it from shaking. He thought of Sowmya's face on the poster down below in the street, the make-up, the smile, and the shiny lips. She was so close, right across from the building, a reminder every day, not a symbol of success but of the deepest of disasters that had befallen all of them. Mani looked over his shoulder at the room behind him.

The ceiling hung low over the room and looked even

smaller from where he sat. Across the room, on the other side, a window opened out into the daylight behind Natesan. A woman was moving in the flat across the street. Screams of children in play came from below. Natesan was standing facing the window, his arms on his hips. He heard Janaki's breathing near him, hovering, her sari pressed to her mouth, waiting for him to speak. He didn't know what to tell all these people but he must speak. He was the one who brought them news.

He cleared his throat. The fluttering within his hands quieted. He talked softly, beginning with the telegram he received at his hostel and about what had happened at the station, as though this was the only way to begin the story, and it was always new to them. Janaki edged closer but Natesan did not stir from his position.

The woman at the Tiruchi station platform had looked him in the eye and denied everything. While he suspected she might be lying, he was also afraid that she might be telling the truth. He had imagined, his mouth filling with sand, Sowmya being dragged back to Thanjavur by Hariharan and Kamala. Then just when the train whistled its way out of the station he saw her.

You saw her? The women asked in one voice.

"They had shaved her hair, completely."

Janaki covered her mouth with her sari. Jaya and Natesan stood still.

He had watched the receding red lights of the train, his face stinging as though slapped by a ghost.

"And then I saw her again one day, at the April art festival in Madurai." "

"Madurai?" Janaki's face emerged from the sari. "Just half a day journey from Ponmalar!"

He almost failed to recognize her with the musicians on stage. He knew the famous Mallika but then he started looking more and more carefully at the young woman seated near the musicians. She wore silk, jasmine in her hair. "

Janaki drew in a her breath. "Jasmine! Always, that girl loved jasmine—"

He hung around at the edge of the temple grounds after the performance, hoping to approach her, although he didn't know what he would say if he did. In the half shade and half-light that dappled the sandy earth under the trees, Sowmya stood with the two women and the rest of the troupe. They were speaking softly. Suddenly Sowmya made a few dance movements, showing the older woman something. Amazed at the way the dance transformed her, he had left without speaking to her, carrying a white hot image of her dancing in his brain. Wherever his work took him, criss-crossing the country, he searched the papers for news about Mallika and then he began to see *her* name. He told them about her debut.

There was silence after he stopped speaking, as though with the power of all their thoughts they had conjured Sowmya up in their midst and terrified of her conversion.

"Why didn't you go and speak to her when you saw her?" Jaya asked.

"*A dasi!*" Natesan interjected. "That is what she has become. Is this what you've all been waiting to hear from this soldier of freedom? You! You can leave now."

"Why do you call her by such names?" Janaki wailed.

"The whole world is calling her that, go ask them! What else do you call a woman who dances on the stage for all the world to see?"

"Who? Who's saying that?"

"Everyone!"

Janaki buried her mouth in her sari and shook her head with vehemence.

From the resignation that Mani saw around Jaya's shoulders he sensed this discussion happened regularly.

"*Look* at us! With one selfish move, she has wiped us out!"

"Appa, what's the point?"

"The point? How can you ask me, what is the point?" His voice was full of anguish. "Him! *He* is the point!" Natesan was pointing to him "*Who* filled her head with foolishness? If she had not behaved like a depraved, a depraved—"

Mani stood up. "Uncle! She has a *life* now instead of living like a ghost for the rest of it! Why can't you see that?"

"She has a *good* life, but she has ruined everyone else's." Jaya said. "My sister should have waited, and my father would have brought her back home. Who knows what could have been?"

"Jaya—"

"My father had women and children in his house. You won't know what that means until you hear a banging at the door in the middle of the night. We have all paid a heavy toll for my sister's happiness. Do you know where Uma lives now? Would you like me to show you?"

He sensed a movement from Janaki, a warning. But Jaya ignored it and went on. "She came home one day with this man from the factory where she works. He's a worker—"

"A Communist! *Hooligan!*" Natesan spit on the floor.

She continued. "He's a Marathi, not our caste. So she brought him right here, into our house, and said she was going to marry him. She wanted my parents' blessing. My father asked her to leave. She left with him that very night, with just the sari she had on. It's been six months since . . ." The twins had always been inseparable. They must have grown up that way. "She lives nearby . . ." Her mouth twisted in a heartbreaking way, and she stopped, pressed her hands tightly to her eyes.

Uma was probably organizing the workers in the mill with this "hooligan." Some of his own friends were involved in dangerous activities with trade unions. This would not be the time to point out that she was doing something important. He did not know how to comfort Jaya. To retrieve what was lost, this was what Jaya wanted for her father, even if she herself did not have a clear idea of what had been lost for him, only an image of it. If only everyone did what they should, things could have stayed the same. He could not have convinced her otherwise. He wondered why she brought him home with her. Was it because he was somebody from that past in which her father lived, who would understand and make the links, set the right? He felt the weight of her expectations.

A movement in the bed. Meenakshi had raised her hand. He extended his hand and held it. Partners in crime, the saboteurs.

Jaya walked with him when he left the flat. They stood at the end of the lane, near a box-shop built against a wall.

"My aunt wants to go on a pilgrimage. She blames herself for everything, for the way she has betrayed my father."

This idea of washing away the sins in a pilgrimage had never meant anything to him but he envied the power it held for those who believed in the idea of redemption and the hope inherent in it.

"I think my sister should come, come see my father, and take my aunt to Kashi," Jaya said.

"Who? Uma?"

She looked at him angrily, as if he was teasing her.

"Sowmya. She needs my father's forgiveness. What's the harm in it? He's her father. She should come and see for herself, look at what she has caused, how we live."

A man stopped by and lit his beedi from the glowing tip of a rope that hung down from shop's frame. Mani touched Jaya's elbow and they moved towards a more secluded spot under a tree.

"Jaya, why can't you feel some sympathy for your sister?"

"Our entire world turned on its head, why don't you see that? Aunt Meenakshi doesn't talk to anybody anymore; it's like she has gone into hiding inside her own self. It's some kind of penance that is what I think. My father—" her words broke off, she looked away for a moment. "Sowmya owes us!" she said fiercely.

"Owes you?"

"Yes. Can you go see her?"

He looked at the girl who was on the verge of turning into a young woman. Jaya would grow old, spent and calloused as though she had become a container for herself, holding everything in and allowing nothing that was tender or hopeful to penetrate. She would become the kind of woman who would look back, with amazement, at her younger self and wonder where she lost her tenderness. He felt ashamed. It would be useless to mention how Sowmya's world had been flipped over. He was an accomplice after all.

"Why me?"

"Why do you keep repeating everything? It's too much," she said.

He saw the weight of all these things on her shoulders, the dreams that she had not allowed herself to dream, the loss of her twin, her father's spirit. He wanted to tell her she was lonely, but held his words. He thought about what lay ahead for him, what the party wanted him to do next. "*Eaargh*!" He slapped a hand to his head.

"What is it?"

"I cannot do this, Jaya. I may have to leave the city suddenly, any time they may call me and no certainty about when I will be back. I don't even know where I'll be tomorrow."

She took a step back. "I am sorry then," she said shaking her head, retreating. "I had no right to ask."

"No, no! Wait!" he said. She stopped. "You can ask me anything. Just give me some time. Let's see what happens. OK?"

He tossed fitfully all night but fell into a deep slumber in the early hours. From the way the room was lit when he became conscious, he knew that it was late morning. The sheet beneath was drenched in sweat. His fever must have broken during the night.

From the way his eyes burned now, and his joints ached, he realized the symptoms had returned. He gave in to the extreme exhaustion in his limbs and fell back on the pillow. When it passed, and it would, he'd call down to Rajaram to bring up a glass of tea.

Ever since his return from the failed attempt at Poona, marchers had been tear-gassed fiercely, shot at, and trampled to death in stampedes. More than sixty thousand people had been jailed. And that was just the official figure. He had returned from a meeting late at night shaking with chills and a headache.

The jangle of trams came from the street below. A low murmur of voices rose up and he faded in and out with its rise and fall, eyes shut against the bright light from the window. For some reason, perhaps because this thought always ran like a stream just below consciousness, he thought of Jaya in the shadows of the Irani café. After his visit to the Natesans house, it had become an unspoken agreement between them to meet at the gates of Lawton & Bowles on Fridays. But when Friday came he would often find himself clear across the city, somewhere else. Sometimes weeks would go by before they met. These meetings, when they happened, were often nothing more than sharing a cup of tea, with short bursts of conversations and long silences, after which, he would walk her to the station and either go on his way or travel back to Parel with her. It was Friday today and he had nothing to do, no particular place he needed to be.

He forced himself to get up and made it to the narrow gallery that overlooked the street. Below, Rajaram's cauldron of tea was simmering on a stove. A brisk line of people waited for their cup.

"*Ey*, Rajaram!"

The old man looked up, waved a skinny hand which could have meant anything, and then turned his attention his back to his customers.

He brushed his teeth and washed up in the bathroom at the end of the gallery. When he returned to his room, a glass of tea had been left on his table, with a saucer covering it. Mani swatted the fly that hovered near and picked up the tea. He sat down on his cot and slowly poured the tea into the saucer. He had not given Jaya a response to her request, and she never asked him again, but he knew he would go see Sowmya. He slowly sipped the sugary tea.

chapter 14 1945

The billboard was at least ten feet high. The men were still at work on the scaffolding. Sowmya looked at the startling approximation of herself. The artist had scaled it as though he was lying at her feet. One foot was lifted off the floor in a dance pose. Her arms were held aloft. Sheathed in a bodice of a shimmery fabric and outlined in a dark border for emphasis, her bust appeared three-dimensional. This huge image of her loomed in front of the car, when they rounded the Gemini Circle, and seemed to be swiveling and grinning at Sowmya even as it vanished behind them. It was being put up to commemorate the continuous run of a hundred days of *Urvashi* at Broadway Talkies.

Sowmya was now heading to a release event of *Wedding Necklace*. A small village community celebrates the wedding of the main character in the film, a Brahmin widow who has been ostracized by her family. They get her married to the village headman, from a lower caste.

"Nobody would believe such a thing," she had said, when Satya first described the plot to her.

"When you see stars up there on the screen, doing these things, you believe. Don't underestimate the power cinema has to shape opinion."

"You are giving them the miracle solution then, social

reform for Brahmin widows and caste problems in one stroke. Gandhiji will be pleased."

"Ah, not exactly pleased. You smirk, but how else do you solve the problem? This caste thing must go. Inter-caste marriages everywhere!"

"But what does marriage have to do with anything? All that my Aunt Meenakshi wanted was to be able to come and go as she pleased, Satya. Not *marriage!* She had already done that."

"You can say that only because— look at the money you make! For our women marriage *is* security."

"So why not show widows making money then?"

"You're such an innocent. The source of a woman's income is always suspect."

Sowmya's jaw dropped. Her contract for *Wedding Necklace* was thirteen lakhs, more money than anything she had made so far. Satya had bargained hard for her. He negotiated for a car and driver, clothing allowance; she would keep all the saris that she wore for the production; a private cottage for her use in the studios for the duration of the shooting, the size of her name and its position on the billing, and the biggest advance anybody had ever received so far. Her name on the bill guaranteed box office returns, he said, and she has earned it. Yet the way she earned her money, as an entertainer, always carried a bad odor. Satya was not lying.

"Sowmya, look." He closed his eyes, took a deep breath. "It will be another hit. Trust me."

She had hoped he would say something, anything, which would make her work valid, make *her* valid.

Wedding Necklace, when finished, got dubbed both in Tamil and Hindi and was released in Madras and in Bombay. The famous Mehrun recorded Kitappa's musical score in both Hindi and Tamil at Satya's sound studio. It was hailed by many Brahmins as an important social reform feature film. Many more called for a boycott, calling it an abomination. The film was going to make everyone involved very, very rich.

The breeze from the window messed up her hair and Sowmya rolled the glass up. She imagined the script for a film about her real life: A Brahmin widow takes a lover. A husband-stealer, the heroine dances to patriotic songs. At one time she would have told this to Mallika and would have gotten a chuckle out of her. But there was not much that made Mallika laugh nowadays.

Sowmya turned away from the window and glanced at Mallika who was leaning against the backseat of the new Desoto, (purchased from a departing American journalist that Satya knew). Other than a nod in acknowledgment when Sowmya's role in a particular film was described to her, Mallika had stopped paying attention to the films Sowmya made or her roles in them: the virgin bride, the virtuous wife, the goddess, the nation's treasure—Mallika paid no attention.

She had refused to accompany them to Bombay for the release. The air and food in that North country would not suit her, she said. Sowmya had packed silently while Mallika went to the temple, and when she returned they dressed quietly for the event.

Mallika had, at first, shown total disregard for the event in Madras as well. Then Satya announced that he had managed to persuade Amritavalli, the widow of the beloved poet from Kanchipuram, to come out of her seclusion to record a song for the inaugural show in Madras. It was a song the poet couple had created together, *We Will Spin our Way to Freedom,* before he died. It was her deep regard for this couple and their long friendship that made Mallika decide to attend. The song would be a hit, Satya predicted, a national anthem. It was also a shrewd political move, as it honored the poet's lower caste community.

A crowd was waiting for Sowmya at the gates of the Wellington auditorium: reporters, fans, and those who had nothing more pressing to do but wait for a glimpse. It was hot in the car. The noise and voices outside rose to a brawl. She imagined their hands reaching in to seize her and resisted the urge to swat at those smiling, brazen faces.

"Kishen Bhatia is a happy man today," Satya said when he saw her. "The film should gross at least fifty lakhs in the first week. This is going to be big!" Bhatia was Satya's major financial backer. Satya had negotiated and finalized the terms for Sowmya. The men mixed Hindi and English in their discussion, neither of which she found a comfortable language to speak in. From where she stood Sowmya saw clearly Bhatia's smile, conspiratorial in its glee at the prospect of another mega-hit. She was choreographing his next film as well with Kumar. She flashed the man her best smile.

A Congress Party leader presided over the film release, which was preceded by a flag raising. Amritavalli, dressed in white khaddar with a green and saffron ribbon of a border, her silver hair combed smoothly back into a soft bun, was escorted to the stage where she stood and sang her song. When she finished Mallika stood up next to Sowmya, and later slowly made her way up to the stage and embraced Amritavalli. Their fingers raked each other's shoulders and back, and the women looked into each other's face speechlessly. What lost peace did their old eyes mourn? Sowmya sought Satya to see if he was thinking the same thing but he was nowhere around.

● ● ●

It was quite late when the car took them back home. Satya had located this piece of prime property, off Nungambakkam Road, for the new house. He drew on his connections at the Cosmopolitan Club and got Roddy Fernandez, the most famous architect in Madras, to design and construct the house. The news made it into the *Talking Pictures,* in a column titled *Psssst!* "Which well-known attorney turned director will be having his sleeping quarters in the new house going up on Nungambakkam Road?"

Mallika and Kitappa had set the direction the front door would face and designed the dance studio when the plans for the new house were drawn. The studio, which stood apart from the main house, was large enough to accommodate several artists, as well as a small audience for a private performance. Windows lined the entire south wall of the studio and several neem trees were planted to flank it. "Neem heals everything that ails the body," Mallika had said. The sea breeze at dawn and sunset did keep the satiny mosaic floors cool, even on the hottest days. At the housewarming, a separate inauguration was held at this studio. Mallika cracked a coconut at the doorstep. Sowmya carried in a plate with a lamp. The icon of the Dancing God was installed in the altar, a niche carved out on the wall. The dance practices that ensued reminded Mallika of the days at George Town, she said. She had found joy at the prospect of the return of those old times that seemed to have been left behind when they vacated the house in George Town.

After the release of *Rajakumari's Dream* (in which Satya had her dancing on a drum, waving a flag) Sowmya was invited to dance at a national art show in New Delhi. Secretaries of the concert halls that had spurned Mallika at one time, now stood in line asking for a booking from Sowmya. At the time of the housewarming she was making a four reeler called *Dances of South India,* for Sun Studios. She was not only choreographing for films she was now also acting in a few with very lucrative advances. The studio was a welcome and thoughtful addition.

With her busy schedule with choreography for film and other productions, Sowmya started bringing the film studio's artists home for practice sessions. Mallika's displeasure at the film dances, and the music they composed for them, turned into open hostility towards the artists. These artists were young and so did not belong to the traditional artist community that Mallika knew. Some were Anglo-Indians and they brought foreign texture to their music, which made for lively music and dance.

"You have taken something I have given you and——— Look! *Grotesque!*" Mallika would tell Sowmya, after they broke up for the night.

When Mallika's outbursts became unbearable, Sowmya decided to conduct these sessions right at the film studios where the shooting took place. The studio manager allocated a space for her, fitted with a sound system. Gradually the dance studio at home fell silent and finally remained locked, except when the housekeeper went in to clean and dust.

At home, after dinner, Mallika asked Sowmya to come see her in her room. She was already dressed for bed when Sowmya came in.

"Amirtha asked me why I don't visit her. I think I will go to Kanchipuram for a few days. After that I will go on a pilgrimage."

Sowmya was silent for a few moments. "Why?" she said.

"What kind of a question is that? I feel a need. My eyes feel vacant, I need to fill them with sacred views, visit my Lord at Thiruvayyaru. I can't breathe here anymore.

Child, why are you crying?"

"When will you be back?"

Mallika looked into the space in front of her.

"When are you coming back?"

"I will know when I am finished. Then I will be home," Mallika said.

Sowmya waited, forcing Mallika with her silence for a proper answer. It did not come.

"You never liked Satya. That's why you are leaving me, because you are angry."

The man who had stopped coming to see Mallika when she refused to give up her dancing was alive still among the livid tissues of her old pulsing heart.

"I am not leaving you," Mallika fixed the pillows on her bed. "Are you happy with what you are doing now? Is all this making you happy?"

"What does that mean, am I happy? Why are you asking me this?"

"Are you happy?"

"Look at this house, the money, car . . . who cannot be happy?"

"Yes." Mallika rose, turned way from Sowmya and began to peel the sheet down on her bed.

"I love him. What can I do?"

Mallika turned around and sat on the bed. She stared at the floor for a minute in thought.

"Are you listening? What do you want me to do? Cinema is important, you don't understand its power."

"You even sound like him."

"Don't go," Sowmya said. "Don't leave me."

"You are an artist. Dance is your work, your religion."

"And stop everything? Walk off all my contracts?"

"Please switch off the light, child. My eyes are so tired."

chapter 15

"Cut!" Satya snapped.

The music stopped. Sowmya left the sun-baked field of packed earth, and collapsed into one of the cane chairs that dotted the tree-shaded part of the studio. The skirt of purple chiffon and the matching bodice and drape were all heavily embroidered with beads and mirror chips weighed a ton. Drenched in sweat and heavy, the dress clung to her, hot and itchy.

A young girl hurried up with a pail. She scooped a mug full of water and poured it over Sowmya's burning feet. Sowmya rapidly waved a reed fan over her feet. It gave the momentary illusion of cooling down her blistered soles. Kazi, the make-up man, approached with his kit. She leaned back on the chair and gave her face up to him, to blot and touch-up. She signaled the girl with her fingers, *more water*.

The sky was a bleached canvas, stretched across the sky, the sun a dim halo. The heat was oppressive. But the sky seemed reluctant to open and pour. Everyone but Satya was hoping for rain.

"Working, working!" Raised on a dolly, his shirt dark with sweat, Satya clapped his hands. "Maybe we can shoot some more footage yet, before it starts raining. Go get Ranjit," he instructed somebody, when the sun broke through for a short stint.

The crew and artists were finishing up lunch, while Satya was shooting her scene. Now Ranjit emerged in full costume, wiping his hands on a towel. A boy trailed behind him carrying a chair, an umbrella, and a water barrel. The crew hustled about to set up for the take. Two small boys scampered up holding large, shiny tin plates, to reflect the diminished sunlight. Ranjit had made his debut with his scatter-shot delivery of dialogue in the historical *Ranjit Kumar,* after which the title became his screen name. No one remembered what his real name was anymore. Thin and handsome, he had an elegant mustache and sideburns. The white collar straining against his neck was stained with melted make-up.

She would be able to rest for about ten minutes, while Ranjit did his part for the shot. She signaled for more water.

The studio carpenters and artists had raised a small village within the studio grounds. A street scene opened out. Houses, and then huts, and the fields beyond that became smaller in perspective, eventually fading into a skyline of temple towers and palm trees. The farm headman's house stood at the edge of the field. A thatched roof capped its short mud walls, which were freshly whitewashed. Plows rested against its sides and two bulls swished their tails, meditatively. She was not sure if the bulls were part of the props or belonged to the studio's groundskeeper. She was choreographing, along with Kumar, for the film. At the moment, Kumar was on one of the floors at the studios getting ready for the rehearsal. When she was finished here she would have to go see him to plan the day's shooting.

She looked up at the sky. The pale sun had vanished.

"Working, working!" Satya snapped his fingers.

Sowmya rose and walked on her swollen soles towards the center of the mound, where Ranjit was waiting for her. Satya was already viewing them through the camera for a good angle. The black chalkboard snapped.

A muffled thunder rolled in the distance, and with that the rain arrived. It poured down soft but steady, filling gutters, making mud-rivers out of streets, and scattering crew and artists to seek shelter in the studio verandah. Without another word, Ranjit got into his Studebaker, make-up intact, and drove off towards Minerva Films for an indoor shoot for a mythological production. The crew waded in the mud colored water, their thin brown shins shiny beneath their rolled up pants, waiting to find rikshaws to take them away. A little while later the rikshaws left the compound, the black flaps let down with much hope to keep the customers dry. The men hauled their vehicles out of the studio compound, shirts sticking to their rain-drenched backs. Quickly, they were swallowed up in the swaying watery sheets. Sowmya went inside to shed the costume and remove her makeup.

She found Kumar in one of the rehearsal halls, in the back of the building. The costume director had brought in a large steel trunk, which was pushed to one corner. Enclosed by a screen that Kumar had set up, this area served as a makeshift green room.

"*Vennilave . . . mmm . . . hmmm.*" Kumar was humming behind the screen, when she came in.

"Kumar?"

"Not *one* showed up!" he called out. "They are a lazy bunch, these women you have hired."

He stepped out with a clutch of safety pins between his teeth, holding in place the carefully pleated piece of chiffon over his left shoulder. He was getting into costume, filling in for one of the girls. A gold-laced skirt gripped his slender hips. Clean-shaven, his hair was slicked back at the temples. With a shake of his head, he could make those locks fall in a cluster of curls over his forehead.

She smiled at him. "You're making me envious!"

"We need a regular troupe, trained and fit. Is anybody listening? If they show up at all, these lazy slobs have no interest in dancing, they can barely keep up to a simple beat."

She went over to the gramophone and wound it up. The plate, already in place on the turntable, started to turn. When she looked around, Kumar was still fiddling with the costume and pins. "Come here," she said.

His head was level with her's. "We cannot keep using bit actors like this. Imagine if we had our own troupe, we could do our own productions, tour . . ."

"Dream on." She took the pin from him and pinned the drape pleats to the blouse, turned him around by the shoulders and pinned the pleats neatly at the waist. "Stand *still.*"

The gramophone hissed when she lowered the needle. She was expecting the music for the rehearsal and instead a band played, startling her. She looked at Kumar.

He grinned sheepishly. He sometimes played his records on the studio gramophone, while waiting for the shooting to start. He would adopt the choreography from an American film, combining the movements with his own from classical dances and create new movements. He would amaze her with ideas that seemed to spool from him like candy floss. "You should be in Hollywood, Kumar," she would tease him and smile at the way his eyes lit up. It was his idea to make her dance on a drum for *Ocean Waves.* It became a hit because of that one scene.

The song played. A woman asked what this thing called love was, why was it a mystery, and why was it making a fool of her.

Kumar closed his eyes, snapped his fingers, and started swaying gently to the song. Suddenly, he grabbed her hand. "Quick- quick-slow," he said.

She let him lead her around the hall, responding to the sweep of the music and its rhythm. She followed him with ease. When he quickly dipped her at the waist, twirled her out and drew her back, she threw her head back and laughed.

Satya came in and stopped at the door.

Without missing a beat Kumar swung her around the

hall. Sowmya lifted her drape like a fan, and grinned at Satya over Kumar's shoulder. He smiled back at her.

The music came to a stop. In a heavy, deliberate way, Satya clapped his hands three or four times. "I'd use a heavier hand with the Max Factor," he said looking at Kumar.

Sowmya laughed. "The extras didn't show,"

"The shooting is a total wash out anyway," Satya said. "Look, the watchman gave me this." He pulled a note from his shirt pocket. "He was busy getting rikshaws and this and that . . . and . . . and I forgot to give it to you."

Something in his voice made her look at his face, as she took it from him. His eyes wouldn't meet hers.

The writing like ants that crawled across the paper, the economy of words. She knew.

"Mani was at the studio during the shoot?"

"I am sorry. He waited, apparently for quite a while. In all the confusion—"

She read each word, went back and read again, then folded the note up. "He has to leave for Mayavaram, he says. He doesn't know when he'll be back again. He was right here. Satya, why didn't someone make him wait and call me?"

"I don't know. The shooting . . ." His voice trailed. "Time is money."

"There's a meeting in Mayavaram tomorrow?"

Satya nodded. He had told her before about how telegrams were flying into newspaper offices, announcing public meetings held in defiance of the government decree. Thousands thronged to meetings that the police, alerted by spies, had not already broken up.

"It's likely that he's being followed. That is probably why he could not wait very long. We may be losing electricity; I need to go check what's going on out there."

After Satya left, she stood reading the short note again.

"Ok, ready?" Kumar said. He had replaced the record on the gramophone and was winding it up. The musical prelude began. "Let's go," he said and took his position, that of the main dancer's friend.

Sowmya moved to center stage, her mind on the message in the note. He would try and see her again. She missed the cue. "Sorry," she said.

Kumar went and reset the record and took his position again. "Ready?"

The music went into up-tempo and she waited. It was the place where from a group of four girls, one breaks away and joins her. Kumar stepped forward in this missing girl's place. Sowmya went through the motions, the movement of her hands, the swaying, the twirl, the flirtatious glance. She was a marionette, pulled by the forces of the song's tempo.

"A twirl and a step . . . one, two, three and a *four*! Three times! Why did you stop?"

Sowmya slumped down on a chair, ran her sari over her face, dabbing at the perspiration.

"We practiced this! What happened?"

She rested her cheek on her palm and looked at Kumar, silently, for a moment. She told him about Mani. "I cannot do this today, Kumar." She threw her head back and looked at the ceiling.

"These film dances," she sat up. "Kumar, they have taken over my very *brain*." She widened her eyes and looked at him. "There is just no time, never enough time to practice my own dance. I wish I could just stop everything for just *one* single minute and take a deep breath."

The rain raged outside.

"Everything, everything I *know* will be expunged from my memory by these--these--. Mallika was right."

Kumar kneeled beside her. "First the girls don't show, then this rain. Now you are crashing on me. This day has turned to mud, sister. What is this? Some kind of a curse?"

"Yes, Mallika's. You know she's planning to desert me, don't you?"

"Don't be so dramatic." Kumar sat back on his heels. "Old people like to go on pilgrimages, that's what they do"

"She's not that old."

"OK," he laughed. After a moment he stood up, snapped his fingers.

"Remember one time you asked me about a mime for a verse, about Parvati and Shiva? I will show you now, and after that we are going to get on with this rehearsal. Alright?"

He demonstrated the feminine first, then the masculine, then the union.

"How's that?"

She shook her head. "Where is the desire that made Parvati enter Shiva, become one half of him? What happened to Shiva's fury?"

"You will see it in a minute, dear heart, when Satya finds out we are not ready. He'll do a furious dance, a tandava, on our heads."

Satya returned a few minutes later and told them they all needed to clear out. Power had shut down. He rode home with Sowmya.

● ● ●

The rain had stopped but the streets had flooded. Four women walked in front of the car. They carried enormous bundles of long grass, balancing the weight with their necks and shoulders. Water dripped from the grass onto their bare shoulders. Their wet sari hung from their hips, which swung with the motion of their stride, their limbs slenderer by hard labor. Sowmya watched them until the car passed them, at which point she looked into their faces, so calm in spite of the effort of balancing the weight and battling the weather.

The new house was off the main road, on a lane that did not yet have a name. Construction of the second floor had halted. Cement had vanished from the market, like every other commodity after the war started. Eventually, a third floor was built onto the house when Sowmya no longer lived there. Now it stood with a flat terrace, edged with a small parapet. Wrought iron gates, designed with two blooming lotuses, welcomed visitors. A marble plaque at both sides of the gate merely said Sowmya, in English and in Tamil. The watchman came running to open the gates, a towel over his head as shelter from the sprinkle of rain.

"What will you do when you find him?" Satya asked.

"Who?" she said.

Satya hooked a finger under her chin and made Sowmya turn and look at him. She did not blink. She saw Mani hurtling down on his bike towards the house in Ponmalar, rounding the corner, a quick glance to see if she was there. She always was, always expecting him.

"He's a friend," she said, pushing his hand down but not letting it go. "I don't know what else to call him. He has been good to me, to all of us. I betrayed him at Tiruchi station."

She scrutinized his face. Was he jealous? *Make me your wife first, then you can claim me.*

"The Quit India movement is catching fire. I have some connections there, I can just ring up—"

"No!" She said. "No." Softening her voice, "He has always taken care of himself."

"If all you want to do is find him—"

"I can wait. One of these days he will find me."

The driver pulled into the portico and Rosie, the housekeeper, opened Sowmya's door.

The partial blackout had sunk the house into total gloom. The house had already seemed bereft to her without Mallika and Kitappa. The siblings were traveling somewhere down south near Kalady, a pilgrimage of uncertain itinerary and indefinite length.

"Somebody's waiting for you," Rosie whispered.

Before going inside, Sowmya scooped up the damp newspapers in the verandah, both in English and in Tamil. She quickly ran her eyes through the headlines and photographs. There was a picture of Gandhi with the poet Sarojini, at the railway station in Poona, with two European police officers in tow. She saw the weariness of a country breaking up hanging around Gandhiji's skinny shoulders.

It was only then that Sowmya noticed a figure in the shadows of the verandah.

"Who is it?" Her heart beat against her ribcage.

"From Bombay. He wouldn't leave," the girl whispered. "He has been waiting for a long time, about two hours. He wouldn't come inside and wait."

The man stepped up. "Namaskaram," he said, clutching an envelope between the fingers that he touched in greeting. Sowmya returned his greeting.

He was on a visit to Madras for his niece's wedding. "I am a colleague of your sister."

"Sorry?"

"Jaya. Your sister?" Slightly in awe of her, or perhaps due to shyness, the man shuffled. He crossed his arms and held the elbows tightly in a posture of respect as he spoke to her. His name was Rao.

"Please," Sowmya said. "Please, come inside."

They went inside, where Rosie had lit a few candles. The man was the head clerk at the same company where her sister worked, he said. "I am bringing this message from your sister, madam," he said in English, "I am taking it upon myself to inform you. I thought you would want to know, the ladies are alone, you see. The gentleman is very sick. Your sister requested me to carry this message to you."

After the man left she sat next to Satya on the sofa in the drawing room, the envelope in her hand. The envelope did not have much, just an address in Bombay. Was it Jaya or Uma, which one of the twins wrote this? The man mentioned he worked with Jaya. There was just an address, and only the imprint of the girl's hand on the paper, so curt in its import. Yet she examined the curve of the script, the angles and the firm horizontals to somehow conjure up the young woman. The twins had arrived premature. Peering into their tiny faces, she had been amazed at the perfectly formed miniature lips that turned greedily when she'd brush her finger against a cheek. Pressing her face into the softness of the voile chemise, she had breathed the baby smell of milk and rubber sheet and something else so distinct, the scent of her mother's skin. "I will keep her," she told her mother, "you can have Uma." Janaki had turned away at this and faced the wall.

The room where they sat smelled of new paint. The workmen had left their tools and cans in a corner, covered with canvas sheets. All the walls were painted the same color, a sage green. The red-oxide stained floor seemed

raw still. It needed the polish that comes only from footsteps walking across it. Green drapery beneath wood
casements ballooned in the rain-wet breeze and then got
sucked back against the window grill. The portico was
splashed with rain. The gulmohar at the edge of the lawn,
near the compound wall, had shed all its blossoms and the
ground beneath was covered with little flames of orange
and red. Sitting in this remote place, how could she possibly believe the voice that talked about her father and the
"ladies," Aunt Meenakshi, her mother, and her sisters. Did
such a world even exist? She tried to see the women, all
connected by blood.

"Before production starts in Bombay," Satya said, leaning over, examining the address in her hand, "if you want
to go see them . . ."

She pictured herself at the address, standing at the front
of a flat in that big city, and was immediately gripped by
terror.

She looked at the handwriting again in the frail light of
the candle. "Look, look at this," she jerked her hand. "No
message, no nothing."

"Sowmya, I know this address. Full of our people from
here, and they live in these... these—you cannot imagine
how tiny these flats are, dingy, airless."

"A typist, the man said." She could not imagine. "How
did my . . . *my* father . . . how did he allow them to work?"

"*You* work! You want to know what I think?"

She looked at him.

"Send some money for now. Send a money order, you have the address."

"It will come right back. He will never accept charity from me."

"Yes. Send it to your sister's office address then. The man told you where he works. All you need to do is put down Lawton & Bowles, Colaba, Bombay. It'll reach. Send a money order to her attention, she can cash it at the post office. Your father does not have to know."

That night, she wanted to dive into the heat of his interior to draw comfort, extract into herself the strength from his muscles. She knew all his smells, his chest, his neck, every part of his body as he moved over her. When he drew her astride over him, she leaned down searching for assurance in the shadows beneath his chin, where she eventually only buried her shameful convulsions.

In the dark, she removed the withered and brown jasmine in her hair. Satya snored beside her. Sowmya turned to her side and watched him. Yamini had left for Shivan Kovil on the thin pretext of caring for her father's step-brother who had broken his hip when a cart fell on him. While he recuperated, Yamini stayed back helping him manage the family's farm and the forty acres of banana orchards. It was now four months since she had left. Occasionally Sowmya would catch a glimpse of Yamini when she was in the city, getting out from a car, or entering a shop in Pondy Bazar. Mortified and confused, her cheeks flaming, Sowmya would turn and walk in the opposite direction, hating herself, hating Satya. He had once told her that Yamini had become accustomed to the murmurs and accusations about her childlessness, the sniggering over his relationship with Sowmya. This did not bring her any comfort because she knew this was a lie. Yamini's yearnings, the absent weight of a child at her bosom, burned in Sowmya's own belly. The terrible loneliness when Yamini would turn over and see the undisturbed side of the mattress and know Satya had left to spend the night with another woman, pressed down on Sowmya's own heart. When she caught the shadow of a smile in some woman's face as she passed, the sort that only fell from being loved as a wife, she would see herself touching the woman's hand, saying wordlessly, *I know you, I have been you before.* These shimmering possibilities would only last a moment, before they broke down and left her hollowed out. She would rush to the mirror, when she came home, and there she would see the eyes of the child peering back at her.

Unable to sleep, Sowmya turned over onto her back. The rained out shooting and the ruined dance practice swirled in her mind. She imagined Jaya writing the letter. She must have, surely she must have, first written a longer version, addressing her as *Akka, my dear elder sister* and then stopped. She must have been unable to proceed in the humiliation of asking for help. Did she then tear up the letter, start another one and at that point decided the address as sufficient, and that the messenger was enough? Is that why it looked as though written with rage? Heart thumping, she stared straight in front of her, all at once remembering her father's eyes, the panic in them at the prospect of her disobedience when he sent her to Thanjavur.

Sowmya rose from her bed.

In the prayer room, in the flickering light of the altar lamp, her hands groped for Mallika's old ankle bells among the gods and goddesses, where they had been retired. She found them and picked them up, held them in her hands as if weighing them. The leather strip that held the rows of the brass bells had softened with age, and rested on her palms worn and tired. Ridges and points on the surface of the brass bells had been beaten down to smoothness by use. She stroked the raised bumps on the leather, the ghosts of missing bells, those that had come loose during Mallika's dancing and not been replaced. Age had mellowed the swiftness and tempo of Mallika's feet but had transferred power to the nuances in the miming, the emotions and signals through which she expressed the stories residing inside her. It was for this that people had come to see her dance. Sowmya stroked the sad anklets, missing Mallika, missing the connection with her that had frayed so badly and finally come undone.

She carried the anklets to the terrace, which was the unfinished second floor. A bright hue had shot across the dark sky, heralding daybreak. It had been a long time since she had watched the sky lighten like this when she had once practiced with Mallika and Kitappa on the terrace at George Town. They would begin with meditation when it was still dark. A breeze would pick up as the sun came up. Even the stickiness of perspiration would be exhilarating after a session of vigorous practice that had yielded gems of inspired dance movements, new expressions. Sowmya could not remember the last time she danced under an open sky while the sun's rays split it. The dance studio in the back was now locked.

Sowmya tied the anklets on. *Ga-jjal, ga-jjal.* The sound of the bells was rich, unlike anything her own sets made.

The rain had left small puddles. She walked across the terrace to the middle, and faced South. The rain clouds had broken up and spread in long trails across the sky. Even a few stars twinkled in the patches of clear sky. She placed her feet together, the bony protrusion of anklebones rubbing against each other. Resting the back of her wrists on her hips, she stood in posture, slightly leaning forward at the waist. The glassy pools of water flickered. The air was full of freshness of trees.

The ancient heady notes in the scale of Bhairavi that she had hummed for Kumar in the morning swirled around her, the melody swollen with its ringing tone.

Ri_Ga Ma Pa Da Nee ...
Saa_ NiDaPa Paa_ MaGaRi Saa...

Elongated by the notes, she dissolved into the spotted sky, into its darkness and light, into the crescent of the moon. Her breath mingled with the expanse of the huge sky. She waited.

It did not begin slowly but with a roar, like rushing waters, a torrent, and pulsed between her ears and behind her eyes and she moved to its rhythm. Her hands formed symbols, the dancing deer, the rising flame, the flashing eyes. She listened closely to the sound that reverberated in her limbs. Its clarity would vanish, she feared, upon opening her eyes, so she kept them closed and moved in the light behind her closed eyelids. Her feet grazed the rough cement. Steps gradually formed a pattern that she recognized and she tried to measure them but they slipped and she had to begin again, and again, capturing her thoughts in the movements of her limbs. Shiva's fury merging in Parvati's desire, the central mystery of the lyric, still eluded. Blood pulsed and crashed through her, thumping in her ears. Finally when she stopped, exhausted, a rosy hue from the east steadily infused the clouds and she watched as they turned a furious red, as though with passion, and lit up the sky.

Satya was leaning on the parapet when she turned, his arms folded over his chest, just the way the he would watch her practice when she was sixteen. A dark patch of hair covered his bare chest but she knew that up close there would be, among the glassy dark, strays of gray. He was lit for her as though by pink studio lights.

A pulse beat steadily in the hollow of her neck. When a sudden ray of light pierced through the clouds, he lifted one arm to shield his eyes and patted the place next to him. She wiped her face roughly with the end of her sari, startled by the speed with which she was overcome with wrath. Images that had earlier formed and given shape to her dance all at once came together and she knew the meaning of desire and fury—they were the same.

Once inside the circle of his arms her sharp anger subsided. Satya tightened his arms and drew her between his legs. She leaned into him, losing herself to him. His breath smelled of Kolynos as he closed his lips over her mouth.

She rested her chin on his shoulder and looked up at the sky, which had now yielded its vivid shades to the whiteness of the morning sunlight that swept the entire terrace.

"Satya. Marry me," she said.

Satya's arms loosened around her so he could see her face.

"OK," he said, "OK, I'll arrange it. We can go before the registrar, swear an oath—"

She shook her head. "With the music of nagaswaram," she said, "with the chanting of mantra, seven steps around the fire, my people around me. Not anonymously in some government office, Satya."

Satya folded her in an embrace again, pressed her face to his chest. Although bigamy was technically prohibited, as he had explained to her once the Hindu Marriage Law the attorney that he was, it applied only to the *second* valid marriage entered into, which is a marriage performed with complete rituals and ceremonies, the seven steps. But if the second marriage was performed omitting the rituals, as in a civil ceremony, he was off the hook. "That's the law, whether it makes sense or not."

Of course, all this would become an issue only if Yamini were to bring charges of bigamy. They looked at each other, seeing Yamini in each other's eyes.

"Sowmya—"

"That's not a wedding."

"I can go to jail," he said.

What could she say to that?

"Look at me," he said. "Sowmya. Look at me. Do you believe I love you? "

She covered his mouth with her hand. He gently pried it off, kissed her fingers one by one.

"Please. Let me finish. I wish it were different, that we lived in Europe, in America, where people can marry for love, again and again. We don't marry for love, so it is forever. I don't know what will happen to Yamini if I divorced her, I simply cannot do that. I owe her, her father, too much. I cannot do this to him."

He pressed her face to his chest. If a fate could be imagined that was worse than widowhood, it was a relationship instantly made illegitimate with a few lines on a paper. A mistress was commonplace, but a non-wife? Who could imagine that?

She kissed his hand, pulled him toward her and kissed him hard on the mouth.

"Let it be," she whispered. "Let it be."

chapter 16

Zamindar's Daughter was nearing completion and, already, Satya was gearing up for a new production. Two months had passed since that note from Mani, and Sowmya had begun to wonder if the whole thing was a dream. But she still expected him to arrive any day and it was on one afternoon, when she had fallen asleep, that he finally did.

She did not have any call sheets that day. She had bathed early, dressed, and waited in the drawing room, not quite sure why she thought he would come that day. It was past mid-day and the room had darkened, in contrast, to the brightness that lit up the portico and the lawns beyond. A woman approached the gate and held up some fruit, "Ripe sapota, *amma?*" She bought some, and forgot them when she came inside and slouched on the couch in the drawing room, from where she heard a bird call in a crazed trilling repetition. Pots and pans clattered in the rear service yard of the kitchen, and the cook called to someone. She tried to distinguish the street-sounds that came over the compound wall: slippers scraping over the pavement, the rattle of a bicycle driven at breakneck speed. Rosie came in and closed the shutters against the heat, and took the fruit inside.

The gate creaked and she was instantly awake. She heard the scraping of feet through the louvered ventilator above the door frame. Was she awake or dreaming still? Rosie's small voice came from near the gate, then Mani's voice in response. Smooth as though moist, his voice carried with it traces of all the distant and terrible places she had imagined him in.

Sowmya jumped up and ran to the door and flung it open.

Mani was climbing the two steps and striding over the distance of the front porch. He looked worn. Grimy with soot from the train, the loose trousers and kurta hung from his frame. Half his face was covered with a beard and his skin was rough with exhaustion. He stopped at the door, clutching a canvas holdall and a small suitcase. A smile widened her face. As had been his habit, he did not return her smile but his eyes came alive with enough elation.

Rosie took the holdall from his hand and hovered near the door while he removed his sandals. He turned and asked the girl if he could have some buttermilk.

His collarbone rose and fell when he spoke and the eyes that once held an almost maniacal gleam were now sunken in the shadows of his cheekbones. But in his small movements were still alive the flash of the young man who had once alighted from his bike and walked into the house with a bag that had books for her, and a few yards of flowers for her mother. Sowmya wanted to laugh with relief, touch him, and feel how coarse his hair had become.

"Salt in the buttermilk, ayya?" Rosie asked.

"Yes, please. And a little sugar."

"I got the note late," Sowmya said as he passed by her and walked into the living room. She followed him. "Why didn't you wait?"

"You were busy and someone was waiting for me. It's all right. We meet now."

He folded himself down on the chair across from her. What did he see? The polish of a million eyes gazing at her in the darkness of the cinema theater? Or Yamini's wrath darkening her skin? She hunched her shoulders.

He looked at the glass of buttermilk that Rosie placed in front of him for a long moment then shook his head as if clearing his vision.

"Please take," Sowmya said.

He drank it down with long sips. His slim fingers, with sad half moon shapes at the base of his nails, held the tumbler unsteadily and trembled when he placed the glass back on the table.

"I saw the *Doll's Wedding*," he said, wiping his mouth with a kerchief.

Her role in it was that of a harlot with a heart of gold. The hero places a kumkum dot between her brows, marking her as his wife before dying of cirrhosis of the liver in her arms. She wipes it away in her grief, sacrificing her youth and beauty and lives in the shadow of his memory as his widow. It was a case for temperance and the rehabilitation of fallen women, all at once.

"The plate with the song *Is My Heart a Glass of Wine?* sold out in the first ten days," she said, watching his trembling fingers as he fumbled with his pocket to put his kerchief back. "Kittappa and Neelam in a duet."

"I hear it everywhere," he nodded. And then he crumpled and collapsed in the chair.

● ● ●

Mani slept through the night and the next day, waking only for water, which he drank deeply straight from the clay surai. He would not stop shivering, even under two blankets, so she placed a quilt on top. Then he burned from fever. The doctor from the local dispensary came in the evening, pronounced malaria, and gave him something for the fever. Sowmya wrung cloths in ice water and placed them on his brow. Taking turns with Rosie, she stayed up with him through the night, changing the cloth frequently. In the early morning his fever broke and he was drenched in sweat. She helped him change his clothes and replaced the sheets with fresh ones, and went into his room every hour to check his temperature. He slept without stirring, which alarmed her into running a finger under his nose.

Before she left for the studio in the late morning, she checked on him. She counted out the pills and instructed Rosie on what to cook for him, to collect his clothes for wash and clean his room while he bathed so as not to disturb him. When she returned in the evening she found him sleeping.

"He ate very little," Rosie said. "There are books and note paper everywhere. When he wakes up that's what he does, writing and reading. Mostly he just slept."

The next day shooting had run late and it was already dark when Sowmya got home. She arrived eager to see if Mani would be well enough to talk. He had trimmed his beard, put on a clean shirt and was waiting for her in the drawing room. She could see him more clearly now, how thin he had become.

"Nice job I did, falling sick on you like this," he said.

She smiled. "You are feeling better."

When she came down after her bath, Rosie had set the table with two plates, iced water, and dishes of steaming sambar with eggplant and onions, curried green beans, rice, and a jar of fresh yogurt. They ate leisurely, in amiable silence, but he merely picked at his food.

After dinner, they sat in the residual light from the dining room that fell into the circular verandah, which looked out into the side garden. Leaves shook in a breeze that lifted now and then. The sky was full of stars.

Sowmya tucked her feet under her in the chair. In the deepest recesses of her bones there was a burn of anticipation, or it could be dread. She observed Mani silently, in no hurry to speak. He had come with a purpose for sure. There would be time enough to speak of that but right now she was content to just have him safe. The bars of light that fell from the dining room imprisoned him, and he looked like he could float away from between them. She wanted to hold her hand out and hold him in place. It had been too long and there was much she wanted to say and hear from him, but most of all she just wanted to feel his proximity.

"I did not expect to fall sick like this, I cannot afford it. I have lost too much time. I need to return to Bombay. Too many things are happening, pulling in opposite directions. There is so much turmoil, particularly in the Punjab and Bengal. The Muslim League is campaigning hard for votes in both these places, hoping for a majority. Jinnah is going around asking Muslims "Are you a true believer or an infidel and a traitor?" People don't know enough to call it the wrong question. Pakistan has become a reality in many minds already. Both Hindus and Mussalmans see it at as better option than a bloody civil war. There is too much fear and insecurity. Gandhiji is the only true believer. Whoever said we are lovers of nonviolence was a joker. Enough of all that, let me tell you right off that I came here to take you back to Bombay with me."

She looked into the night without answering him. The sky suddenly appeared spotted with brilliant tiny holes, instead of stars.

"Your aunt has been sick for a while now and you need to go see her. See your father, you need to fix this between you both. Your sisters need you."

"Did my father say he wanted to see me? Did he send for me?"

"You know your father, Sowmya. He would never say such a thing, but you must still come with me. Jaya asked me to bring you, to come and see him. She thinks you owe it to them, but that is Jaya. I think you should come, but for other reasons, for your sake."

She rose and walked up to the verandah's railing. The breeze from the sea had abruptly stilled and the trees were a dark and still shape in the night. After that one letter from Jaya, Sowmya had waited with some anxiety for the money to be returned angrily. But the money order took and she had been sending money monthly. They were never acknowledged. The signed receipts were her only connection to this invisible sister, so inscrutable, so silent.

"Mani, tell me about my sisters."

"I met Jaya by an amazing accident. This is what happened. It was when Gandhiji had started his fast at the Agha Khan palace in Poona, and the government was afraid he might die on them."

I want freedom immediately, this very night before dawn, if it can be had. Gandhi's words had made her chest swell with grief and joy at the same time. She nodded.

"They wanted me to go to Poona for satyagraha. I had borrowed some European clothes from my friend Gopal who works in Colaba . . ."

● ● ●

"I left behind a lot of dirty business for them to mop up," Sowmya said, when Mani finished. "Look at what I left for you and my aunt Meenakshi to bear on my behalf."

"Who said change is cheap? It is bloody. But so is not changing."

"You have all paid a heavy price because of me."

"Everybody pays a price when there is injustice. Everybody. Change is hard and people resist, but when it is over, when all the wounds are healed, life goes on. People accept as if it was always this way. This is how we survive, always have. Your father could also accept this. He's made some mistakes as well. He did not have to send you to Thanjavur, there was no need, and yet he made you go. Disaster followed. Maybe there was some fear involved, something else, and he is ashamed to admit it and accept blame. It is easier to be angry, so he's angry."

"My father was a brave man, Mani. He faced the whole village with courage, telling them off, as long as I was in his protection. As long as I obeyed the rules he set, things were fine. I should have gone back home, he had a right to expect that I would be patient. Instead I disobeyed him, leaving behind so much shame, such disaster. Jaya is right to blame me."

"Yes, maybe. But what kind of a thing is it, to be cut off at the knees when you are fifteen? It simply does not make sense, and it would have only gotten worse for you if you had returned. Once Ramki's parents had altered you that way, it would have stuck, that state, the shorn head, the ascetic life, would have become the normal. It is *not* bloody normal. It is unnatural; they wanted you to do something unnatural. And your father knew all this, Sowmya. He knew of the cruelty and yet didn't know how to resist it. Where was his model? *That* was your father's problem. He did his best. It is because there *are* no rules, you see, they are only what we make of them. His anger is as much about himself, his own helplessness, as it is about you. Now he cannot forgive you for making him so helpless."

He fell silent.

"I am figuring all this out for myself as I am speaking to you," he said after a while.

She then told him about Jaya's note, about the money she had been sending to her address. "I could not understand this curt silence, I always sensed these great feelings behind it. Now I know," she said.

Mani shook his head, laughed. "I shouldn't be surprised. You don't know Jaya. She . . . You have to know her, she's a beauty." He then told her about Uma. "I am leaving the day after tomorrow. Come with me."

She did not answer him. She imagined standing at the building in Bombay, the stairwell and the tiny flat, all of this that Mani had evoked so fully in her mind, even raising her hand to knock. Courage failed her when she imagined the rage she would have to endure.

Rosie called to ask if Sowmya needed anything.

"Just switch off the lights, Rosie. Go to bed."

Within a few moments the lights in the dining room clicked, leaving the verandah enveloped in the silky night.

"In the train, I heard everything between Mallika and you," Sowmya said after a while. "I could not come out and face you, I was terrified of the decision I had made, but also afraid you would talk me out of it. Only when the train began to move …You came as promised, I failed you."

Mani did not move in his chair. She was grateful for the darkness. If it was annoyance that was in his eyes she did not want to know.

"Hmmm."

"Was your friend disappointed?"

"Disappointed? I don't know. When I went to fetch him he was waiting with his bags all packed. He refused flatly to go with the plan. He took the Boat Mail directly for Danushkodi and did not stop at the junction. Last I heard, he had joined the seminary and become a priest over there," Mani said.

"A priest! Aren't catholic priests supposed to be celibate? Poor man. And you were trying to get him married!"

"It was a reckless idea, I should have known better. I am ashamed of it now. I was such a fool."

They grinned at each other in the darkness.

"What would you have done with me then, if I had gotten out at the station?"

"Are you asking me if I would have taken you back to Thanjavur? or Ponmalar?"

"No."

He was silent and she waited.

"Whatever was necessary. Whatever I had to give would have been yours."

All he possessed then, besides the arrogance and the defiant courage that comes out of simply being young, were his books and a bicycle. She doubted he had much more today.   But he would have done exactly what he said.

"You would have made me your wife?"

"If you considered me worthy I would have thought it my fortune."

"You should write dialog for Tamil cinema. You know, Mallika's convinced that marriage will destroy me. It is a good thing that I did not get out at the station. I would have destroyed you as well."

They sat silently for a while.

"Mani, if it wasn't for that address on the notebook I would have never had the courage to leave as I did. Everything that happened— if it's anyone's fault, it's mine. Please stop blaming yourself."

"It's not about blame, Sowmya. I did consider all the consequences of sending you off to Ceylon. And yet, if you ask me, under the circumstances I would do it all over again, that is the truth. Your father has a right to feel that I violated his trust. I did. He holds me responsible for destroying his family, and he is right. Change comes about only through destruction, and it is always bloody. Forests grow from charred remains, it's not painless. I am not blaming myself for trying but I hold myself responsible for the pain it has caused."

The breeze had died down completely. Seated among the still shapes of shrubs and trees around them, it felt as though they both had merged into the landscape.

"So, are you coming with me tomorrow?"

In the morning Rosie packed a basket with food that would keep well in the heat, a flask of coffee, and a small surai of water. The train was leaving mid-morning.

He traveled with two sets of clothes, well worn as was the owner. Sowmya had sewed on the missing buttons from his shirts, and mended the seams that were coming apart before sending them off to the laundry. They were now neatly packed in his small suitcase, which sat next to the holdall he arrived with.

"Let me take you to Chellaram's," Sowmya had said. "They can stitch up your order and have it here by the time you leave," she said.

He shook his head. "I have everything I need."

When they reached the station, Sowmya waited in the car and watched helplessly as he turned in the first class ticket she had reserved for him. He then stood in line at the third class window for his ticket. She bid good-bye to him at the gate. He gave her his address in Bombay.

"When are you coming?"

She did not tell him how frightened she was to face her father. "Not now, I have dates for shooting, commitments. Mani, tell my aunt Meenakshi to hold on, *please*.

I will come, I will come to see her."

When she got into the car and asked the driver to go home he turned to her with a surprised look.

"Madam is not going to the studio?"

"No, madam is not. Let's go home. Just garage the car and then you can also go home. I'm not going anywhere today."

Sowmya did not want to enter the house right away, when she returned from the station. She would only face the relentless silence. She kicked off her slippers and walked over the lawn, into the garden. Hot sunlight cast pools of shade everywhere, the grass warm and moist.

She should really go inside and call Balram at the studio, to explain why she could not come for the shoot that day. What would she say? Would she tell him that she had forgotten what she did before this, before she had become imprisoned in the body of the dancing star, the dreamgirl actress? That she had become a mere shadow, rendered over and over on the smoky screen, lasting only as long as the film reeled itself out in the darkened hall. What was left of her after the lights came on? Could Balram tell her that, please? Beauty, she would tell him, the beauty Mallika said would be hers, where is it now? She thought of the expression on Balram's doughy face, if she were to say all this to him. *Please get into costume, amma. See? It's getting late.*

She collaborated with Kumar over imitations. All this work only generated more images of her that frightened Sowmya with their vacuousness when she confronted them. The production of these images took all of her energy and there was no space left anymore to search for the right lyric, the perfection in its expression. How intense those dance sessions with Mallika and Kitappa once were. It was as if her breath had left her for a moment and from the next moment she had breathed a different air, full of exquisite beauty and sound. She had hurled herself into a cycle when she accepted her place in the cinema, not knowing, or caring, the full extent of what she had committed herself to. And now she felt like she could not breathe. Is it any wonder then that Mallika needed to go in search of places where she could breathe a different air?

Sowmya took the keychain that was hanging at her hips and walked towards the back, where the dance studio was. It was detached from the house, connected to the main building by a breezeway. She opened the padlocked door. The windows, designed to let air and light in, were all shut tight. Rosie swept it clean and dusted every day, so the dark room was spotless, and smelled cool. She recalled the day this room was used for the first time. The lamp was lit twice daily for the Dancing God, at sunrise and at sunset.

The polished brass image of Nataraja shone in the dark niche. Somebody had forgotten to replace the lamp after scouring it. The niche was lifeless without the daily adoration that animated the sacred space.

Sowmya turned towards the center of the empty room and called out a beat.

Dheem-tha, dheem-tha, dheem-tha, dheem-tha,
thare-naa!
Nathra dheem-tha thana thare-naa dheem!
Nathra dheem-tha thana thare-naa dheem!

The jubilant beats returned to her with a thin sadness, from the corners of the hall. Her insides went still as though they had forgotten how to sing. When she tried calling out the beats again it was so hollow, it made her want to weep.

Sowmya walked up to a window, unlatched the hook and flung the shutters open. Sunlight poured in and formed a bright hot pool on the floor. The neem trees planted along the windows were still, as though they had lost the will to move in the oppressive heat. She went to the next window and opened it, then the next, and the next and soon her fingers were tugging at the bolts that were stuck, tearing her nails. The heat was like a furnace blast on her face and she was perspiring from the effort. It seemed this was an important step to something else and she needed to get all these windows opened and let the light stream in, so it could flush out the massive absence in the room and replace it with sound before anything else could happen.

She stopped only after the last shutter was opened. With the end of her sari, she wiped her streaming face and neck. Sweat immediately beaded over her upper lip, and it streamed down her back and pooled at the hollow of her back.

She went to the center of the hall, stood erect, threw her shoulders back and pressed her wrists against her hips. She closed her eyes. Her head swirled with the swollen notes of raga Bhairavi:

Saa RiGa-RiGa SaaRi . . .
Paa – aa
DaNi SaaRi . . .

Dancing deer, the rising flame, the flashing eyes. She focused on the icon at the altar. Behind her, there was frenetic action. A crowd of people was pressing behind her and among them was Neelam and Mallika, Kumar and the make-up man Kazi, Naidu from the jewelry store, Satya with his eyes so sad and his smile so sweet, Aunt Meenskhi and her mother, her father, and the children, Uma and Jaya, making mud-cakes in that hazy beautiful light falling on her father's courtyard. Behind them, more people poured into the hall and they climbed and wandered across the four walls of the hall as though they were searching for something. She did not recognize these people, she did not know their names. Behind them all stood the girl by herself, the girl whose face she always saw when she looked into a mirror.

chapter 17 1946

The first telegram arrived late July. *Appa seriously ill.
Come soon.*

Appa! Sowmya silently called out the word for father
as though testing it for the first time. She saw herself
standing in the same room with Jaya. Her sister's brow
would be creased with worry as she hurried home from
her office, bringing her father his dinner and measuring
the medicine. She imagined several people walking into
the room and passing through her, as if she were only a
shadow. Sowmya gestures with her hand to say something but no sound comes out of her mouth. Where
is her father? Among the shapeless and rumpled sheets
her fingers cannot find the density of his. Yet his eyes
are open and watching her. What's the expression in his
eyes? She did not want him to die that way, full of so
much hardness.

She wished Mani were at her side. She had waited for
several weeks, which turned into months, to hear from
him and there had been nothing. All the reports that
came from Bombay kneaded her stomach with dread.
The year, 1946, began with the strike by the Royal Indian
Navy in February. Protest quickly became a mutiny that
raged from Karachi to Calcutta, and through the wireless

spread quickly to every port in India. In Bombay, guns were trained at the *Taj Mahal Hotel* and mail delivery had stopped. In a comical gesture, anyone white was pulled off their cars and asked to shout *Jai Hind!* In July Muhammad Ali Jinnah, suspicious of Nehru's motives, rejected the invitation to form the interim Government with the Congress party. At a press conference, in his home in Malabar Hills, he declared Muslims could never get a fair deal in a Hindu dominated India, and called for a direct action to demand a state for Muslims. The Muslim League led protest marches through the city streets, with black flags. A man was stabbed fifteen times and thrown across Flora Fountain, in central Bombay. British and Indian police troops fired into mobs that were swinging clubs and bottles. Additional troops of the Gurkha and Sikh regiments were called in. Killings continued unabated and twenty-four hour curfews were imposed on the terrorized city. Where could Mani be amidst all this? Arrested as he got off the train in Bombay somewhere, caught in a mob, killed. She went to bed thinking of him in a city gone mad, and woke up in the morning with the same thought.

Even a response to Jaya's telegram was doubtful as delivery was not guaranteed. Train service to the north of the country had become erratic. Waylaid with boulders placed on the tracks, carriages were set on fire. Engineers shot past stations without stopping. Airplanes were not an option as the aerodromes were shut down except for official flights.

A second telegram arrived. She decided she would just go to the station and take the first train out, in the direction of Bombay. She sent a cable to Jaya anyway, not knowing if it would reach, asking for Mani to meet her at the station.

Satya was in Karaikudi, directing a film for the Shanmukha Brothers. She was going purely by what felt right within her bones. She did not know whether they were right decisions, she only knew that her breathing somehow depended on making them. Satya would have questioned her. *Why cancel all the call sheets, why not continue with things until she knew her mind better?* The trouble was she didn't know if she could find her mind anymore. He had no patience for this; cinema and its production absorbed all his attention. No, it would not be possible to explain her actions, and Satya, always one step ahead, would have insisted she confront the consequences.

The next day, when he returned from his trip, Satya brought Kitappa with him as they were working on a sound recording at the studio and they both were busy all day. Sowmya blamed her busy schedule for not having time for him to visit her that night.

That afternoon when she returned home from an errand, with packages in hand, she saw his car in the portico. Rosie peeped from the interior. Her worried mouth telegraphed Satya's mood. He was pacing the floor inside.

Balram had called him and complained bitterly. How could she do this to him? Has she forgotten how he had giver her an opening in his production when she was a nobody? Is this anyway to treat someone who had come through when she had needed him? Does she even understand all the financial deals that are tied in with this production? Has her head become so swollen with pride that she has lost her mind?

"I had to calm him down, told him I would talk to you. You simply cannot walk out of contracts like this, this is so unprofessional. Why would anybody hire you again?"

She silently handed the packages to Rosie to put away and then asked her for some tea.

"Would you like some?" She asked turning to Satya.

"What is the point of all this?" he said. "You want to go see your father, go. Bring your aunt *here* if that's what you want! They will *never* understand you, you can be sure of that. You can talk until you're hoarse but it will be like screaming at the wind."

"They don't have to understand me."

"What then? *What*, Sowmya?"

She sat down and kicked off her slippers. Satya was standing over her, perspiring copiously, his face red and puffy. He should cut down on the drinking. How carefully she needed to think now about what to say and how to phrase it to him. Instead of such impatience, if he would just listen with his heart, which was from where he understood her the best, she would need to explain nothing. She needed to let her father see her, see her as she was, without having to avert his eyes. This Satya would have understood. In his heart, he would surely know that it was not about approval but about redemption. Her father, too, needed her forgiveness as much as she needed his and she found that the hardest of all to give. But the way Satya was now, he would only ask her *how long?* How long will you ache for his approval? That was all that he would allow.

"Can you make that fan go faster? It is so hot," she looked up at the fan.

"The blasted thing is on high." He scowled.

Rosie brought the tea in. Satya finally sat down and took his tea from her.

"I got two telegrams. He is dying. My aunt Meenakshi needs me. She wants to go on a pilgrimage, Mani says, to Kashi. I want to take her."

"How long do you plan to be away?"

"As long as necessary." She didn't tell him that she wanted to get herself to a place where she could find her way back to her dancing. She would allow nothing and no one to chip away pieces of this dream that was still forming.

"What sort of an answer is that? Do you have any idea what this will cost you? The studio will *sue* for damages!"

Sowmya drained her tea. She was still thirsty.

"The studio doesn't own me," she said. Where did *that* come from? From *him,* something he would have said in a distant past, blowing smoke rings. "We'll handle it," she said, again echoing him, not at all sure how.

"You're a *fool!*" Satya jumped to his feet. "What do you know about any of this, to *handle* it?"

Sowmya looked at his eyes that were bloodshot, due to lack of sleep or booze, she was not sure. All he ever thought about was cinema, advances and contracts, box-office. What happened to the *Bicycle Thief?* He never talked about the kinds of films he would make, but only what would be hits.

She held his eyes for a full moment and waited for his expression to change. Satya bent down, gripped her wrist and pulled her up to her feet.

"Don't look at me like that, Sowmya."

"Let go," she said. He roughly dropped her hand.

"I am glad Mallika is not home," she said, rubbing her wrist. "I could not have possibly dealt with both of you at the same time. You all think you own pieces of me. Satya, please go home now. I cannot talk to you when you're like this."

She took the empty tumbler from his hand, stacked it into hers and took them inside. When she heard his car start up, she got out of her sweaty clothes and bathed.

That night, after dinner, she sat down with Kitappa and asked him if he would go and fetch Mallika from wherever she was at the moment.

Kitappa laughed. "Just hold her by her hand and bring her home? How long have you known my sister?"

"I need her here, elder brother. This is where she needs to be and she is gone, traveling from place to place, temple to temple. Please, you must go. She needs to come back. I need her to come back. Please, you have to do this! Convince her, only you have the courage to do this, nobody else. You know she will not pay any attention to what I say."

Kitappa sat quietly for a while, looking at his open palms as though studying them.

"Child, you know her heart as I do. She is healing it. She is healing it, you see?"

He looked sad to Sowmya. The siblings were so totally different, often disagreeing with each other, but he looked as incomplete without Mallika, as she herself felt.

Sowmya got down on the floor, next to the chair where Kitappa was sitting, and held both his hands in hers. "Please look at me, please brother."

"Yes, amma."

"She needs to come back, she is the one person I cannot do without right now. I cannot do this without her."

Kitappa was silent for a moment.

"Satya was bloody angry when he left."

"I will take care of him. He will be all right."

Kitappa looked at her slightly surprised.

"He will be all right," she patted his hand.

The next morning Sowmya called in the workers and gave orders for the studio to be painted fresh and mirrors installed all along two walls of the studio. She ordered several sets of new anklets, in different sizes, from small to large. The lamp returned to the altar in the studio. She lit it before she left for Central Station.

chapter 18

When she alighted at the Bombay Victoria Station, a man stood on the platform but it was not Mani. He must be running late as usual. He must come, he must. She paced the length of the platform, while the porter waited with her suitcase and watched.

The platform thinned out, the passengers and those who came to meet them dispersed. The engine disengaged and hissed off to the railway yard. Cleaners who came to wash the train down looked at her with interest. Finally, her limbs growing heavy and cumbersome with worry, she signaled to the man. He picked up her suitcase and she followed him off the platform.

Near the ticket collector's window, she saw Mani. His kurta swung loosely on him, as he hurried through the station gates. Unshaven and even thinner than she remembered, he was bounding towards her. He ran past her without looking.

"Mani!"

He stopped in his tracks and turned around. His expression did not change when his eyes found her, as though his face had forgotten how to register surprise or delight. But as he approached her in long, unhurried strides, she saw his mouth relax into a smile.

"Good. Your train arrived early actually," he said, catching his breath. "Curfew at 6. We'll get a taxi. A little safer. If at all we get one."

Mani got in the back seat with Sowmya. The stores were all shuttered, the streets were eerily calm and deserted.

"How far is the hospital?"

"What hospital. He's *home*."

"What?"

There was nothing they could do for him anymore, the hospital told them, and they needed the beds. Mani was just coming from the hospital himself, where he had taken a man who had been severely beaten.

"Who? Someone you know?"

"My chai-walla, Rajaram. He ran his tea shop right below where I lived."

Mani had arrived at his building in the evening when it had become quite dark. The streets were quieter than usual, there was always some movement here. He first noticed the large aluminum kettle in which Rajaram cooked and cooked his tea all day long. Upside down in the dust it was lying in the middle of the street. The tea shop, only a shack with a tin sheet over sticks that were braced with bricks and rope, was destroyed. Mani looked for the kettle lid in the dark, found it and picked up the kettle which was dented and mangled so badly the lid would not fit anymore. With shaking hands he banged it on the platform to somehow twist it and make it fit again. But it was useless. The two large Primus stoves had been smashed and there was the smell of kerosene. He put all the scraps of his findings in one corner, his chest thumping with pity and horror. Rajaram was nowhere.

The doors to his room were ajar. Mani looked up and down the short gallery but the doors to the other two rooms were bolted and padlocked. His neighbors had fled, he hoped. He pushed the door open and stepped inside. In the darkness he found Rajaram squatting on the floor. His head was a pulpy mess of congealed blood. It was hard to tell what exactly had happened to his face, there were gashes and flesh hanging from it. Blood had streaked down his neck and stained his shirt-front. He was still breathing.

"They had beaten him with I don't even know what. He had a key to my room, in order to collect things for me sometimes. He must have hidden there but they found him."

She clutched at her throat, brimming with grief, for her father, for Rajaram, for Mani, for this woebegone city. "*Why?*"

Mani stared out the window without answering and they rode in silence for several minutes.

"We tried to get your father back in the hospital, my friend Gopal has connections. But he refused. 'Just let me be,' he said."

Her father demanded so little, which is what made refusing his wish so impossible.

"You came. Good," Mani said, looking at her. "Good."

A moment later when she turned toward him to say something, he was sprawled on his seat, his head thrown back, his jaw slack, snoring.

The car moved through the thinly populated streets. She was surprised to see people still around, going about their business. The handsome actor, Dilip Kumar, was smiling on posters above a building. They drove through the wounded and shuttered streets and yet, here and there she saw a store open. A grotesquely blue sky and a canopy of lush green converged down upon a defiant city that had been terrorized in so many different ways.

Even when she knew that her father had moved the family to Bombay, in Sowmya's mind they were still back in the central space of her father's house in the village, redolent with the smell of morning—a mingling of water and blossoms and trees. She turned and looked across the seat at Mani. She wished she could shake him awake but didn't have the heart to. She was terribly alone and frightened.

Mani asked the driver to stop at the top of the lane where the family lived. Sowmya got down from the car and stood on the street. Like the rest of the city here too it looked like unfinished business – life quickly withdrawn from the street and waiting, still ticking.

Sowmya looked at the buildings cramped together on both sides of a narrow lane, almost touching each other across it. Mani picked up her suitcase in one hand and slung the bag that contained a flask and a tiffin-carrier over his shoulder. Sowmya followed him and they walked down the deserted street, their footsteps causing a small disturbance.

A small crowd had gathered at the entrance to the building. Some of those who stood outside the building entrance seemed tenants of the building. Sowmya felt in her stomach, *too late, too late*. They recognized Mani and nodded to him. As their attention shifted towards her coming up behind him, the expression in their eyes changed. A murmur went up among the crowd when they recognized the famous actress.

Mani immediately paused, hung back a bit, and signaled Sowmya to get in front of him. The crowd parted reluctantly to let her pass. Mani stepped up behind her and followed her closely as they went up the stairs.

The front door to the flat was flung wide open, as if it was useless anymore to try and secure anything. Sowmya stopped at the door. A few people had huddled in corners and were leaning against the walls. A young woman, her eyes red and swollen and still weeping, separated from the crowd that seemed intently discussing something. Immediately, and without hesitation, Sowmya recognized Jaya. She felt Mani taking her hand and she let him lead her to the middle of the room where Natesan lay in a cot.

Natesan looked as though he was sleeping peacefully, except for the cotton balls placed at his nostrils, and his toes that were tied together with a piece of cloth. Illness had aged him in ways Sowmya had not imagined. She touched his thin fingers. They were stiff and cold and she fought the impulse to jerk her hands back. How often had she clutched these hands, which now at death repulsed her. She was five or maybe six, on the night of the quarter-moon festival. Her father had raised her and cousin Niru onto his shoulders, one on each side, high above the crowd of heads so they could see the temple chariot. Two dozen men were pulling it, shouting in unison, Govinda, Go-vinda! The huge temple cart rolled with a fearsome grinding sound, carrying the deity for the evening stroll around the temple precincts. Later they had gone past the temple shops that shimmered with toys, mirrors, ribbons and tassels, setting Sowmya's eyes ablaze. She had clutched her father's firm hand then, and skipped with glee, firm and sure of her place on the earth on which she walked. A bright image from a distant past sprung unsullied by any sorrows, like a gift.

Sowmya took her father's shrunken hands into hers. She let go of her grief and it flowed and rushed through her, this searing, cleansing grief, like a stream swollen with the monsoon rain clearing out everything in its way, making little debris out of all the other grievances and regrets that had lodged in her, and leaving in its wake only the crystallized brilliance of his love and tenderness for her that she had known, which would always be true.

A touch like the flutter of a butterfly, on her shoulder. Sowmya turned and looked into her mother's pale, colorless eyes. She had once looked into these very eyes that were made brilliant with kohl. What happened to the blooming lotus that was her mother's face, the sparkling light of diamonds at her ears? She looked at Janaki's shrunken cheeks, the sparse gray hair that hung at her temples. Fifteen years could age someone so much? She held her mother's hand.

"Amma."

"He waited as long as he could for you, Sowmya. Finally this morning, right after he had his coffee . . ."

She had been aware of so little of what had passed in her mother's daily life. She had only seen her mother brimming with life, giving life, and watching over the destruction of her daughter's life like a prison guard. It was impossible to have seen the grief and loss, the tight grip guilt and insecurity had on her mother's emotions. How hateful she had seemed then and how helpless she seemed now.

"Anyway, she's here now." It was Jaya. She had a cup of coffee in her hand and she held it out to Sowmya. "Did Mani show up on time?"

Sowmya smiled and took the coffee. She could see how Mani must have so easily recognized Jaya, the resemblance to her was striking.

How could she tell them the fear that held her back without seeming selfish? Would she ever be able to connect with her sisters? Uma, she learnt later, had refused to come when informed. But she would find her in this great big city that can absorb death and destruction and acrimony, and keep blooming like those blood red blossoms of gulmohar.

"Aunt Meenakshi is asking for you," Jaya said.

Meenakshi was in a small bed made on the floor. Sowmya kneeled down. Meenakshi opened her eyes and looked at her for a few minutes, trying to focus. She then reached for Sowmya's hand, took it in hers and kissed it.

They came with the funeral bier just before noon. When they took Natesan out Sowmya held on to Janaki who stumbled, her legs buckling beneath her. The men did not have much difficulty getting the bier out the apartment's door and down the stairs. Natesan could not have weighed much. The funeral procession waited in the street.

Mani came out of the bathing room, dripping water from the wet funeral clothes. He would accompany the funeral procession to the cremation ground, where he would do the last rites and light the pyre.

Jaya was determined to go to the cremation ground as well. There was fear that the procession may be waylaid by a mob, but she could not be dissuaded and left with Mani. Sowmya stayed back with her mother and aunt and waited.

"I am sorry I arrived too late," Sowmya said.

"It is not safe to travel anywhere anyway," Meenakshi said. "It is very bad here right now in the city, Muslims and

Hindus roaming the streets with daggers and machetes, breaking everybody's heads. We will have peace only when the white man leaves."

Even on her sick bed she had an opinion. Sowmya smiled.

She imagined her father here, in this apartment in a foreign city. She thought of what Mani had told her, about disparate regions coming together as a nation. And yet how difficult it must have been for Natesan to transact these borders, the courage it took to make it in a place so far and so different from where he was born and raised, to lose one daughter to one city and another daughter in another city. Once she left with the man she wanted to marry, Uma never returned. Not even for the funeral. The city had transformed everything that her father possessed, even himself.

Janaki moved closer to Sowmya and stroked her head, stroked her hair, as if getting reacquainted with her.

"Appa was very angry, none of us could talk to him about you. But once he got sick everything changed," Meenakshi said.

"Did he ever ask to see me?"

The women were silent.

"He never said anything, but he wanted to see you," Janaki said after a while. "He wanted to resolve everything."

"Ask forgiveness," Meenakshi said. "Guilt is a big burden. Everybody wants to shed their weight when they are staring at death."

"I needed his forgiveness too," Sowmya said. "I wanted him to say it, that it was all right, but I know, I know he would never—"

Meenakshi stirred and slowly sat up in her bed.

"Look. There are no words to describe what happened to you. I am trying to work out the part I played in this too, setting up everything with Mani. A nice mess we all made. But you know," her voice started shaking with the effort to catch her breath. "I don't regret it. Not anymore. What have we lost by what you did? Nothing, absolutely nothing. Look at Uma, she is lost to us forever. She does not want to have anything to do with this family. At least you came back to see your father, even if only like this. She never—," Meenakshi shook her head, her voice breaking.

At night Meenaskhi did not have any appetite for dinner. They persuaded her to eat a small banana in some milk.

Mani, Jaya, and Sowmya ate the food neighbors had brought in. The electricity had been cut off so they ate in darkness.

"I came here for another reason also," Sowmya said.

All faces turned to her.

"I want to take Aunt Meenakshi to Banares," she said.

"Yes, good. Something my sister has been wanting for a long time," Janaki said.

"You can also drop you father's ashes there," Mani said.

"So we'll all go," Sowmya said.

"Not me. I cannot take anymore leave," Jaya said.

• • •

Ashes from Natesan's remains were brought back from the cremation ground on the third day. Janaki removed the only piece of jewelry she wore, the gold pendants that she wore since her wedding day, and dropped it into the urn.

The government's efforts for relief at the refugee camps were so poor that Mani's work, coordinating the volunteer efforts, was essential. Jaya had exhausted her leave with Natesan's illness and she could not afford to go.

"I'll talk to Gopal," Mani said and the next day returned with a letter sanctioning Jaya's leave, and four tickets in the *Kashi Express*.

They arrived at Banares, the holy city on the river Ganges, a one day journey in normal times, three nights and four days after leaving Bombay.

epilogue

The narrow street snakes and winds its way down. On either side of the lane are high, solid walls broken by small storefronts. Festooned with bright silks, they sell items for worship: flower garlands, sweet burfi and peda in large glass jars smeared with fingerprint. Dark, shiny Banarasi betel leaves are folded around fragrant, sweet, and acrid things that the vendor scoops up from the dozen or more shiny brass and glass containers arrayed in front of him. Tightening her hold on Meenakshi's arm, Sowmya passes on the shopkeepers' plea to come and do business.

As the women approach the ghat at the riverbank, a clutch of children converge around them. The children raise their spindly arms and shiny eyes toward her. They draw her into their circle that swirls with the hunger in their rag covered bodies and, because they are children, hilarity. They touch her sari and move closer. She picks up the pieces of sweets from the basket she has bought for the offering at the temple and places them one by one into their hands. But there are more hands than sweets, so she moves on when she runs out.

The sun sinks behind them among the temple towers. A group of six or seven Buddhist monks in crimson robes pass. The women begin to descend down to the Dashaswamedha Ghat. Jaya gets in front of them and goes down the steps first. Sowmya holds on to Meenakshi's arm securely to steady her, and Janaki holds her other hand. The steps are broad, ancient, eroded but still solid under foot.

The river is seemingly tranquil on the surface. Only by the objects floating on its gray-brown massive waters is its rapid current evident. The river bends here at the temple for Lord Vishvanatha, forming a crescent shape before flowing north again, on its course toward the delta where it empties finally into the Bay of Bengal.

The west bank, where Sowmya stands, is choking with large and small temples, personal dwellings built long ago by wealthy merchants and maharajas, now offering free lodging for the pilgrims. The buildings, dressed in colorful paints, seem as though they have been here as long as the river itself. Wedged between these buildings are small forts, ashrams, a temple for some minor deity. Balconies hang precariously over the network of narrow gullies that run beneath them.

To her right the riverbank stretches for miles cutting across the city of Banares, towards the ghats of Harishchandra, Hanuman, Jalasi and on towards the end where the tributary Assi meets the main river. At this junction is the Manikarnika, where the dead are cremated. This is sacred ground, this west bank of the Ganges. This is where all quests end.

Across the river there is nothing but wilderness that spreads outwards towards a blond sky that is losing rapidly to the night. The woods remind her of a picture that she thought she had forgotten, a picture of the woods that opens out behind the divine Sri Krishna in the dimming evening light. Its details had once conjured up profound nostalgia in her young heart, a longing for a place she had never seen. And now here it is, *this is the place!* How did these woods become part of her memory before she ever saw them? She looks for a long time at the stillness of the gray-green density, where nothing moves.

A dozen pigeons coo and flutter, hop on the steps and cluster over the buildings.

The light offering for the river is getting underway below them near the water. A large stage that hangs partially over the water's edge is being decorated with garlands. Sounds like that of an elephant's trumpet but muted, come from the various small temples along the banks. They are blowing the conches inside. Tiny pennants on top of the several temple towers in the distance flutter in the wind, as though preparing to charge for battle.

Meenakshi and Janaki flank Sowmya and the women sit down at the steps of the ghat and rest their tired feet. Jaya skips down the steps to the river. Her sari ruffles in the wind and she smoothes it down, her hair coiled neatly at the nape. She buys a basket of clay lamps and a flower garland from a girl who runs up to her. She then approaches the boats moored on the banks and calls something to a man who is reclining in his boat. He flings his beedi, still smoking, into the sacred waters and jumps down.

"Watch," Meenakshi says. "Nobody bargains like our Jaya. Poor man has no chance!"

They watch Jaya where strings of lights glow in the fluid darkness that is falling. Jaya looks up at them and calls from below, waving an open hand. Behind her a dozen or so women, all dressed in white, go down the steps and into the river. A moment later, their heads bob in the dark waters, saris clinging to their shaven heads.

Janaki suddenly sways and the women hold her between them. They descend the steps to meet Jaya for the worship of the river goddess, Ganga mai.

The light offering at the bank is led by ten priests. Fire burns in the cauldrons that are lined up against the ghat steps. Glowing strings of lights criss-cross above them causing a luminescent dome. They chant in unison the verses that adore the Fragrant Lord, in rhythmic aspiration and intonation like breath itself. The verses roll in the air, over the waters and across to the other banks, where the woods dark and silent absorb the text that had become sound and become silence again.

Om Tryambhakam Yajamahe
Sugandhim Pushtivardhanam
Urvarukamiva Bandhanan
Mrityor Mukshiya Maamritat

Like a ripe cucumber from the vine, let me separate tenderly from these bonds. Verses at once full of beauty and profound sorrow.

The women descend into the water's edge where a boy helps them float the leaves bearing the lamp on the water. The leaves, tiny boats, carry the lights away and the river goddess glimmers as hundreds of flames float on her dark body.

● ● ●

The boatman is waiting for them when they arrive at four in the morning at the top of the ghat. He greets them and leads them down to the river and into his boat. He has a thin angular face, made handsome and younger than he is by a mustache and a mop of curly dark hair.

The sun is a shot of brilliance above the waters, gradually becoming a shiny disk, as it rises higher in the violet mist. Its elongated reflection shimmers on the waters.

Just as they are ready to push off the bank, a priest calls to them and runs towards the boat. Bathed and in his robes, his brows smeared with sacred ash, he briskly explains to the women why they need his service. He asks the boatman to give him a hand, climbs in and sits on the seat behind them.

"Always, there are ways to allow for life's irregularities," he says, as he arranges around him somehow the small brass plates and oil lamps that he brings out from an old and frayed bag, "such as the lack of a male heir."

"It requires an extra propitiatory side step before proceeding with the main event," he says, which is to send her father off on his voyage to the other world, beyond this one, floating on the waters of the sacred Ganga.

Starting with an invocation, he begins to recite the verses. He is middle-aged, his face holds the beauty that comes from his complete immersion in the certainty of his work. His competent instructions to them are soothing. Do this he says, like this, recite three times, pour the water over to the right after circling your head with it. The daughters do what he bids them. Janaki starts to cry a little, but it is a quick wave of grief that ebbs and then flows. The boatman turns his vessel around, faces east.

Sowmya touches the urn that she holds in her lap. She has so little of her father now, just this. She bites back her grief and fights off the waves of anger and tenderness that rise in rapid succession. If she sifts through the scenes that occupied her all these years, that of her father's eyes the last time she saw him, the fear and anxiety in them, if she could for a moment set that aside, what does she have? Just glimpses that have faded, a slice of an expression, a bit of a voice, the feel of his hand. This is what is left of him. Her father would have wanted his past returned to him, something to assure him that his life had not just been fractured pieces, blown to dust. Sowmya's hand slides over her abdomen, there's a fluttering that she has revealed to no one, not even to Satya. A fragile and sweet thing, a miracle, and she has held on, counting and recounting days, keeping it to herself like a treasure. She could see the baby, her eyes blackened with kohl, silver bells tinkling on her chubby ankles. Sowmya sees her being passed from hands to loving hands, gladdening every pair of eyes that looks upon her-- her mother breathing in her milk skin, Mallika's ancient eyes, her sisters singing to her. . . . Oh Satya!

The sun climbs rapidly into the sky, burning the mist, and suddenly the woods are in view and lit up as though somebody had turned the spotlights on them.

Dance to that heat, she would tell her daughter. Look slightly above their heads. Don't forget to smile!

The End

Acknowledgement

Among the many people I want to acknowledge for the birth of this book, I have to remember the women of India, known and unknown to me. These are the women who have managed to keep their hopes and dreams while working within a crushing framework of cultural and social encumbrances. Their courage and fortitude is what inspired this book.

I wish to thank Peggy Rambach who showed me where to find the story and how to tell it; Ellen Bryant Voigt for the amazing phone call inviting me to attend the Program for Writers at Warren Wilson College; all my gurus at the program; Joan Silber and Wilton Barnhadt for their continued support throughout my journey; Zohra Saed, of Upset Press, for her friendship and her faith in this book.

I wish to also thank Theodore S. Baskaran for not only his book on Tamil cinema, The Eye of the Serpent, a rich source material, but also for the conversations we had and his kindness in facilitating my visit to the Roja Muthiah Libray, Chennai.